Love in Spades

LOVE IN SPADES

The Ladies' Wagering Whist Society, Book 7

Meredith Bond

Cover Art by QuarterbackTB,

https://qtbdesign.wixsite.com/qtbdesign

Logo by Calli Pryor,
https://twitter.com/calliclassic

Edited by The Editing Hall,

http://theeditinghall.com

Published by Anessa Books,
For more information please visit
http://anessabooks.com

Dramatis Personae

Christianne Ayres (previously Lady Norman): Founding member of the Ladies' Wagering Whist Society. She is featured in *A Hand for the Duke*.

Lydia Welles, Lady Welles née Sheffield: member of the Ladies' Wagering Whist Society. Heroine of *Jack of Diamonds*.

Diana Crowther, Lady Colburne née Hemshawe: member of the Ladies' Wagering Whist Society. Heroine of *The Games She Played*.

Claire Tyne, Lady Blakemore: member of the Ladies' Wagering Whist Society. She is featured in *A Trick of Mirrors*.

Alys, Lady Gorling (previously the **Duchess of Kendell)**: member of the Ladies' Wagering Whist Society. She is featured in *A Bid for Romance*.

Penelope, Duchess Bolton, (previously Mrs. Aldridge): member of the Ladies' Wagering Whist Society. She is featured in *An Affair of Hearts.*

Cynthia Montley, Lady Sorrell: member of the Ladies' Wagering Whist Society. She is featured in *Love in Spades*.

Ellen Aston, Lady Moreton: member of the Ladies' Wagering Whist Society. She is the heroine of *A Token of Love*.

Joshua Powell, Lord Wickford: owner, Powell's Club for Gentlemen. Hero of *King of Clubs.*

Tina Bronley, Duchess of Warwick née Rowan: Christianne and Liam's natural daughter. Heroine of *A Hand for the Duke*.

Robert Bronley, Duke of Warwick: Hero of *A Hand for the Duke*.

Margaret Douglass, Lady Rossburk, née Bronley: Warwick's sister. Heroine of *A Bid for Romance*.

Liam Ayres, Lord Ayres: Christianne's husband and Tina's father. Featured in *A Hand for the Duke*.

John Welles, Lord Welles: Hero in *Jack of Diamonds*.

Andrew Crowther, Lord Colburne: Hero in *The Games She Played*.

Beatrice Adler, Lady St. Vincent, née Kendrick: Lady Blakemore's niece. Heroine in *A Trick of Mirrors*.

Isabelle Pike, Lady Conway: née Kendrick: Lady Blakemore's niece. Heroine in *A Trick of Mirrors*.

Edward Pike, Lord Conway: Hero in *A Trick of Mirrors*.

Paul Adler, Lord St. Vincent: Hero in *A Trick of Mirrors*.

Elizabeth Aldridge, née Adler: Lord St. Vincent's young step-mother. Heroine in *An Affair of Hearts*.

James Douglass, Marquess of Rossburk: School friend of Joshua Powell. Hero in *A Bid for Romance*.

Charles Aldridge: Mrs. Aldridge's son, watchmaker, and businessman. Hero in *An Affair of Hearts*.

Cassia Benton: Sister to Cynthia Montley, Lady Sorrell. Heroine of *Love in Spades*.

Archibald (Archer) Fitzwalter: Hero of *Love in Spades*.

Christopher Pennyston, Viscount Pennyston: Hero of *A Token of Love*.

Gwendolyn Sherman: School friend of Cassia Benton, and the twins Bee and Bel. Heroine of *King of Clubs*.

Chapter One

~March 31, 1808~

Cassia Benton wiped at the soil muddying her skirt, wondering what color roses would bloom, if any, on the bushes she'd planted last autumn. She'd spent the entire morning tending the few plants that had sprouted of the more than thirty she'd started. She was trying to create a pink, hardier, strongly scented rose.

Last fall she'd done all the hard work involved in hybridizing her roses, and now that it was finally spring, she was waiting and watching each and every day to see what would grow. It was slow work that required more patience than skill. Mentally, she made a list of all she still needed to do: note down the growth—

"Cassia! Are you even listening to me?" her mother snapped, her voice getting uncommonly loud.

Cassie's head jerked up. The sudden movement caused the last pin holding her heavy brown hair to fall. Her wavy locks tumbled past her shoulders. She quickly twisted it into a knot on top of her head and retrieved the pin from the floor. Shoving it in, she hoped it would hold. "I'm sorry, Mother, I was just thinking—"

"About your roses, as always! What am I going to do with you?" The exasperation in Lady Benton's voice was palpable, leaving Cassie shifting guiltily on the sofa. Her mother turned to Cassie's older sister, Cynthia, who had come home for a visit. Their mother frowned as she caught Cyn trying to slip Cassie a pin from her own deep mahogany hair—perfectly coiffed as always. "Do you see what I have to deal with?"

"She's always been this way, Mother," Cynthia said with the utmost patience. Cassie appreciated her sister a great deal. She'd always been understanding of Cassie's passions, much more so than their mother. It was odd. Her mother was frustrated but understanding when it came to her father's scientific work and even her older brother's—if you could call digging up old bits of pottery science—but she never extended the same courtesy to Cassie. It wasn't fair.

"I know," Lady Benton said with an exaggerated sigh. "Cassia, can we have your full, undivided attention for just a few minutes? Please?"

Her mother was reduced to begging? Maybe this was serious. Cassie forced herself to focus. "Yes, Mother. I'm sorry. What is it that you wanted to speak with me about?"

"Your debut, for the twelfth time," Lady Benton said. She tilted her head and looked meaningfully at Cassie, widening her stormy, green eyes—the same eyes all three Benton children had inherited—so as to stress the importance of the topic.

"We've discussed this, Mother. I'm not—"

"Yes, yes, you are," her mother said, interrupting her. "If you'd been listening to me for the past quarter of an hour, which now, I see, you were not." Her mother pressed her lips together for a moment, clearly holding back the words of anger she so wanted to unleash on her youngest child. She closed her eyes, took in a deep breath, and started again. "You are now twenty-one years old. You're practically on the shelf! You will be making your debut this season, and I expect you to be engaged by the end of it. Is that understood?"

"But, Mother!" Cassie started to protest.

"No! You no longer have the luxury to argue with me nor take more than a year to find a husband. I have let this go for long enough. I have put up with your arguments and allowed you entirely too much license. That stops now! You will go to London with your sister, and you will make your debut. There will be no arguments and no further discussion. Now you are excused to go and pack." Her mother paused to look her up and down pointedly. "And for goodness' sake, change into a clean dress! You are filthy. Why are you not wearing the apron I gave you?"

Cassie kept her eyes lowered so her mother couldn't see the anger in her eyes. "I forgot. But, Mother—"

"You are dismissed!" her mother said, interrupting her again. "Cynthia, please accompany your sister to her room and assist her in packing."

Cynthia stood up like the dutiful daughter she'd always been. She gave Cassie a small, encouraging smile.

Cassie had no choice but to follow her sister out of the room.

Once they reached Cassie's room and closed the door, she turned on Cynthia. "There's got to be a way—"

"No. She's right, Cassie. It's almost too late as it is. You'll be coming to London and making your debut," Cynthia said, sounding much too much like their mother for Cassie's peace of mind.

"But Cyn, my roses! I can't just leave them," Cassie argued.

Cynthia shrugged. "Bring the ones you can, but you don't have any other option. You need to marry, my sweet. Not only will it give you access to your inheritance, but you don't want to be known as that crazy lady in the village, now do you?" she asked with a little smile.

Cassie gritted her teeth. "Is there nothing—"

"Nothing! Listen, I knew this was coming, and I did a little research," Cyn said, opening the trunk someone had conveniently left at the foot of Cassie's bed. Drawers were opened, and her sister started pulling clothing out and placing it carefully into the trunk. "You, of course, have heard of the Royal Society of London?"

"Of course! It's the most prestigious society for the natural sciences in the country," Cassie said.

"Yes, well, they meet most Fridays at Burlington House in London. I don't see why you can't attend."

Cassie froze. "I... I can attend their meetings?"

"Yes. They're open to the public," Cyn said, continuing with her packing of Cassie's things. She finished with the last drawer and moved to the wardrobe. "I don't think you should bring very many of your dresses. Maybe just a few of your older ones to garden in. We'll buy you a new wardrobe for the season," she said in the most off-hand way.

"Garden? How can I garden in London? My plants are here!" Cassie said, feeling her throat tighten once more.

"You have a number of roses in pots. I've seen them. You can bring them along with you. I don't have a greenhouse, naturally, but my breakfast parlor is very sunny. I imagine you could put a number of your plants there. We'll set up a table for them in front of the window. And then, of course, I would love for you to plant some of your roses outside in my garden. Would you mind very much, sharing some of them with me?"

Cassie widened her eyes in surprise. "You've never wanted any of my roses before!"

"Yes, I have. I asked you for some last Christmas," Cyn said.

"At Christmas! What was I to do, dig them up from the garden in the middle of winter? How ridiculous!"

"You said you would give some to me this spring, if you remember?" Cyn pointed out.

"Oh, yes. Yes, I did." Cassie had forgotten, actually, but she would be very happy to give some to Cyn now—especially as it seemed she was going to be moving to London for the spring whether she liked it or not.

What Cassie didn't share with anyone—nor would she ever—was the other reason she did not want to go to London: Philip Bowlette, Viscount Kineton, the man Cassie had fallen deeply, madly in love with when she'd been seventeen years old. He'd been one of her father's students at Oxford, and she thought they'd had something special.

They'd met during Cassie's summer holidays from school, spent three blissful months together punting on the river, going for picnics, and gardening together. When Cassie had returned home for Christmas, he'd been there happily waiting for her under the mistletoe with the most adorable grin on his handsome face. But when she returned again the following summer, he was gone. She later heard he'd graduated and married some wealthy chit in London.

He hadn't said goodbye! Not in person. Not in a letter. He hadn't even left a message with her father! Cassie had been devastated.

She was certain she would meet him in London if she went. She knew he was there. She knew he always attended the ton events. Even Cynthia had mentioned seeing him a few times, just enough to rub it in her face that he'd left her without a word—not that her sister did so intentionally. She'd never known what Cassie and Philip had shared, and she never would! But Cassie didn't know what she would do if she met him now. She could only hope she didn't throw herself at him either in tears or with her fists flying because she was still angry. Either one was a distinct possibility that Cassie didn't even want to contemplate.

"There is no possible way I could convince Mother..." Cassie started. She stopped speaking because Cynthia had turned around to glare at her in a most mother-like way.

"Right." Cassie sighed dramatically. She turned on her heel, saying, "I guess I'll go and gather up my gardening things and decide which roses to bring with me." She opened the door. "I wonder how my new seedlings would do if I moved them from the garden..." she started more to herself than anyone else, especially since she'd left Cynthia behind in her room to decide which dresses would go to London and which could safely stay behind.

Cassie certainly had no opinion on the matter. Her sister could choose for her.

~April 1~

Archibald Fitzwalter strode confidently down the

gangplank from the ship that had carried him, five other passengers, and a hold full of goods from Bombay to London. It had been a long journey, and he was very happy to be on solid ground once again, but clearly not as happy as Mr. Rowley, who was down on his knees and looked ready to kiss the dock itself.

Archer burst out laughing. "Really Rowley, was it that bad?" he asked the fellow who was probably just about five years older than himself.

The man looked up, tilted his head a little as he considered Archer's query, and then shook his head. "I suppose not," he said as he got back to his feet. "It just feels so damn good to be off that ship! Not that it wasn't wonderful spending time with you, Fitzwalter, it was. Honestly, I don't know what I would have done if you hadn't been there to—

"My boy!" Lord Lonsdale came up from behind Archer and slapped him on his back. "You heading off? Must come 'round to visit. Yes, yes, must come 'round," the older man said through his overgrown walrus of a mustache. "Want you to meet my daughter. Told you about her, didn't I?"

Archer laughed. "You did, my lord, a number of times. I can't wait to meet her. She sounds like an absolutely lovely girl."

"Not just lovely, but smart," the man said, tapping a finger against the side of his gray-haired head.

"I would expect nothing less of a daughter of yours, my lord," Archer said with a slight bow.

The man burst out laughing. "Indeed! Indeed." He shook his head and patted Archer's shoulder again. "Always the charmer, you are. Going to charm the shoes right off my little MaryAnn's feet."

"I will be more than happy to assist her in putting her slippers back on again," Archer said with a wink.

The man burst out laughing again. His attention was caught by a man in livery coming up to them. "Eh? Oh, that's me. Recognize the livery if not the man," he told Archer.

"Well, it's been an honor, my lord. I do hope you enjoy being home again after your long journey," Archer said.

"I'm sure I will. Say, can I drop you someplace?"

"Oh no, thank you so much, my lord. Mrs. Tilbury said she would see me to my friend's home in Mayfair," Archer said.

"Oh ho!" the man said with an exaggerated wink. "So there is something there after all. And you've been so gentlemanly and denying it all these months, you old rascal!"

Archer laughed, but shook his head. "No, no, my lord. Truly, she is only being kind. I believe she said her sister lived very close to Lord Kineton, with whom I will be staying until I can find lodgings for myself."

"Uh-huh." The man sniggered and then went off with the footman who'd already loaded his lordship's luggage onto his carriage. "Now, remember, you will be coming to meet MaryAnn. I'll expect to see you in my lady's drawing room before the week is out."

"Thank you, my lord, I look forward to it."

"You're really going to meet his daughter?" Mr. Rowley asked after the carriage had rolled off.

"Of course! Why not? He says she's quite pretty," Archer said.

The man gave a shrug.

"Mr. Fitzwalter, sir, where would you like your trunk?" a sailor asked, coming down the gangway with the enormous piece of luggage in his big, beefy arms.

"My goodness, Harold! You didn't need to carry it down by yourself," Archer said, jumping to help the man.

"No, no. No worries. I won the coin toss and got the privilege of bringing it down." He deposited the trunk on the ground and then held out his hand. "It's been an honor, sir, having you on board. I know the captain is coming down to thank you himself in just a minute. I believe he's helping Mrs. Tilbury with her things."

"You all have been too kind," Archer said, grasping onto the man's hand. "Thank you for all you've done to make this journey most enjoyable."

"The pleasure has been ours, sir." He turned to walk back up the gangway, but turned back and whispered loudly, "If only all of our passengers were as kind as you, it would make these trips a lot more pleasant." He tipped his hat and then went back aboard the ship.

"Nice fella," Archer said. "In fact, all the sailors were, don't you think?"

"I can't say I met many of them," Mr. Rowley said. "You did, though?"

"Yes, I met a number of them as I strolled about on the decks."

Finally, Mrs. Tilbury, the sweetest middle-aged lady, made her way slowly down the gangplank, a basket in one hand, the other hand gripping tightly onto the rope to steady herself. Archer jumped forward to assist her to the ground.

"Oh, thank you so much, Mr. Fitzwalter. Thank

you. I just... ugh, that gangplank terrifies me," she said, looking back at the offending bridge that extended from the ship down to the dock.

"Well, just think, you'll never have to walk on it ever again. You're home!" he said happily.

She sighed with a big smile on her face as she looked around the docks. "Yes, home!"

Two sailors came down after her carrying her trunks followed by the captain.

"Is your carriage nearby, Mrs. Tilbury?" the captain asked, looking around.

She turned and then smiled. "Yes, yes, there it is." She pointed toward a bright red coach. "You may see my luggage and Mr. Fitzwalter's put on top. I'll be driving him to Mayfair."

The captain gave a bow and then saw to it, coming back quickly. "May I say what an honor it's been having you both on board." He suddenly noticed Mr. Rowley standing there and quickly added, "Er, the three of you, I meant to say."

Mr. Rowley gave a little snort of laughter. "I'm sure you meant exactly what you said, sir. You hardly saw me at all the entire journey. I was so horridly ill."

"Yes, I am sorry about that," the captain said.

"Thank goodness Fitzwalter was there and kept me company a good bit," Mr. Rowley said, giving Archer a nod.

"He kept you company in your quarters and me on my daily walks around the deck. Honestly, Mr. Fitzwalter, I don't quite know how you did it. What a busy journey you must have had," Mrs. Tilbury said with a little laugh.

"You all made it so very pleasant. I would have been bored beyond belief if not for both of you. And Lord Lonsdale, of course," Archer said.

"Well, thank you again," the captain said with a tip of his hat.

"Shall we?" the lady asked, about to start toward her carriage. "Oh, Mr. Rowley, do you need a ride as well?"

"Thank you, ma'am, no. I'll get a hack. I'm going in a different direction. But thank you." Mr. Rowley reached out a hand to Archer, who shook it happily.

"I do hope we'll see each other again," Archer said.

"As do I."

Archer then followed Mrs. Tilbury to her conveyance, ready and eager to see what his time in London would bring.

Chapter Two

Cassie watched the scenery pass by outside her sister's traveling carriage window. The city was beginning to creep up on them. She'd only been to London a few times, but she could already tell they were getting close.

"Are you ready?" Cynthia asked as she stretched her feet out on the seat next to Cassie. Normally, her sister would never put her feet up on the seat, but there wasn't any room on the floor for them to put their feet down. Cassie had filled all the available space with her pots of roses.

Cassie shifted slightly to face her sister. Her feet were tucked up next to her. "I don't think so."

Cyn gave her a small, encouraging smile. "Don't worry. It's going to be fine, you know."

"I just don't like meeting new people. I can be so awkward," Cassie admitted.

"I completely understand the feeling, believe me. You will have two things to make it easier, though."

Cassie tilted her head to the side and waited for her sister to continue.

"One is the Ladies' Wagering Whist Society. We're all very good friends, and all the ladies are truly kind and supportive. They will help you without you even needing to ask."

Cassie smiled. "You are so lucky to have such good friends."

Cynthia nodded. "I am. And that's the other thing you have—friends."

Cassie frowned. "You mean your friends?"

"No, I mean yours. The Kendrick twins—or well, they are Lady Conway and Lady St. Vincent now—but Bee and Bel are both going to be in town for the season."

Cassie gasped. "I'd forgotten that! Oh, my goodness! How wonderful! I can't wait to see them again!"

"I figured you would be eager to do so. I invited them over for dinner this evening."

If she could have, Cassie would have hugged her sister. Since she couldn't even put her feet down on the floor, she reached out her hand. Cynthia took it in her own. "You are the best of sisters, do you know that?"

Cynthia laughed. "Well, I knew this wasn't going to be easy for you and... well, I just did for you exactly what I wished someone had done for me when I'd made my debut."

Cassie could only shake her head. "You are too good, Cyn. Thank you."

Now she actually had something to look forward to. Maybe this season wasn't going to be as bad as she'd feared.

~*~

Archer jumped down from Mrs. Tilbury's coach and turned to thank her once again while the driver lifted down his trunk.

"It has been such an honor, Mrs. Tilbury. I do hope we have a chance to meet again," Archer said through the open carriage door.

"Entirely my pleasure, sir. And yes, I'm certain we shall." She gave a wave, and Archer closed the door and turned to tip the driver.

After watching the carriage continue down the street, Archer turned and strode up the three impressive steps to his closest friend's home. He paused to admire the columns flanking the sharp black door before lifting the brass knocker and letting it fall loudly.

The door was answered immediately by a footman in bright blue livery. "May I help you, sir?"

"Yes, I am Archer Fitzwalter, here to see Lord Kineton." He passed over a visiting card which, unfortunately, stated that he was from Fort St. George, Madras and a lieutenant of the East India Company Army, Madras Presidency, neither of which were currently true.

The man bowed and allowed him entrance to the house. "If you would wait here for one moment, Lieutenant Fitzwalter. I will see if his lordship is at home."

"It's just plain old mister, now, but thank you. He should be expecting me," Archer said with confidence.

The man bowed and went to check, nonetheless.

His good friend came bounding down the stairs a few minutes later. His straight, dark blond hair bounced with every step, his brilliant blue eyes danced with laughter. "You've come! It took you long enough," Kineton said, reaching out for Archer's hand and giving his shoulder a friendly slap.

"Well, it does take some time to travel nearly

half-way around the world. My apologies for the slowness of the tide," Archer said, laughing. He gave his childhood friend's arm a squeeze. "It has been a long time!" he said, looking his friend over.

The last time they'd seen each other was three years earlier, just before Archer had left for India. Kineton had been at Oxford when Archer's father had bought him his commission.

"You haven't changed a bit!" Kineton said. He narrowed his eyes a bit. "Was your hair always that blond?"

Archer laughed. "That hot Indian sun has bleached it a bit," he admitted. "Combined with my tanned face, it looks lighter, I imagine."

"Yes, that must be it," his friend nodded. "And you're still taller than me! I was hoping I would have caught up by now."

Archer laughed again. "In three years? Have you grown since I left?"

"A little," his friend hedged.

"Well, I've always been taller than you, always will be."

Kineton just shook his head, but his smile didn't waver. "It's not fair, you know. The girls always did go for you at the dances."

"I never left you behind! Always made sure you had a partner too. And besides, who's the one married now? It's not me!"

"No, but we're going to fix that, aren't we?" Kineton wiggled his eyebrows suggestively. "But let's not stand here in the foyer. Come up and meet my wife."

"Yes, yes! Oh, er, my trunk is outside. You did say it was all right if I stayed with you until I could find rooms of my own. Lady Kineton won't mind, will she?" Archer asked.

"Don't be ridiculous, of course she doesn't mind!" He turned toward the footman, standing discreetly by the door. "Fetch Mr. Fitzwalter's trunk and put it in the green room," he directed the man. The fellow nodded and went off to do his bidding.

Archer paused. "That trunk's rather heavy, maybe I should—"

"Don't you even think of lifting a finger," Kineton protested. "If he can't manage, there are two more footman to help him. Now, come upstairs."

Archer nodded, but watched as the footman went out to get his trunk, worried about the man lifting something that heavy. The sailor had been used to lifting heavy loads; he didn't know about this footman, no matter how broad his shoulders.

"Coming?" Kineton's voice pulled his thoughts back to what he was supposed to be doing—following his friend up to meet his lady wife. Archer jogged up the steps after him.

Lady Kineton was a beautiful petite thing with pale brown hair and large brown eyes. When she stood to greet him, Kineton towered over her.

"My darling, here is my dearest childhood friend, Mr. Archibald Fitzwalter."

"Mr. Fitzwalter, how lovely to meet you," she said, inclining her head and extending a child-sized hand in his direction.

He quickly took a few steps forward to take it in his own and allow his lips to hover over the back of it. "It is an honor, Lady Kineton."

"I understand you will be spending the season with us," she said, smiling at him, her eyes crinkling ever so slightly.

"Hopefully, it won't take me quite that long to

find someplace to stay. I promise to be out of your hair as soon as possible. I do thank you most sincerely for your hospitality," he said, bowing once more.

Kineton waved a negligent hand. "It is no trouble at all. And do not rush to find rooms, we're very happy to have you stay as long as you want."

"No trouble at all, truly," his wife agreed. "We have plenty of room, and it will be lovely to get to know Kineton's good friend. You'll have to tell me every embarrassing thing you can remember about my husband." She gave a tinkling little giggle.

Kineton burst out laughing. "Oh, no, Archer wouldn't do that! If he did, I might have to tell some tales myself."

Archer smiled at them both but stayed quiet. He was certain Kineton wouldn't appreciate him sharing embarrassing stories, just as he wouldn't. As Kineton was being so kind as to put him up, he was not about to jeopardize his friendship in any way. He was also hoping to use his friend's contacts to find the financial investors he needed to get his new company up and running—the entire reason he had come. No, no, he'd be telling no tales, that was for certain.

"Well, we will leave you to your stitching, madam, and go down to my study for some gentlemanly talk," Kineton said, giving his wife's cheek a quick buss.

Archer gave the lady another bow and followed his friend out the door and back downstairs. In his study, which was a refreshingly masculine room of dark wood paneling and paintings of horses and the countryside, Kineton handed Archer a glass of amber liquor.

Archer sniffed at it.

"Brandy," Kineton said.

"Ah! It's been a while since I've had anything so refined," Archer said. He lifted his glass to toast his host and then took a sip. It was sickly sweet but burned pleasantly down his throat.

"What do you drink in Madras?" Kineton asked, taking a seat on the red leather sofa and indicating Archer sit in the matching wing-back chair across from him.

"Very bad wine, when we can get it. And my superior is a Scotsman who always has a few bottles of whisky handy. I think he brings it over by the barrel."

Kineton shook his head. "Ugh! Can't stand whisky."

"I've actually developed quite a liking for it."

"Well, tell me all about this new endeavor of yours. You're planning to undercut the East India Company?"

Archer choked on the sip of brandy he was taking just at that moment. When he stopped coughing and laughing, he said, "No, no! Not undercut. I couldn't possibly do that. I want to start a business that actually pays a fair price for the goods purchased. It'll be a small endeavor that will simply export spices from Southern India. The East India Company is much more interested in cotton and silk. They won't even notice a small spice merchant."

"I thought you worked for the Company," Kineton said, frowning.

"I am in their army. Or, well, I was. I quit."

"So you could start this business?"

"Because I had problems with some of their

policies. Just before I joined, there was an uprising near Madras where over 600 men were murdered for standing up for their religious practices. Once I learned about that, I... I just couldn't stomach the Company's rule any longer. They don't pay a fair price for their goods in order to squeeze out as much profit as they can, and they don't treat the native people well. It just... well, it floors me how they can treat people that way," he said with much more heat than he'd intended. "I'm sorry, but it infuriates me."

"So, in your typical fashion, you're going to do something about it," Kineton said with a laugh.

"I don't know what you find amusing about poor people being hung out to dry," Archer said, putting his glass down with some force.

"No, no. No offense meant. I can see this is something you feel very strongly about," his friend said, immediately holding up his hands. "You just tend to... well, you tend to jump into things."

"I'm not jumping into this. I've thought it out, and this is the best way to help these people. Philip, you haven't seen the way the Indians live—if you can even call it that," he said. He shook the image of the poverty he'd seen out of his mind's eye. It was too disturbing, especially when he was sitting here in his friend's luxurious home in London, enjoying a glass of fine liquor that probably cost Kineton a pretty penny.

"You know I would..." Kineton started.

"No, no, I told you in my letter I'm not asking you to invest," Archer replied quickly. It was one thing the two boys had in common while growing up—both their fathers had been in difficult financial situations. They figured it was the boggy land the neighbors were attempting to farm, but they hadn't known the particulars. Of course, now Kineton had inherited his father's land. Archer didn't know how well he was doing with it, but it couldn't be much better than Lord Fitzwalter who, Archer knew, was always struggling, living on the edge.

"Well, you know, all I have is thanks to Martha-aaah!" Kineton snapped his fingers, his eyes lighting up with excitement. "But of course! That's just what you need!"

"Martha? Er, your wife?" Archer was confused.

"Yes, Martha's my wife, so you can't have her. But you need someone just like her—an heiress! I'll introduce you to all the girls who are known to have large dowries. That's where you will get the funds for your business." Kineton sat back with a very self-satisfied grin.

Archer just laughed and shook his head. "No, thank you. It worked for you because you're very happy living here in London, playing escort to your lovely wife, but I'm going back to Madras as soon as I get the money I need. I can't marry someone, take her money, and abandon her here."

"You could bring her—"

"And I would not submit a gently born young lady to the trials of living in India. No! Honestly, all you need to do is introduce me to some of your wealthier gentleman friends, and I'll do the rest. I'm certain I can convince a few people to invest in this business. It's a sound idea."

Kineton shook his head sadly. "You're making a mistake, Archer. You're young and not that bad looking. I'm sure you could find a very willing miss—"

"Thank you, no!" Archer insisted.

His friend sighed heavily. "Very well." He sat up again as another thought seemed to strike. "What about a wardrobe?"

"Are you referring to mine? I've been living in a uniform for the past three years."

"Just what I thought. I'll take you 'round to my man. He'll get you fixed up in no time."

"Excellent!" He looked down at his coat and breeches and then over at Kineton's clothes. It was painfully obvious that Archer hadn't seen a tailor in some time, and certainly not one who had been on Bond Street recently. And besides, who didn't like getting new clothes?

"And don't even think of laying out the ready for them," Kineton added. "I know you're strapped for funds. I've got a good allowance, and I just won a monkey off of old Merriton a few nights ago."

"You have an allowance?" Archer asked.

Kineton's cheeks turned slightly rosy. "Er, yes. Howden—that's Martha's father—keeps a tight fist on his money. I'll get a good chunk in the end since Martha's an only child, but for now I have to put up with him."

"Didn't you get ten thousand pounds when you married? I remember you writing me about the fantastic dowry you received."

Kineton shifted uneasily in his seat. "Yes, but it all got divided between my estate, trust funds for Martha, and any children we might have as per the terms of the marriage settlement. I actually saw very little of that. I tell you, Howden's a sharp one."

Archer gave a little laugh. "In other words, he arranged it so you couldn't possibly squander his blunt."

"Yes." Kineton clearly wasn't happy about the arrangement, but he had agreed to it, so he truly couldn't complain.

"Well, I appreciate you lending me a hand for now, and I will pay you back just as soon—"

"No worries, old man! No worries!" Kineton sat forward again. "I can't wait to introduce you to society. I tell you the ladies are going to be eating out of your hand. You'll have your funding in no time."

"Kineton, I told you, I'm not marrying—"

"Right, right, so you say. Just don't... don't dismiss the idea completely, all right?"

Archer sighed. "Fine. I suppose it's always good to have a contingency plan."

"That's my boy!"

Chapter Three

That evening, Isabel, Lady Conway—better known simply as Bel—let out an ear-piercing squeal the moment she walked into Cynthia's drawing room. Running up to Cassie and giving her a big hug, she said, "I can't believe you're finally here! We are going to have the best season! I can't wait to introduce you to everybody and, oh, my goodness, I will introduce you to every eligible man I know. Now granted, that's not a lot, but we'll find more. I promise. We are going to have so much fun and—"

"My goodness! Take a breath, Bel!" Cassie laughed, interrupting her good friend.

Bel just giggled.

"Yes, friends, this is the esteemed Viscountess Conway," Lord Conway said, looking lovingly at his new wife. He turned back to Cassie. "Miss Benton, it is wonderful to see you again."

"Oh, Conway!" Bel laughed and playfully swatted at his arm. "I don't have to be on my best behavior with Cassia. We went to school together." She turned toward Cassie's sister. "Thank you so much, Lady Sorrell, for arranging for this dinner party. I am so thrilled to have Cassia here, as you might have been able to tell," she said with a giggle.

Cynthia nodded. "It's my pleasure. I do so want my sister to feel comfortable and be happy here this season. You know it's going to be difficult for her. I wanted to be sure she was at least surrounded by friends."

"Absolutely! I couldn't agree more. I so wished I could have had my friends here when I'd made my debut. Goodness, I almost didn't even have my sister!"

"You almost didn't have me where?" Beatrice, Lady St. Vincent asked coming into the room. Even though the twins no longer lived together, they still looked completely identical. Cassie wasn't certain, but it almost looked as if both girls' deep red hair was done up the same way, with the same curls gently framing their pretty creamy complexions. Only Bel's giggles and Bee's gentle smiles made it so Cassie could tell them apart.

"Oh, Bee, how wonderful to see you." Cassie walked up and gave her other closest friend a hug.

"You're looking well," Bee said, looking her over.

"Thank you. I was just thinking the same of you. Marriage agrees with you, I think," Cassie said with a broad smile. She turned to Bee's new husband and curtsied. "Good evening, Lord St. Vincent."

He bowed slightly in return. "Good evening. It's very nice to see you again, Miss Benton." He turned to their hostess. "Lady Sorrell, how are you this evening?"

"Well, thank you, my lord. Welcome." Cynthia said with a broad smile.

"I was just saying that I don't know what I would have done if I hadn't had you with me at my come-out," Bel said, finishing what she'd been saying earlier.

"Oh, yes? Well, I'm glad you think so. It certainly took me long enough to convince you of that," Bee said.

"No, that's not true—" At a look from her sister, Bel stopped and gave a little giggle. "Oh, well, all right, maybe it is. But the point is, Cassia shouldn't have to make her debut alone. We'll be right by her side the whole time."

"Ah, and here are more people who will be right by your side, I'm certain," Cynthia said, coming forward to greet four more people who'd just come in.

Cassie didn't know them so she took in a deep breath to ready herself, placed a polite smile onto her lips, and came forward to curtsey to the newcomers. She knew she was going to have to be dealing with a lot of strangers, but she had rather been hoping her sister wouldn't force them on her so quickly. She supposed this would help her for what was to come. Meeting new people in a comfortable setting was easier, she supposed.

"Lord and Lady Welles, Lord and Lady Colburne, may I present my sister, Cassia Benton?" Cynthia said, giving them all a broad smile. She turned to Cassie and said, "Lydia and Diana are two of my closest friends. I do hope they become yours as well."

"Thank you, Cynthia!" Diana said, reaching out and giving Cynthia's arm a friendly squeeze. She turned to Cassie. "And don't you even think of calling us anything but our given names."

Cassie laughed, relaxing a touch. "Thank you, and of course, you'll call me Cassia. You're both members of the Whist Society, aren't you?" she asked.

"We do have that honor," Lydia said with a smile. "And just two short years ago we were exactly where you are now."

"However, we had something which very few young ladies just making their debut have—the support of the Ladies' Wagering Whist Society," Diana said.

"True, but you do have that, Cassia, so consider yourself very lucky," Lydia agreed with a giggle.

"I couldn't agree more," Bee said, coming over to greet the newcomers. "I don't know what I would have done without the Wagering Whist Society." She gave Lydia and Diana a happy smile before turning back to Cassie. "So, are you nervous about making your debut?"

Lifting one shoulder a touch, Cassie said, "A bit." She looked over at her sister who was looking at her skeptically. "Oh, all right. A lot!"

"She's been fighting this for years," Cynthia said with a laugh.

"Finally had no choice in the matter?" Lord St. Vincent asked with a little chuckle.

"Precisely, my lord. My mother didn't give me any other option this year," Cassie answered.

"Why, may I ask, have you not wanted to make your debut?" Lord Welles asked.

"I'm just not very good with people," Cassie admitted. "And I'm certain I won't find a husband who..." she paused.

"Will allow you to continue with your experiments?" Bee finished for her. Cassie felt a rush of gratitude for having friends who knew and understood her.

"Yes. How will I ever find a gentleman who will be tolerant of my work?" Cassie asked, feeling her stomach tighten with nerves.

"This is your work with roses?" Lydia asked.

"Yes." Cassie started.

"She has the most incredible plants. You should see her garden!" Bee said to the room at large.

"She brought a good number of them here," Cynthia interjected.

"You did? How wonderful!" Bel said, turning to her with a big smile.

"It was the only way I could get her to come!" Cynthia said with a laugh.

"I couldn't just leave them all behind," Cassie explained.

"Of course not!" Lord Colburne said, understanding immediately. "Especially plants. They need constant care and attention, I imagine."

Cassie nodded. "Not only that, but I've got new—"

"I think you can explain all about your latest experiments over dinner," Cynthia said, interrupting her. She turned to the footman who was standing at the door and gave him a nod. "Have you informed Lord Sorrell that it is time for him to join us?"

"He is no longer at home, my lady," the footman said. "He sends his apologies. He was called away to attend a meeting at Parliament."

"Oh." Cynthia frowned. She turned awkwardly toward her guests who were all watching the interchange.

"It's quite all right. I'm sure we'll see him soon enough," Lord Conway said quickly.

"Yes, of course," Lord St. Vincent agreed.

"I do apologize. He said he had some work to do this evening, but had hoped he would be able to join us for dinner," Cynthia explained.

"It's not a problem at all," Diana said.

"Well, then, I don't think there's any need for a formal procession to the dining room, is there? We're all friends here," Cynthia said with a nervous smile.

"Our numbers would have been uneven anyway," Cassia pointed out.

"Of course, you're right. I didn't invite a gentleman to even them out. It was meant to be an informal party," Cynthia agreed. "Shall we?" She indicated the door, and they all made their way to the dining room.

Cassie grabbed a hold of her sister's arm. "It's all right, Cyn. I know you're more used to formal evenings, but this is wonderful just the way it is."

Cynthia gave her a smile and squeezed her arm gratefully.

~April 4~

A few days later Bee and Bel were once again on the Sorrell's doorstep. This time they were there to see to the very important business of shopping for Cassie's wardrobe.

"Is Tina going to be joining us?" Bee asked as they all piled into Cynthia's carriage.

"Who is Tina?" Cassie asked.

"The Duchess of Warwick," Bel answered.

"She used to be a modiste and has an excellent fashion sense," Cynthia explained.

"Oh, yes! You've told me about her," Cassie said, now remembering the fantastic tales her sister had written to her the year before. She could hardly believe they were true!

"No, Bee, I didn't invite her. I thought maybe we could handle Cassie's wardrobe on our own. I always feel bad because Tina is only ever called upon to help with fashion dilemmas. I'd like to call on her just as a friend rather than asking for her help," Cynthia explained.

"Oh! Of course!" Bee said immediately, looking a little chastened.

"Perhaps we could invite her out for a ride one afternoon," Cassie suggested.

Her sister gave her a bright smile. "That's a wonderful idea. Or perhaps to see your roses."

"Oh, yes—if you think she'd be interested," Cassie said a little hesitantly.

"I'm sure she would. You have incredible flowers," Bel said.

"Many are still very young," Cassie commented.

"Will they flower anyway?" Bel asked.

"I expect so," Cassie said, "but most likely only one or two blooms."

"I'm sure she'll enjoy seeing them anyway," Cynthia said.

They pulled up to a shop just then so all talk of roses ceased. Within moments, they were whisked inside and elbow deep into fabrics and fashion plates. Cassie's attention was pulled this way and that by the three other women who wanted her to look at this or feel that. She was made to stand in front of a mirror, and then pulled to the window for the very best light, so colors could be matched with her overly tanned complexion. It was exhausting and confusing, and Cassie felt practically dizzy from it all.

After trying on two half-made gowns, she was

getting dressed once again when there was a squeal, quickly followed by another and another. She urged the woman helping her to hurry, so she could go to the front of the store to see what all the excitement was about.

"Cassia! Cassia! See who's here! You will not believe it," Bel said, dragging her forward the moment she emerged from the curtained dressing room.

Standing in the middle of the shop, speaking with Cynthia and Bee was... "Gwendolyn!" Cassie said enthusiastically, coming over to her very good friend from school. It wasn't the excited squeal Bel had uttered, but for her, it was high excitement indeed.

Gwendolyn turned and engulfed Cassie in a big hug, squeezing her tight. "Oh, it's so good to see you!" Gwendolyn pulled back and looked her over. "Something's different."

She let go and walked around Cassie taking her in from all sides. "What..." She snapped her fingers. "I know what it is. You're not covered in dirt!" She grabbed Cassie's hand and looked at her nails. "Clean!"

Cassie laughed and pulled her hand back from her friend. "It's Cynthia's fault. Can you believe? She forced me to bathe and clean under my nails."

"Oh, good." Gwendolyn breathed a sigh of relief. "So, this is not normal? Please tell me it's not."

With a giggle, Cassie shook her head. "I promise, it's not! But you are looking fabulous as always." In truth, Gwendolyn had always been the best-dressed of all the girls at school. She loved fashion and looking good. Her pale blonde hair was always perfectly done, even after hours of chatting and giggling together. It had driven Cassie to distraction, especially since her own hair slipped free of its pins at the slightest provocation.

Gwendolyn had always insisted it was because first impressions were so very important, but even after they'd become the closest of friends, Cassie had never seen Gwendolyn rumpled or mussed in any way. They'd lived next to each other for three years, and never once was she not impeccably dressed.

"Oh, thank you, but actually I'm here to get a new wardrobe." Her bright blue eyes widened. "Don't tell me... are you making your come-out this season?"

Cassie laughed. "I am. And you?"

"Yes!" Gwendolyn said. "You two convinced me at your wedding that it absolutely had to be this year for me," she told the twins.

"I am so glad you listened to us!" Bel said.

"But who is sponsoring you?" Bee asked.

Gwendolyn gave a negligent shrug. "No one. I don't need a sponsor, I'm sure."

The twins looked at each other and then back at their friend with identical worried expressions on their faces. "You do, Gwendolyn. I know you think your wealth will open all doors to you—" Bel started.

"And it might, but—" Bee interjected.

"But you do need a sponsor. We would do so, but we're still too young and not very well established ourselves," Bel finished.

"Maybe Cynthia..." Cassie started.

"I don't know, Cassie. I'm going to have my hands full with you," Cynthia said apologetically. "You understand, Gwendolyn?"

"Of course! Don't give it a second thought,"

Gwendolyn said with a wave of her hand and a smile.

"Maybe our aunt who brought me out last season can help," Bel said.

"Yes! She was expecting to have me to sponsor this season, but since I was here last year—" Bee started.

"And are now married," Gwendolyn said, giving Bee's arm a squeeze.

Bee's smile blossomed over her entire face. "And am now married," she agreed. "I'll ask her."

"But I don't want to inconvenience anyone, and I don't even know your aunt," Gwendolyn said.

"Well, why don't you come over tomorrow, and I'll introduce you," Bee said.

"Do you think...?" Gwendolyn asked hesitantly.

"I'm sure she wouldn't mind at all. And if she's not available, I wonder if Mrs... I mean, Duchess Bolton wouldn't mind," Cynthia said. "She's a good friend of mine and would probably love to sponsor a young lady such as yourself."

"A duchess?" Gwendolyn breathed.

"She just recently became a duchess, and before that she was plain old Mrs. Aldridge, widow, whose husband was a watchmaker," Bel explained.

"A watchmaker?" Gwendolyn turned toward her friend with raised eyebrows.

"Yes! So, maybe she would be the perfect person to sponsor you. That's an excellent idea, Lady Sorrell," Bee agreed.

"Could I possibly meet her?" Gwendolyn asked hesitantly.

"I would be happy to introduce you," Cynthia said.

"Thank you," Gwendolyn said with some relief.

"Have you finished choosing your gowns, Cassia, or are you just getting started?"

"We're just finishing, but we could probably stay and help you," Cassie suggested, noticing that Gwendolyn was alone except for her maid.

She was rewarded with a broad smile. "I would like that above all else!"

Chapter Four

~April 6~

$\mathcal{K}$ineton's tailor had done an incredible job making a dark blue coat and white formal breeches in record time. He was especially pleased with the waistcoat which was of a lighter blue with dark blue embroidery. Archer was certain his friend had paid dearly for the convenience, but Kineton had refused to allow him to see the bill, let alone help pay it. Now, decked out in his new finery, Archer followed his good friend into what he expected would be the first of many such events as he scoured the haute ton for potential investors.

It wasn't just the candles which glittered throughout Lady Kershaw's ballroom but people as well. Dozens of ladies dazzled in their finery with their fans gently waving, while a hundred or more gentlemen pranced about showing off like peacocks.

This was what Archer had missed most being in India. He just stood near the entrance taking it all in. It had been a very long time since he had attended a party. There were simply too few ladies in Madras to make it a regular occurrence.

Lady Kineton had abandoned her husband and Archer, going off to find her own friends the moment they'd walked in the door, but their arrival was already turning heads.

He nodded to a few beautiful women who were gently waving their fans in an attempt to hide the fact that they were staring at him. He was about to start toward the ladies when Kineton grabbed his arm.

"I'll point out the girls with large dowries," Kineton said, squinting a critical eye as he looked around.

"Thank you, but I told you—" Archer began.

Kineton's narrowed eyes pierced him with their intent stare. "Do you want to fund your business or not?"

"Of course—"

"Then you will make pretty to the girls I introduce you to. Come along," Kineton said, striding off into the crowd.

Archer had no choice but to follow. He gave a slight shrug to the women who were still watching him, now giggling to each other.

A moment later, Kineton was all smiles as he bowed to a woman in a purple turban with two white ostrich feathers nodding gently over her head. "Lady Penderton, how lovely you look this evening." He turned toward the young lady at her side. Her dark blonde hair was drawn up into a complicated arrangement that involved feathers and sparkling diamonds. "Miss Penderton," he nodded toward the girl. She gave a small, polite smile revealing front teeth that looked too big for her mouth.

"Good evening, my lord," the girl whispered, giving him a small curtsey.

"And who have we here, Lord Kineton?" the lady asked, looking Archer over as if he were a horse for sale at Tattersall's.

"May I present my good friend, Mr. Archer Fitzwalter, son of Baron Fitzwalter of Etting," Kineton said.

Archer bowed to the ladies.

"Fitzwalter of Etting? Isn't the Earldom of Bedworth..." the lady began.

"Yes, my lady. My family did hold the title for some time, but no longer," Archer explained. He might not be in his current situation if his family still held the title. He wasn't entirely certain how it had been lost—something to do with a royal mistress he thought—but... well, bygones and all that.

"Hmph." The woman's feathers trembled over her head as she calculated his answer. "I see."

Archer wasn't certain what it was that she did see, but he wasn't going to question her. He turned to her daughter and smiled warmly. She looked to be about sixteen or seventeen years old, still practically a child. "Is this your first season, Miss Penderton?" he asked, certain of the answer.

Her cheeks took on a rosy hue, and her gaze dropped to her hands clasped tightly in front of her. "Yes."

"And how are you enjoying yourself so far? Or... this couldn't possibly be your first ball, could it?" he asked gently.

Her color heightened even more. "Yes, it is."

"Well, you must be so very excited. I have to say that I am." He leaned in a little closer and said in a loud whisper, "It's my first ball too."

Her eyes shot up to his in surprise. "It is?"

"Well, not the very first ball I've ever been to, but the first one I've attended in a very long time," he admitted. "I'm not entirely certain..." The sound of the orchestra beginning to play reached his ears above the hubbub of chatter all around them. "Ah! There we are. Would you care to dance, Miss Penderton?" he asked, bowing and holding out a hand.

She paused and looked to her mother who gave the slightest nod.

"Thank you, sir. I would enjoy that a great deal," she said, a shy smile growing on her lips.

"How is it that you know Lord Kineton," Archer asked as they took their positions on the floor.

"I met him last week at a small soirée," the girl said. It was the longest sentence she'd uttered so far. Archer had hoped the dance wouldn't be as painful as he'd feared.

~*~

Cassie tried her best not to fidget with the ribbon dangling down from the waist of her new gown. It was a very pretty, rich green ribbon that wound twice around her rib cage before ending in a pretty bow with the rest of the ribbon falling down to her ankles. Next to her, her sister was chatting with her friends. Cassie had already forgotten the names of most of them. How could she be expected to remember so many names all at once? It was even more difficult than memorizing the Latin names of the different types of roses, and those she loved. These ladies... well, she had yet to say more than two words to any of them, so she didn't know if she would even like them or not.

"You do not have your sister's unfortunate predilection for knowledge, do you, Miss Benton?" a sizeable older lady asked looking down her nose at Cassie.

Cassie swallowed hard. "I... I am a botanist, my lady."

"Your Grace," the woman said confusingly.

"I'm sorry?"

"You should address me as Your Grace," the woman said.

"Oh! I do beg your pardon! Cynthia introduced everyone so quickly, I'm afraid I didn't..."

"It is quite all right," the woman said, giving her the slightest smile. "I am actually soon to lose that title, but I have had it for so many years... well, I have to admit it will be odd to be addressed as 'my lady'."

"When is the wedding, Duchess?" Lydia asked. She had been standing on Cynthia's far side, speaking with her. It had been such a relief to meet at least two people she knew; Cassie had lost count as to the number of times she'd silently thanked her sister for having that dinner party the night she'd arrived.

"We were thinking of holding a small ceremony on May Day," the duchess answered, her cheeks turning ever so slightly pink.

"How wonderful!" Lydia said.

"It will be very small, very private. We don't want a fuss, not at our age. You understand, Lady Welles," the duchess said.

"Oh, yes, of course! So it will just be you, Lord Gorling, Mr. Hershawn... and anyone else?" Lydia asked.

"Lord Gorling's other children will be there as well, and Lord and Lady Rossburke. Lady Rossburke is like a daughter to me, you know," the duchess said, a warm smile lighting her eyes.

"Did I just hear you say that Lady Margaret will be here?" a rotund older lady asked with some excitement as she joined their group.

"Yes, Lady Rossburke has come for the season. I don't know if we'll be seeing her tonight, but I do know that she and Lord Rossburke got into town a few days ago," Her Grace said.

Cassie turned and was relieved beyond measure to see Gwendolyn join them as well.

"Gwen!" she breathed like a sigh of relief.

Her dearest friend was looking beautiful in a fine white muslin gown with white embroidery. Not surprisingly, the girl herself looked nearly as white as her dress. The expression on her face nearly made Cassie give her a big hug. Gwen was as nervous as she was.

"Ladies, may I introduce Miss Gwendolyn Sherman? I will be sponsoring her this season," the older lady said, looking around the group. "Miss Sherman, this is the Duchess of Kendell, Lady Welles, and of course you know Lady Sorrell, and may I assume this is your sister, my lady?"

"Yes, Miss Cassia Benton, Your Grace," Cynthia said before giving Gwen a nod and a small smile.

"How do you do?" Cassie asked, sinking into a curtsey. She assumed, then, that this was Duchess Bolton who Cynthia had suggested as a sponsor for Gwen. She was so happy that had clearly worked out well.

The Duchess gave Cassie a kind smile and then resumed their earlier conversation. "You must be especially excited to see Lady Rossburke, Lady Welles."

"Absolutely! She, Diana, and I would go riding in the park regularly," Lydia explained to Cassie and Gwen.

"Yes, and then last year we were so happy to include Bel into our group," Diana added, joining into the conversation.

"Miss Sherman, this is Lady Colburne," Duchess Bolton said, interrupting.

"Yes, er, we've met," Gwen said with a touch of awkwardness. The lady, however, was very kind and gave her a smile.

"Well, I imagine sometimes it was Bel and sometimes Bee accompanying us on our rides, but we didn't know that at the time," Lydia said, giggling.

Cassie knew her good friends had hidden the fact that they'd both been in London last season when it was supposed to have only been Bel. It was Cassie who Bee was supposed to have been visiting when she'd been here instead of watching out for her sister. So now Cassie smiled and nodded, understanding the dilemma these ladies had had. "If it makes you feel any better, I've known the Kendrick twins for five years now, and I still can't tell them apart."

"No, I don't know that anyone can if they aren't wearing their bracelets," Gwen agreed.

At the other ladies' obvious confusion, Cassie explained, "Bel has a bracelet with a little bell attached, and Bee has one with a bee. They wear them so that people will know who is who."

"How very clever!" Duchess Bolton commented. "The four of you went to school together?"

Both Cassie and Gwen nodded.

"Well, we sincerely hope you and Miss Sherman will be able to join our happy little riding group," Lydia said.

Cassie was touched that they were including her. "Thank you," she said, placing a hand to her chest. "That is very kind of you, truly."

"Of course! We understand how difficult this

season is going to be for you both," Diana said.

"So this is where the most beautiful ladies are all hiding," said a gentleman with wavy locks of rich brown hair, coming up to them. He paused to bow.

"Mr. Hershawn! How lovely to see you," Diana said, giving the man a big smile.

"You've let your hair grow," Lydia exclaimed in delight.

He pushed the waves off his forehead, giving an embarrassed little laugh. "Thought I'd see what it would be like. What do you think, Duchess?" he asked Gwen's chaperone.

"I will reserve judgement," the duchess said diplomatically but giving him a little wink. "Have you met Lady Sorrell's younger sister, Miss Benton? And this is Miss Sherman who I will be sponsoring this season," the lady said, indicating them both.

"No, I don't believe I've had the honor," the gentleman said. He took Cassie's hand and bowed over it and then did the same for Gwen.

"Mr. Hershawn is a good friend of ours and soon to be the duchess's stepson," Lydia said.

"Not me, the Duchess of Kendell, soon to be Lady Gorling," Duchess Bolton explained quickly.

"This is getting very confusing," Gwen said, her gaze following the direction the duchess was looking and seeing the other older woman who Cassie had first been speaking with. She'd moved on and was now talking with another older lady in a dark blue silk gown who looked vaguely familiar. She would have to explore that turn of thought later.

Duchess Bolton gave Mr. Hershawn a nod and moved to join the other group as well. Gwen gave her a little shrug and followed.

"Very," Cassie said under her breath. She turned

back to the gentleman to whom she'd just been introduced, giving him a curtsey. "It's a pleasure to meet you, sir."

"Are both you and Miss Sherman making your debut this season, Miss Benton?" he asked.

"Yes. This is my first party, although I imagine if my sister has her way, not my last," she gave a little laugh.

"Of course not your last!" he said, almost appalled. But then he gave a loud laugh. "You must be funning! Oh, my, you are too droll!" he exclaimed.

Cassie pressed her lips together, holding back the words she longed to say—but he probably wouldn't take her seriously if she commented that she truly wished it were her last party. She didn't see how Cynthia did this every year—spending months doing nothing but attending social functions and such. There were so many people. So much noise. It was all rather overwhelming.

"I do believe the first set is forming, Miss Benton. Would you do me the honor?" the gentleman held his hand out for her to take.

"Oh! Er, I'd be honored." She curtsied again and took his hand. As he led her onto the floor, she wondered if she should have asked her sister's permission first. Oh well. It was too late.

Mr. Hershawn kept up what Cassie supposed was witty banter for the duration of the dance and afterward brought her back to where her sister had been. They were both looking around for her when they were joined by the one man she'd most wanted to avoid.

"Cassia? Is that you?" the deep, rich voice of Lord Kineton approached, turning Cassie's stomach into one big rock of tension.

Chapter Five

There was no way she could avoid him now. If she'd seen him coming, she could have turned and gone in the other direction, but now with this strange Mr. Hershawn next to her, there was nothing she could do. "Philip! How... er... wonderful to see you here! What a surprise," she said, plastering a polite smile onto her face.

"It certainly is! You aren't making your debut this season, are you? Aren't you a little, well..." He gave an embarrassed laugh. He turned to Mr. Hershawn. "You weren't about to lead her out for a dance, were you?"

"No. Just looking for her sister, Lady Sorrell," Mr. Hershawn admitted.

"Ah, well, I'll be more than happy to lead her out. Give us a chance to catch up. We're old friends as you might have guessed," Philip told the gentleman.

"Oh, of course, of course." Mr. Hershawn bowed to Cassie. "It has been lovely."

"Yes. Thank you for the dance," Cassie said, almost wishing he wouldn't go and leave her alone with Philip. Politeness demanded that she take Philip's outstretched hand and allow him to lead her back onto the dance floor.

"You're looking remarkably well," he said, after they'd bowed to each other at the start of the dance.

Cassie laughed. "You mean you don't remember me looking quite so clean."

He chuckled. "Now that you mention it, that is what was missing. I couldn't quite put my finger on what was different."

She was happy the movements of the dance took them apart for the moment. She had to unscramble her thoughts. How she had even been able to speak with such civility so far, she had no idea. All the mixed-up feelings warring inside of her, and her tongue still managed to work, her brain was still able to put words together and form intelligible sentences. It amazed her.

The last time she'd seen Philip...

She nearly missed taking his hand again as the dance brought them back together.

"You're thinking about our last picnic on the banks of the river, aren't you?" he practically whispered into her ear. Luckily, she was forced to move past him with the steps of the dance, otherwise he would have seen her face. She could feel her cheeks burn.

When they came together again, she hoped they had cooled enough so as to not give her away. "It's not nice to remind a lady of her indiscretions," she pointed out.

Ha! Indiscretions didn't come close to describing the kiss they'd shared that afternoon. And if she recalled correctly—and she knew she did—his hand had somehow found its way down the front of her bodice as well. Thank goodness, she'd managed to stop the other one from climbing up the inside of her skirts. He'd begged her to allow him to give her a "special" gift, but she'd been adamant and had refused.

When she learned the following summer he'd left for London, she'd been grateful for her restraint. Reading the announcement of his engagement in the paper, she'd briefly wondered if he'd been caught with his hand up this other young lady's skirts. But she wouldn't think about that now.

"How is your lady wife?" Cassie asked as Philip turned her in a circle, his eyes on her décolletage rather than her face.

His gaze jumped to her eyes, and a smile broke out onto his lips. "So, you heard about that, did you?"

"It was announced in the papers," she pointed out. "Merely a month after you disappeared from Oxford."

"I didn't disappear. I graduated," he pointed out. He moved to turn the other lady in their quartet. When he came back to her, he nodded toward the side of the room. "See the woman with the light brown hair in ringlets, laughing and fawning over the fellow in the bottle-green coat?"

Cassie looked in the direction he'd nodded. A very beautiful young woman was laughing, standing very close to the gentleman she was speaking with—so close she had her hand on his chest in the most intimate manner. "The one in the deep red gown?" Cassie asked.

"That's her."

"It doesn't bother you..." Cassie stopped. This was none of her business.

"We have an agreement. She does what she wants with who she wants, and I do the same. It's all very amicable," he said, raising his eyebrows a little at Cassie.

She didn't like what he was implying, but she kept her mouth closed and was grateful that the dance moved them apart again.

"If I had known when we were... ah, friends... that your father was rolling in it, I can assure you, that could have been you there," he said, with a little nod of his head toward his wife.

"Rolling in what?" Cassie asked, picturing the manure they used to fertilize their garden.

Philip burst out laughing. "Money," he clarified. "I married my Martha for her dowry. You do know that, don't you?"

Cassie had to work to keep her mouth from dropping open.

"She did the same. I mean, her father would give her only the most meager pin money until she married. Now we both get a very handsome allowance every quarter," he explained.

"Do you have no feelings for each other?" Cassie asked, rather appalled at his honesty. She'd heard people married for money or convenience, she just never expected to be told as much and so blatantly.

"Of course we do! Actually, we like each other a great deal. We're rather similar," he admitted.

"Well, that's good to hear, I suppose," Cassie said. She refused to allow her mind to dwell on the thought that it could have been she who he'd married, as he'd just indicated, if he'd known the size of her dowry. No, she would definitely not go down that winding path. She'd been in love with him once, but those feelings were long gone, she told herself.

Actually, now that she thought about it... they were gone, especially now that she knew his actual intentions. With her eyes opened to his true colors, she knew she had been very lucky he'd left when he did. His ignorance had probably saved her from a lifetime of unrequited love.

She curtsied to him almost in relief.

She turned to go in the direction where she'd last seen her sister, but he took her arm and led her in the other direction instead. "I think my sister…"

"There's someone I'd like you to meet first, then I promise, we'll find your sister," he said, leading her away. She had no choice but to go with him.

He led her to the side of the room and then turned to wait. A moment later, a very tall, extremely good-looking man came and joined them. The smile on his face grew wary as he looked from Philip to her.

"Mr. Fitzwalter, may I have the pleasure of making you known to an old friend of mine, Miss Benton?" Philip said, introducing them.

Cassie curtsied. It was so nice to meet a man she had to look up to. Much to her embarrassment, Cassie had always been about the same height or maybe an inch shorter than a good number of gentlemen. But this man with his pale-blond hair, tanned, rugged-looking face, and deep blue eyes was so tall that she had to turn her face up to speak with him. "It's a pleasure, Mr. Fitzwalter."

"The pleasure is mine, Miss Benton. Sadly, I'm afraid I just came over to tell you that I have been invited into the card room," the gentleman said.

"What? But you need to dance…" Philip protested.

"My apologies, Miss Benton. No, I need to be in the card room," he said, as if it were something significant.

Philip huffed unhappily. "Very well, if you must."

"Yes. It's been a pleasure." The man bowed and went off, leaving Philip frowning after him.

Cassie didn't see how he could have come to that conclusion when he hadn't said more than a dozen words to her. "May we find my sister now?" Cassie asked, pulling Philip's attention away from his rude friend.

Philip pouted, but nodded.

~April 7~

Archer was just finishing up his breakfast the following morning when Kineton walked into the room. Seeing his host, he immediately folded the newspaper he'd been reading, putting it back together the way it had been when he'd taken it from Kineton's place at the head of the table.

"Good morning. Ah, thank you," Kineton said, accepting the newspaper as he sat down.

"Sorry, I didn't think you'd mind if I read it before you came down," Archer said, giving him a cheeky little smile.

Kineton indicated to the footman that he'd like coffee. "No, not at all. Anything interesting?"

"Not much." Archer scooped up the last of the egg on his plate and popped it into his mouth.

"What about last night?" Kineton asked. "Any success in the card room?"

"Oh, yes! I spoke with a number of gentlemen. Most weren't interested, of course, but there were a few who asked me to speak with them again today. And a few who offered names of others who might be interested," Archer said after swallowing down his food.

"Excellent! Well done!" Kineton said, leaning back as the footman put a plate of food down in front of him.

"Yes, I'm quite pleased. I've got a few letters to write this morning requesting appointments, but I think I did quite well for my first foray into society," Archer said before biting into his third piece of toast.

The footman entered and presented a salver to Archer. "This came for you, sir, in the morning's post."

Archer snatched up the letter. "Thank you." He paused to look at it and then felt his stomach sink. The handwriting was all too familiar.

"Getting mail already!" Kineton commented with a little laugh.

"I left yours on the table in the study, my lord," the footman told his employer.

"Yes, yes, that's fine. I don't need to look at it just now," Kineton said, dismissing the man. "Who is that from?" he asked Archer.

"My father," he frowned. "I told him I'd be staying with you. I hope you don't mind."

"No, not at all." Kineton went back to reading his newspaper and eating his breakfast.

Archer had no desire to see what Baron Fitzwalter wanted of him, but he supposed it was better to get the pain over with quickly, rather like having a bad tooth pulled. He broke open the seal and unfolded the paper.

Dear Son,

I hope this letter finds you well.

I was extremely disappointed to hear that you have resigned your commission in the army. After merely two years, you cannot have learned the discipline and respect I wished for you to get out of your time there. Considering that you have resigned and returned to England with yet another one of your hair-brained schemes proves this to be the case.

I am still of the opinion that I should have bought you a commission in the English army to fight on the continent, rather than in India. Only your mother's entreaties for your safety convinced me otherwise. I am now regretting giving in to her feminine sensibilities.

Please know that I am extremely disappointed. Your mother insists that all will be well, but then she has always jumped to your defense. I will believe it when I see it.

All here is the same.

Your esteemed Father.

Archer sat back in his chair and ran his hand down his face as if he could wipe off the bitterness of his father's letter. Lord Fitzwalter had never had a kind word for his only son, and it didn't look like anything had or, indeed, would ever change. Hair-brained schemes! As if helping the poor of Southern India was a lark that he was doing for fun.

Clearly his father had no concept of the reality of India. Maybe one day, Archer would be able to convince his father to travel there to see it for himself—after Archer's business had become a successful venture. Maybe then Baron Fitzwalter would give Archer the respect he deserved.

"Everything all right?" Kineton asked, startling Archer from his thoughts.

"What? Oh, yes," he sighed.

"You are frowning fiercely, not to mention the heavy sighs," Kineton said with a little laugh.

Archer held up the letter. "My father..."

Kineton held up a hand. "Say no more."

Yes, his friend knew. He'd even been witness on more than one occasion as Lord Fitzwalter expressed his honest opinion of his son.

Archer glanced back down at the letter still in his hand. "All here is the same," he read aloud. He looked up at his friend. "That means things are not well. I wonder if he and my mother are wanting for anything. Has there been more flooding in the area, do you know?"

Kineton gave a snorting laugh. "Has there been flooding? In Warwickshire? You must be joking. That's all there ever is."

Archer frowned and shook his head. "I'm certain they can't be having an easy time of it, then."

"It's been a bloody mess, I have to tell you. I've had my fields drained and irrigation put in at least twice in the past few years. The land is nothing but a bog. Hardly anything grows!"

Archer tilted his head and looked at his friend.

"What?" Kineton said, peering at him.

"You know quite a bit about this. I'm impressed," Archer commented, trying to keep the laugh from his voice. Kineton had never shown any interest in his father's estate when they were growing up.

"Well, I have to, don't I? My father's estate is now mine and, believe it or not, I studied botany at university," Kineton said defensively.

"That's right! I'd forgotten about that. And you actually learned something. I am definitely impressed!" This time Archer couldn't hold back his laughter.

Kineton frowned at him, and Archer could just picture him as a little boy sticking his tongue out at him.

"What are you going to do about your father?" Kineton asked, like a sudden downpour of cold rain.

Archer sighed again. "I don't think there's

anything I can do. He doesn't want help, and even if he did, he certainly doesn't believe I could provide any." He paused and thought about it.

"I suppose you'd better find that funding for your business quickly and get that started," Kineton commented. "Once you prove to him you can do that, perhaps…"

"Ha! Perhaps! Yes, and perhaps the swallows will fly backwards," Archer said with a bark of laughter. "And besides, the whole purpose of the business is not to support my father but the people of Southern India. They, I know, will appreciate my efforts. My father certainly never would." He sighed and ran his hand down his face again. "Starting this business is going to take some time. And it will take time for it to become profitable." Archer said, toying with the fantasy of being able to rescue his father's estate with the profits from his business. He stood. "I guess I'd better get writing those letters and asking for appointments, then. If you'll excuse me?"

Kineton gave a nod and went back to reading his paper as Archer headed for his friend's study.

Chapter Six

"I beg your pardon, Miss Benton," a maid said, coming down the garden walkway. Cassie looked up from the rose she'd just finished planting. "Yes..." She searched her mind for the young woman's name. It was either Sally or Penny, she couldn't remember which. They both had thin faces and green eyes. "Penny?" she tried.

The girl smiled. "I'm Sally, Miss, but thank you for trying."

"Ah! I'm sorry, Sally. I'm trying to remember."

"I really appreciate that. I don't even think his lordship knows any of our names," she said with a shake of her head.

Cassie could only shake her head. Her brother-in-law probably wasn't home often enough to know one maid or footman from another.

"Speaking of which, his lordship isn't at home at the moment, and he's got a visitor. I'm afraid Mrs. Brown, the housekeeper, thinks you should come in and entertain the gentleman for a little until Lord Sorrell returns," the girl said.

"Entertain him? What about my sister? Can't she do it?" Cassie asked.

"She's not at home either."

"Oh, that's right. She went to the milliner's to get a new hat." Cassie sighed. "Well, that will teach me to avoid shopping with my sister," she commented to herself. She looked up at Sally again. "Are you certain he needs entertaining? Can't he just wait in the drawing room by himself?"

"Mrs. Brown said it would be better if you were to meet him. More proper-like," the girl said apologetically. "I'm to sit with you while you do so."

"Ugh! But I'm busy, and I'm sure you are too," she started.

Sally gave her a look as if to say, This would be the right thing to do.

Cassie heaved a sigh and stood, brushing the dirt off her hands. "Very well." Her skirt was covered with streaks of mud—she'd forgotten to wear her apron again. Oh, well, he was just going to have to accept her as is.

She clomped into the house in her work boots, pausing to knock some of the dirt off them just inside the door. She didn't want to make the staff angry for leaving a trail of mud on the nice clean floors.

A gentleman jumped to his feet as Cassie entered the room. She paused to curtsey after seeing Sally, out of the corner of her eye, take a seat in the corner of the room. Cassie immediately recognized the man from the ball the previous evening. How could she possibly forget that height, that handsome face, and such broad shoulders? She tamped down her excitement, however, sternly reminding herself the rudeness that went with the beauty, not to mention the fact that he'd just had her pulled in from the garden. "Oh! You're Philip's friend. We met last night."

"Er, yes. Fitzwalter. Archer Fitzwalter," he said,

bowing to her.

"Right. Mr. Fitzwalter who needed to rush off to the gaming room the moment we met," Cassie said, and then supposed she shouldn't have reminded him of his bad behavior. She gave a little mental shrug. She was certain he wasn't the sort of man she wanted to marry anyway, not unless he turned out to be a scientist, which was highly unlikely. It was almost a shame, considering how her stomach flipped just looking at him.

Ugh! How shallow can one get, Cassie reprimanded herself. She was not going to allow herself to get distracted by a pretty face.

"Er, yes. I apologize for that. I needed to meet some people," he said. He paused and then added, "I didn't mean to disturb your gardening."

Cassie looked down at herself and shrugged. "No? Oh, well then, if you don't mind, I'm going to go back to it. I don't know when my brother-in-law will be home. Did you have an appointment?"

She caught Mr. Fitzwalter snapping his mouth shut after it dropped open a touch. "Er, yes. Yes, I did. I do."

"Oh, well then, I'm sure he'll return—"

"Mr. Fitzwalter, I do apologize," Lord Sorrell said, coming into the drawing room. He stopped and looked at Cassie. "What in God's name... Why are you covered in dirt?"

"I was planting Cynthia's roses. I promised her I would do so today," Cassie explained.

"Oh." Her brother-in-law still looked confused.

"Sally, the maid," she explained, certain Sorrell wouldn't know who she was speaking about otherwise, "insisted I come in and entertain Mr. Fitzwalter until you got home."

"And you thought to do so covered in dirt?" her brother-in-law asked in astonishment. "Well, at least you didn't sit down!"

"You're welcome," Cassie said in a huff. She didn't need him insulting her too. There was nothing wrong with a little dirt, and she knew better than to sit on the clean sofa when she was covered in it. "Be happy I hadn't gotten to fertilizing the flowers yet—I always use unadulterated manure." With that parting shot, she turned and strode from the room.

~*~

Archer had the hardest time not bursting out laughing. Miss Benton was definitely unusual—manure! Yes, indeed, he was very grateful she'd been called in before she'd gotten into that.

Never in his life had a young woman seemed more upset to have been in his company. Clearly, she'd been forced to leave her gardening to come inside. But whereas most young ladies would have hidden their annoyance at such a disturbance, Miss Benton didn't feel the need to do so. Well, he supposed he should appreciate her honesty.

He turned to Lord Sorrell and shifted his thinking to the reason he was here.

"I appreciate you taking a few minutes to meet with me, my lord," he said, turning to the extremely fair man. His hair was even more blond than Archer's, and his skin was quite pale. It made Archer wonder if the fellow ever got outside. He, himself, enjoyed getting out for two to three hours a day to ride, but he supposed not everyone was as athletically minded.

"Not at all. I do apologize for my, er, sister-in-law and for being late, naturally. Lord Gorling can be rather long-winded. Why don't we go into my study?" Lord Sorrell led the way.

When they were both comfortably seated, Lord Sorrell turned to Archer and asked, "So, how may I help you?"

"I have a proposition, and I've been told you might be interested," Archer started. He continued through his planned speech, concerning both the spice trade and the living conditions of the farmers who he intended to help. He did leave out the unfair practices of the East India Company, considering he was in the presence of a nobleman who might very well have a vested interest in the company.

Lord Sorrell had maintained an interested expression throughout Archer's explanation, but now he frowned. "It sounds like a fascinating business proposition. I assume you would not be infringing on the monopoly established by the East India Company?"

"No, my lord, naturally," Archer answered quickly.

Lord Sorrell gave him a small smile. "Naturally. If you were, I can't imagine you would have come to an MP with your proposal."

Archer gave a little chuckle. "No, my lord."

"You do know that I am quite involved in Parliament?" his lordship asked.

"I did not, but I assure you, this is all above board. As I'm sure you're aware, the East India Company, which was my employer for many years, is currently more concerned with nation-building than trade. I have been in their army for the past two years. They have divested themselves from a number of areas, leaving open business opportunities for people such as myself."

Lord Sorrell nodded. "Still, I can't help but feel it would be a conflict of interest for me even if I were interested in investing in your company."

"But you are not?" Archer had to ask.

"No, I'm afraid I am not."

Archer nodded. A dead end. It was not the first, and he was certain it would not be the last. Truly, he was just getting started. "Would you happen to know of anyone who might be interested in such an opportunity?" Archer asked. He always did so. It was how he'd got Lord Sorrell's name to begin with.

The gentleman thought for a moment, then shook his head. "I'm afraid I don't." He stood. "But I do thank you for telling me about this interesting project you are embarking upon. I feel it's good for me to be aware of such things."

"Of course. And I appreciate your time, my lord."

Archer bowed himself out.

~April 8~

Cassie was so excited. She took a good thirty minutes to get dressed the following evening. She needed to look just right—not too fashionable and yet not overly ordinary either. She needed to look intelligent, but perhaps not too much of a bluestocking. It was a difficult balance, but the most important thing was that she was going to be attending a talk at the Royal Society of Natural Sciences. It would be a highly intellectual evening where she would get to meet and speak with other natural scientists.

This evening's talk was on the subject of electricity, specifically its effects on organic matter. The following week there was to be a lecture on botanical findings in Scotland, but Cassie hadn't wanted to wait even a week to hear the society's lectures, no matter what the topic. After only attending one party, she already worried she was losing her scientific edge. No, she needed—and desperately wanted—the intellectual stimulation this talk would provide.

She was walking down the stairs, thinking about the delights of the evening to come, when voices echoed from the hallway below her.

"Sorrell, how could you? You promised you would join us for dinner. I knew you wouldn't be interested in attending the lecture with us, but at the very least—"

"I am sorry, Cynthia, but something came up. Something much more important than having dinner with you and your sister," Cassie could hear her brother-in-law say.

"But you haven't even had dinner with us once since Cassia came to London. Honestly, what sort of host—"

"Cynthia, that's enough. We're discussing your sister, not some esteemed guest. I know you are disappointed, but really, you should be aware that my schedule can change at any moment," he said, sounding tired and annoyed.

"Yes, I am aware, and it always seems to change when it is something I wanted to do." Cynthia, too, was beginning to sound irritated.

"That's not fair. It's not even true. I've done plenty of things with you that I had no interest in at all."

"Really? When? When was the last time you escorted me to any sort of society—"

"Oh, come now! My time is a great deal more important than attending some silly party. Really, I've had enough of this. I will see you tomorrow."

"But Sorrell," Cynthia's began to plead.

"Goodnight, Cynthia." Lord Sorrell's footsteps sounded firmly as he left the room and proceeded down the stairs, to the front door which could be heard opening and then closing.

Cynthia had come out of the room to watch her husband leave. When she turned to go back into the drawing room, she caught sight of Cassie standing there on the step. Her face immediately turned bright red. "Oh, Cassie, I didn't see you standing there."

Cassie continued down the stairs, feeling her own face heat with embarrassment at having been witness to a private, marital spat. "I haven't been here long. Er, was that Sorrell I just heard leaving?"

"Yes. I'm afraid he won't be able to join us for dinner after all. Something came up," Cynthia said, walking over to the window.

"Oh, that's a shame," Cassie said. She noticed her sister swipe at her cheek and added quickly, "But not a problem at all. In fact, I'm rather happy he won't be joining us. That gives us the opportunity for you to tell me more about your Wagering Whist Society friends. You know even after I met them at the ball a few days ago, I'm still completely confused as to who's who."

Cynthia turned and gave her a forced smile. "Yes, I did notice that you accidentally called the Duchess of Kendell 'my lady'."

"I did, ugh! I was so embarrassed when she corrected me," Cassie said, going over to the sideboard and pouring out a glass of wine for her sister and herself.

"You should listen more carefully when people are introduced to you," Cynthia said, accepting the wine.

"You're right. I should, and I will definitely try harder next time. Actually, perhaps this evening will be good practice. What do you think?" Cassie asked, happy to see her sister distracted from her troubles.

They had a pleasant dinner and then took Cynthia's carriage to Fleet Street where the Royal Society held its meetings.

The hall where the lecture was to take place was surprisingly small. It only held, perhaps, one hundred people and was only about a quarter-full when Cassie and Cynthia arrived.

"Have you ever been to one of these lectures before?" Cassie asked her sister as they took their seats in the middle of the room.

"Just once," Cynthia admitted.

"Was it this empty?"

Cynthia shook her head. "I believe more people will be coming in late."

Cassie continued to look around, noting there were a few other women besides themselves. That was good. It would have been beyond awkward if they'd been the only females present.

"Good evening, gentlemen and, er, ladies," a gentleman said, approaching the lectern. "We have a fascinating talk for you today by an esteemed physical scientist."

The man droned on for another ten minutes, introducing the speaker who would be talking about his experiments with electricity. The speaker himself was, thankfully, quite animated about his subject. Otherwise, Cassie wasn't entirely certain she could have kept awake for the entire hour-long lecture. She only had to give her sister a nudge once when Cassie noticed her eyes had drifted closed.

"Wha—" Cynthia said with a start when Cassie

elbowed her in the ribs.

"Shhh!"

Cynthia looked around quickly. "Oh." She straightened herself and returned to concentrating on the lecture.

The man finished his talk to polite applause. There was one person who clapped much more loudly and enthusiastically than anyone else. The speaker looked over at him and gave a nod of acknowledgement.

The original speaker then got back up and said, "Thank you, sir, thank you very much for that, ha-ha-ha, electrifying speech." He gave the audience a big smile, and a number of people dutifully chuckled. He cleared his throat and added, "There will be refreshments in the hall. Thank you for joining us this evening."

Cassie stood, along with most others in the room. Her legs were stiff with sitting still for so long.

"Do you want to stay for the refreshments?" Cynthia asked.

"I would like to for a few moments, if that's all right?" Cassie asked. She didn't have any particular reason in mind, but just thought it would be the polite thing to do.

"Yes, of course."

Chapter Seven

Cynthia led the way, following in the wake of a number of other people. They each took a glass of lemonade that tasted more like water that had had a lemon pass within a few feet of it.

"Well, it was quite an interesting talk," Cassie said generally.

"Yes, indeed," Cynthia agreed while looking around at the assembled people.

"Interesting? It was absolutely brilliant!" a gentleman said. He must have been the enthusiastic clapper. He was about the same height as Cassie, with straight black hair and sparkling green eyes.

"Do you study the phenomenon, sir?" Cassie asked.

"I do indeed," the man said. "It is absolutely fascinating. I like to think of myself as following in the esteemed footsteps of Benjamin Franklin, Luigi Galvani, and Alessandro Volta."

"Do you work with animals or metals?" Cassie asked.

The man smiled at her understanding of the burgeoning field. "I work with various types of metals. While Mr. Galvani's experiments with the legs of frogs was fascinating, I am more interested in this concept of holding onto electricity for future use."

"I'm afraid I don't know of these experiments with frogs," Cynthia said, looking a little confused.

"Oh, it was quite interesting if a bit gruesome," Cassie said with a little laugh. "He ran electricity through a frog's legs and they jumped."

"The frog jumped?" Cynthia repeated.

"There wasn't actually any frog attached to the legs," Cassie explained. "It was just the legs of a dead frog."

"Galvani believed all living beings have electricity within their bodies which is what allows us to move," the man explained. "Volta's experiments have shown that the reason the legs jumped was due to the metal used in the experiment."

"It's quite fascinating," Cassie agreed. "But don't you believe there is some validity to Galvani's theories?"

"I do, actually. It has been shown that all living beings, even man, will twitch when electricity is run through them. I don't know if I believe we are walking sources of electricity or possibly stores of the phenomenon," the man answered.

Cassie nodded and wondered whether the same would be true of plants, if they would move on their own if electricity was run through them.

"I am Humphrey Crome," the man said, giving her and Cynthia a bow.

"I am Miss Cassia Benton, and this is my sister, Lady Sorrell," Cassie said, taking the lead since it had been her that he'd mainly been speaking with.

"Miss Benton, Lady Sorrell, it is a pleasure," he said. "Your knowledge of the natural sciences is quite impressive, Miss Benton."

"Thank you. I like to keep abreast of what is going on in the world of natural philosophy," she said.

"I do as well, but I suppose my reading has fallen sadly behind in the subject," her sister said.

"Well, it's hard to keep up with everything," Cassie said.

"And you've read all the scientific journals, I suppose," Cynthia commented.

"Naturally."

"Do you consider yourself to be a lady scientist?" Mr. Crome asked curiously.

"I dabble in botany," Cassie admitted.

"Dabble is not the word. My sister is being modest. She does incredible work with roses, sir," Cynthia said, giving Cassie a proud smile.

"Well..." Cassie said demurely.

"How fascinating! And an entirely appropriate subject for a young lady," Mr. Crome said approvingly.

"I am working on attempting to breed new variations on the species," Cassie said, wondering if he would think it appropriate for a young lady to work with the sexual organs of the plants as she did.

"Really, how very nice," the gentleman said with a vague smile. He clearly had no idea of the implications of breeding flowers. Perhaps that was just as well.

He then spent the next ten minutes attempting to explain his work to her and her sister in overly simplistic terms. Cassie appreciated his thoughtfulness, if not the implicit assumption that neither she nor Cynthia would understand the complicated nature of his studies. His detailed explanation was cut short however when the speaker passed them. "Oh, sir, sir..." Mr. Crome said, beginning to call after the man. He briefly turned back to Cassie to say, "I beg your pardon, ladies. It was lovely meeting you."

"And you—" Cassie started, but a moment later she would have been speaking to empty air.

"Well, that was interesting," Cynthia said, leading the way out of the hall.

"Indeed, and Mr. Crome seemed to be a fascinating man doing important work as well," Cassie agreed. She did sincerely hope to meet him again the following week when they returned for the next lecture. She thought she might like to further this acquaintance.

~*~

"How was your meeting today?" Lady Kineton asked that evening at dinner. Archer's friend had had another engagement, so it was just Archer and the lady. It was only slightly awkward since they didn't know each other very well, but he supposed he should be grateful she hadn't ordered a tray to her room instead of keeping him company.

"It was interesting," Archer admitted, cutting a piece of meat on his plate. He loaded up his fork but didn't pop it directly into his mouth quite yet.

"Who was it with?" she asked, giving him a smile. "Kineton told me you were out at a meeting earlier but didn't give me any details."

"Oh!" Archer returned her smile. "It was with Lord Sorrell." He ate the food off his fork.

"My, my, you are reaching high, aren't you?" she said, impressed.

"I don't know about that..." he started after

swallowing.

"Lord Sorrell is quite prestigious within Parliament. Some have even wondered if he wasn't positioning himself to move into a minister's position."

"Really? Well, I was simply there to ask him if he'd personally be interesting in investing in my business."

"And was he?" she asked, taking a sip from her wine glass which had just been refilled by an attentive footman.

"No, sadly, he wasn't," Archer admitted.

"I am sorry. But he was an interesting person to speak with?" she asked, probing a little before continuing to eat her own dinner.

"He was, but I have to admit it wasn't specifically my meeting with him that I found most interesting about my time at the Sorrell home."

"Oh?"

"I had the, er, pleasure of meeting Miss Benton, his sister-in-law, while I was waiting for his lordship." He couldn't help the smile that grew on his face. He hid it behind his wine glass as he lifted it for a drink.

"Oh-ho," the lady said with a lift of her eyebrows. She leaned forward. "Tell me more."

Archer laughed. "It's not at all what you may be thinking. The young lady was apparently called in from the garden to entertain me while I awaited Lord Sorrell. She made it abundantly clear she was not pleased."

"What? How unusual!"

"I thought so myself," he admitted. "Never have I been made to feel more insignificant by a young lady. You would think she had absolutely no interest in men or finding a husband, despite the fact that Kineton, himself, introduced us last night at the ball. I am pretty certain he did so because he knows she is on the look out for a husband."

"But not you?" the lady asked with a little laugh.

Archer shrugged. "I guess not. Although, being dismissed like that only makes me all the more eager to get to know the lady better."

"Ah, so you're that sort, are you?"

"What sort is that?"

"You like a challenge," she said, smiling behind her own wine glass. "Kineton isn't like that. He likes a sure-thing. It was almost too easy to bring him up to scratch."

Archer laughed. He knew precisely why his friend was so eager to marry this woman and, sadly, it had nothing to do with her personality. But she must be aware of that. He knew of the agreement Kineton and his wife had—both free to pursue their own interests so long as they were discreet. It was far from a love-match.

"I do like a challenge," he admitted to his friend's wife. "Not only that, but for her to find gardening more interesting than me? No, no, it's too much. I simply can't allow such a slight to just sit."

Lady Kineton laughed. "It's a wonder that you're willing to waste your time on such a mouse when you are so much more of a lion." Her eyes widened ever so slightly before narrowing seductively.

Archer, however, was not going to get caught in that trap. He'd seen what sort of woman his friend had married, and he wasn't going to join the ranks of men willing to cuckold Kineton. He returned his attention to his plate instead.

The lady clearly wasn't going to be put off, however. "So what are you going to do about it?" she asked, leaning forward provocatively.

"I believe a charm offensive is in order, don't you?" he asked, keeping his gaze from where it had no business being, despite the fact that the lady's charms were on full display.

She leaned back again and nodded, understanding that he was not going to play her game. Still, a smile spread across her perfect, bow-shaped lips. "Indeed, I do."

~April 11~

Archer walked into Lady Bradmore's ballroom, pausing just inside the door. His eyes found the quarry immediately, and he allowed a smile to spread slowly across his face.

Miss Benton was standing not too far off with her sister and some other ladies. Her eyes were scanning the room as she listened to one of the other women speaking. He could see the moment she caught sight of him because her beautiful lips parted ever so slightly, and she immediately turned back to her friend, pretending she hadn't seen him.

"Good evening, Miss Benton," he said to himself. "Challenge accepted."

It wouldn't do to seem overly eager, however. Archer knew that much. He sauntered over to a few men he'd met at the last ball he'd attended. "Good evening, gentlemen," he said, giving them all a slight bow.

"Ah, Fitzwalter," one older man said, giving him a nod and stroking the thick sideburns that reached toward his mouth.

"You look like you're on the hunt," one of the younger men said with a laugh.

"You saw that too, Hershawn? The way he stopped, took stock of the room, and then came over here?" Another fellow, a Lord Featherington if Archer wasn't mistaken.

"It was hard to miss," Hershawn said with a laugh.

"I cannot deny your acute assessment, Mr. Hershawn, Lord Featherington," Archer said with a conspiratorial smile.

"So, who is it you're after?" Featherington asked.

"Miss Benton," Archer said, nodding in her direction.

"She's Lady Sorrell's younger sister, isn't she?" Hershawn asked. "Met her the other night. Had a dance with her. Nice girl, if a bit quiet. But is she really your type, Fitzwalter? She's a bit of a bluestocking."

"A bluestocking?" Archer asked. He wasn't sure how he felt about intellectual girls. Well, at least she would be able to hold a decent conversation, if she ever deigned to speak with him, that is. "I'll give it a try. Wish me luck," he said with a shrug.

Featherington laughed. "Don't think it's luck a fellow like you needs."

Archer turned back and gave the fellow a wink before making a beeline toward the ladies.

"Good evening, Lady Sorrell," he said, joining them. "Miss Benton, how lovely to see you again, and looking so clean too," he said with his most charming smile.

She gave a little snort of laughter.

At least she has a sense of humor, he thought.

"Clean? Cassia? Rarely," another young lady

giggled.

"Mr. Fitzwalter, may I introduce my very good friend, Miss Sherman? She knows of my predilection for dirt. Gwendolyn, this is Lord Kineton's friend, Mr. Fitzwalter," Miss Benton said.

Gwendolyn gave him a curtsey as he bowed. "It is a pleasure, Mr. Fitzwalter."

"The last time Mr. Fitzwalter and I had the pleasure of meeting, I had been called in from the garden. I'm afraid I didn't have time to change before my presence was required in the drawing room. Otherwise, I would have been clean. I am trying to mend my ways," Miss Benton explained.

"And of course, you'd forgotten to wear your apron, hadn't you?" her sister asked.

"When have I ever remembered?" Miss Benton responded with a laugh.

Lady Sorrell just shook her head and sighed. She turned to him. "My apologies, Mr. Fitzwalter. My sister is incorrigible."

He smiled at them both. "It's perfectly all right. I simply wanted to apologize for having pulled the young lady away from her occupation."

"Well..." Miss Benton started.

"I'm sure it was perfectly fine," Lady Sorrell said, giving her sister a significant sidelong glance.

"Pulling Cassia away from the garden?" Miss Sherman asked in disbelief.

"Yes, even that. When duty calls, it doesn't matter what you're doing, does it, Cassia?" Lady Sorrell asked her sister pointedly, sounding more like a mother than a sister, but perhaps that was the way older sisters sounded. Archer didn't know. He was an only child.

Chapter Eight

"Well, in any case, I did want to try to make it up to you. Would a dance suffice?" he asked.

"For time from my roses? I don't—"

"She would be honored to dance with you, Mr. Fitzwalter," Lady Sorrell said, cutting Miss Benton off.

"Indeed, she likes dancing a great deal and is very good at it," Miss Sherman added before Miss Benton herself could say anything further.

She looked from her sister to her friend and back again before finally turning to Archer. She gave him a resigned look and said in an almost rote manner, "I would love to dance, thank you so much, sir."

"If you'd rather not..." he started, not knowing what to make of this girl. He was wondering if she would be worth the challenge.

"Oh, no, she would truly love to. Don't listen to her," Miss Sherman assured him.

Miss Benton gave a little shrug, so he offered her his hand, and she gracefully placed her own into it.

Luckily there was a set just forming, so they joined in.

"I don't seem to be able to do anything right in your eyes, Miss Benton. Please tell me how I can fix this?" he said, giving it another try after bowing to her at the start of the dance.

"It's not that you're doing anything wrong. I'm afraid I'm just not good at all this socializing," she admitted. "I'm sorry if you have misunderstood my reluctance as anything directed against you, personally. I assure you, it is me, not you."

"That is very kind to say. I have to admit, I haven't had a great deal of experience with this sort of thing myself. You know, I've only just recently returned from India," he said. The fact always seemed to fascinate girls.

"Oh, really? How interesting!" she responded as all had. "What was it that took you to the subcontinent?"

"I was employed by the East India Company," he said. Normally, he would have told her straight out that he was in the army, but with this girl, he imagined she wouldn't be so impressed with valor and uniforms as most.

"Ah, in the managing of their territories or on the business side?" she asked with more knowledge of the situation than he expected.

"I was a lieutenant in their army," he admitted. "My father purchased a commission for me, hoping I would learn restraint."

"And did you?" she asked, looking highly amused.

"What I learned was that the East India Company cares very little for the people of India," he admitted.

She blinked up at him. "But is that not to be expected? Don't all colonizers treat native populations as if they were not worth the dirt on their boots?"

He gave a nod of agreement as the dance took them apart again. This girl was most definitely of a different sort, and yet, Archer found himself absolutely fascinated by her brutal honesty and keen understanding.

"So what made you decide to leave the army, if I may ask?" she asked when they came back together again.

"An overwhelming desire to do something good for the people of Southern India," he said. "I'm going to start a business to import the spices they grow there and pay them appropriately rather than the pittance they are receiving now."

"I can't imagine that will be very profitable," she pointed out.

"I'm going to do my best to make it so, by cutting costs in other places. I've got plans," he told her succinctly.

She seemed to accept that this wasn't the place to get into the details. As they turned in a round-about she said, "They do have incredible spices there, don't they? I have to admit, I have only tasted a very few—the salt and pepper, of course—but there are so many more. Mustard, anise, coriander, cumin, and what else?" she asked before the movements of the dance took them in opposite directions.

"You are clearly very well informed," he commented when they moved back together again. "There are a great many more spices than that. We don't use half of them in our cooking, but there is a growing demand for a number of them here in England."

"I do like to keep up with what's going on

around the world," she admitted. "Wasn't there a mutiny of sorts in Madras a few years ago?"

They moved apart once more, but when he took her hands to move her about in a circle, he said, "Yes! The Vellore Mutiny. You are remarkably knowledgeable. I don't think many gentlemen I've spoken to remember or even knew of that."

She gave a little shrug and gave him a smile.

This girl was a great deal more intriguing than he'd guessed. He was definitely going to have to get to know her better.

They discussed Madras and what it was like living in India for the rest of the dance. It was definitely the most fascinating experience he'd had since he'd arrived back in London. They were just returning to Lady Sorrell when Miss Benton stopped for a moment. She took in the gentleman standing by her sister's side and then nearly ran the rest of the way. "Mr. Crome! What a great surprise this is!" she exclaimed as Archer followed behind her.

"Ah, Miss Benton, how lovely it is to see you again," the man said. He smiled much too warmly for Archer's taste. In fact, he didn't like how she was smiling at this fellow, either.

"I didn't realize you came to society parties," Miss Benton said.

"I don't, usually, but after meeting you and your lovely sister the other night, I thought I might do so. Of course, I know the Bradmores, so they were kind enough to allow me to join the party."

Archer couldn't believe this brilliant girl was more interested in Mr. Boring than himself, and yet, she was practically salivating on the man. He didn't like this development at all.

~*~

Cassie was so amazed to see Mr. Crome here at a ball! She hadn't realized he was a member of the ton but was very happy to meet him.

It was Cynthia who recalled Mr. Fitzwalter's presence and introduced the two men. They shook hands and then Mr. Fitzwalter asked, "Where did you have the pleasure of meeting these lovely sisters?"

"At the Royal Society meeting," Mr. Crome answered, but Archer didn't know what this Royal Society was. He looked to Miss Benton for more of an explanation.

"My sister and I attended a fascinating lecture on conductive metals used in electricity," she explained, "and met Mr. Crome afterward." She turned to the gentleman in question. "Do you know, I'm still thinking about that talk and wondering whether conductivity of copper makes it easier or more difficult for Mr. Volta's battery—"

Lady Sorrell began to laugh and cut her off. "My sister can get so very involved in these sorts of discussions, but naturally, they're not exactly your usual topic of conversation at a ball. Mr. Crome, do tell us how you know the Bradmores."

"Oh, er, of course." The man looked flustered for a moment, then said, "Bradmore and my brother were in school together and became close friends. Eton. Naturally, I chased after them as most younger brothers do, trying to ape them. Er, my elder brother is Earl Midton." He then turned to Cassie and added, "I do hope we'll be able to continue our discussion at a more appropriate time."

"As do I," she agreed.

"Earl Midton? Isn't he the gentleman Lord Colburne resuscitated the year before last?" Cynthia asked.

"Yes! Why, yes, indeed, that's right," Mr. Crome said, giving her a smile.

"He's a brilliant doctor, Lord Colburne. Lord Midton collapsed at a party, but luckily Lord Colburne was there," Cynthia explained to Mr. Fitzwalter. "And how has your brother been doing since then?"

"Quite well, actually. Lord Colburne has continued his care and, while my brother has had to watch his diet and go a bit easy, he's doing very well. Thank you for asking," Mr. Crome said, giving her a slight bow.

"How very fortunate Lord Colburne was there and able to do something. I had the pleasure of a long conversation with him when he and Lady Colburne joined us for dinner not long ago," Cassie said.

"Indeed!" Mr. Crome agreed.

Cassie suddenly remembered when she and Mr. Crome could meet. "My sister will be having an at-home tomorrow, Mr. Crome. Perhaps we can continue our conversation then?"

"That would be lovely."

"And perhaps, I can show you my garden," she said, giving him a warm smile.

His return smile contained all the enthusiasm she could hope for. "That would be wonderful! I would like that a great deal."

Mr. Fitzwalter gave a little laugh. "You're quite attached to your garden, aren't you?"

Cassie frowned at him. "Yes, I am. Do you have a problem with this, Mr. Fitzwalter?"

He sobered up immediately. "Er, no, not at all.

If you'll excuse me, I see a friend of mine. Enjoy the rest of your evening."

"What a very odd man," Mr. Crome commented after he'd left.

"Yes. I'm not entirely certain what to make of him. But he has had some very interesting experiences in India," Cassie admitted with a slight shrug. She was much more interested in Mr. Crome, however, and looked forward to getting to know him better.

That joy looked like it was going to have to wait as Cynthia's friend, Lydia, and another woman joined them.

"Good evening Lady Sorrell, Miss Benton," Lydia said, giving them both a smile. "Miss Benton, do you know Lady Moreton? She's another member of the Whist Society."

Cassie gave the woman a curtsey. She looked to be about Cynthia's age, maybe a year or two younger.

"And this is Mr. Crome," Cynthia said, introducing him to her friends.

They exchanged greetings and then Lady Moreton asked, "Was that Lord Kineton's friend who was just here speaking with you?"

"Yes, it was," she answered. "Did you want to meet him? He's very nice." Cynthia gave the lady a broad smile.

"Oh, no!" The lady gave an embarrassed laugh. "I was just wondering. I was speaking with some other ladies, and they were asking about him, seeing as he's new to town."

"And has been seen dancing with quite a few young ladies," Lydia added with a little giggle.

"Including quite a few wallflowers, which is quite lovely," Lady Moreton added.

Cassie's good opinion of the man ticked up a notch. Any gentleman who paid particular attention to the shyer girls of society was a good man.

"I'm sure a gentleman such as he isn't overly discriminating," Mr. Crome said with a slight smile.

Cassie looked at him and wondered what he meant by that. "I think it's wonderful that he does so. It's a true affliction to be so shy that you can't put yourself forward."

The man sobered immediately. "Oh, indeed! I just meant... well, I, er, too, find myself feeling quite shy at times. It's, er, why I don't come to many society parties."

"I'm very sorry to hear that. Perhaps if you tried to come to more parties and got to know more people, it would help," Cassie suggested. "I've always thought of myself as rather shy, but now that I know people, coming to parties is becoming easier."

"Really?" he asked, giving her a sweet smile.

"Yes, although, I do still become a little overwhelmed at times," she admitted. She was about to mention that a walk in the garden was the perfect remedy for that, but refrained from doing so, lest she look as if she were asking for such an invitation—which would be highly inappropriate.

He gave her a slight bow. "I completely understand, Miss Benton. Thank you for your understanding. I think I might begin to attend more functions, especially now that I know you... er, and your lovely sister, of course."

Cassie did her best to hold back her giggles, but she shared a look with Cynthia. The gentleman was doing his best to be charming, and she greatly appreciated that.

~April 12~

Cynthia had just given orders to the maid to bring up the tea and cakes when already there could be heard a knock at the door. She looked over at Cassie. "I wonder who that could be so early?"

Cassie widened her eyes at her sister and gave a little shrug. "I suppose we'll find out in a moment," she said with a little laugh.

Mr. Crome was announced a moment later.

He paused just inside the door to bow to the ladies and look around at the large, empty room. "Oh, dear, I seem to have arrived too early," he said with some embarrassment.

"No, no, you are right on time," Cynthia said, coming over to meet him.

"I'm afraid I'm not very practiced at these sorts of things. It's been a while since I took part in society," he admitted.

Cassie gave him a little curtsey, and Cynthia invited him to take a seat.

"You said last night that your brother is Lord Midton, so presumably you have had some experience..." Cynthia started.

"One would think," Mr. Crome admitted. He gave them an apologetic little smile. "However, as I was always rather, er, shy. I kept to myself a great deal as a young man, focusing on my studies instead of socializing as most do."

"I completely understand," Cassie said. "The only reason why I know how to go on properly is because my mother sent me to a school for young ladies where I had no choice but to attend classes in deportment, dancing, and such."

"All the things young ladies are supposed to know," Mr. Crome said with a smile and a nod.

"Precisely," Cassie agreed. "But which I had absolutely no interest in learning, I can assure you."

"And yet, you did very well there and now know all that you should," Cynthia pointed.

"Thanks to my friends. I'm sure I would have gotten myself kicked out if it weren't for the Kendrick twins and Gwendolyn," Cassie admitted.

"Sent down? Certainly not! They wouldn't have—" Mr. Crome began.

"It was entirely my intention to be sent home when I was forced to attend against my will," Cassie admitted. "But as I say, I made friends, and then I didn't want to leave."

"Thank goodness for the twins and Miss Sherman! I never realized what a debt we owe to them!" Cynthia said with a little laugh.

"So much more than you realize," Cassie said. "On the other hand, if it hadn't been for me, Bel and Gwendolyn would certainly have failed their classes in Natural Philosophy."

"So it was a fair exchange," Mr. Crome said, nodding his approval.

"Miss Sherman and Lady St. Vincent," the footman announced, coming into the room.

Chapter Nine

S peaking of whom," Cassie said, jumping up to greet her friends.

"Whom?" Bee asked, coming into the room and giving Cynthia and Mr. Crome a small curtsey.

Gwendolyn followed her lead and looked expectantly at Cassie for her answer.

"You and your sister and Gwendolyn," Cassie explained. "I was just telling Mr. Crome how I couldn't have gotten through school without you."

"Oh," Bee nodded.

"Goodness, no!" Gwendolyn agreed. "She was just awful and hardly even tried in so many of the classes—deportment, music, water colors..."

"I'm not that bad in water colors," Cassie protested.

"So long as you were painting roses, you were fine," Gwendolyn agreed with a laugh.

"Ah, speaking of which, you were going to show me your garden, Miss Benton," Mr. Crome said.

"Yes, I was." Cassie turned to Cynthia. "Do you mind?"

"No, but only because most people haven't arrived yet. But don't take too long, all right?" her sister said.

"Do you want to come?" Cassie asked her friends.

"No, thank you, we'll, uh, we'll see it another time," Bee said quickly before Gwendolyn could answer. Bee gave Gwendolyn a significant look.

Gwendolyn raised her eyebrows a touch and then smiled at Mr. Crome. She said nothing, so Cassie gave them both a nod and turned to Mr. Crome to indicate he should follow her.

She knew what her friends were doing, and she appreciated it. She did want to have some time alone with the gentleman.

She led him down to the breakfast room where most of her plants were enjoying the sunlight on the dining table, which had been pushed closer to the windows.

~*~

As Archer was shown into Lady Sorrell's drawing room, he was at least assured he would be greeted with a bit more enthusiasm than he had the last time he'd been there.

"Mr. Fitzwalter, how lovely to see you," Lady Sorrell said, welcoming him.

He paused to bow to her. There were four other men in the room and a number of ladies, many of whom he didn't know. Noticeably missing was Miss Benton. "Thank you so much, my lady. I do hope your sister isn't feeling any ill effects from last night's party?"

"Oh, no," the lady said. "She's just showing Mr. Crome her roses. I believe you were there when she promised to do so last night?"

"Yes, indeed, I was," he admitted. What was it with this girl and flowers? "She seems to be inordinately fond of her garden. Is Mr. Crome a botanist or some such thing?" he asked, realizing he was beginning to sound a touch peevish.

"No, he studies electricity, so I understand. My sister, however—"

"They aren't alone, are they?" he asked, interrupting. If he were into the physical sciences, then what was she doing showing him her garden? It just didn't make any sense.

"They are, but knowing my sister, she has nothing else on her mind but her roses. At least not when she's showing off her latest—"

"How unusual," he said, trying not to sound as if he were accusing the lady of being a bad chaperone, when in fact that was precisely what he meant to say. "Perhaps I should join them."

"Oh, I'm sure they'll be back any moment," the lady said, and indeed, as she did so, Miss Benton and Mr. Crome walked into the room. They were both smiling and laughing at something, making Archer practically growl with annoyance. No, clearly Lady Sorrell was being entirely too lax in her duties. There was nothing he could say, however, so instead he joined the couple, forcibly pulling the corners of his lips up into a smile. "Miss Benton, how do you do?"

"Oh, Mr. Fitzwalter, you came! Goodness, look at how many people have arrived." She turned to Mr. Crome with a bright smile. "I suppose we took a little longer in the garden than we should have."

"But it was most interesting," the gentleman said. "Your roses are adorable."

Adorable? How could flowers be adorable? Archer was confused, and clearly Miss Benton was as well because her smile faltered ever so slightly.

"If you would please excuse me, I should greet

the other guests," she started. Her sister came over just at that moment, perhaps to remind Miss Benton of her duties.

"Before you do so," Archer said, capturing her attention again before she ran off. "I was wondering if you were available tomorrow for a ride in the park?"

"Oh! Er," she hedged.

"Of course she is," Lady Sorrell said, quickly filling in the gap. "I think that sounds like a wonderful idea. Cassia loves the park, and getting some fresh air and exercise is just what you need, isn't it?" she asked turning to her sister with a meaningful look.

"Yes, yes, of course," Miss Benton said. She clearly had no other choice but to do so, but Archer would accept that.

So long as she was entirely his for an hour or so, he almost didn't care how she got there. Of course, he was fully confident that once he had her alone, he would be able to make her forget entirely about the scientist. Honestly, could a man get any more boring than that? "Excellent. I'll pick you up tomorrow around this time?" he asked.

"All right. That sounds lovely, thank you," Miss Benton said, giving him a polite smile.

He watched her walk away, quite pleased with himself. Crome might have had fifteen minutes alone with her, but he would have an afternoon.

~April 13~

Cynthia entered Lady Ayres' drawing room on Wednesday afternoon and looked happily around at the ladies who'd gathered for their weekly card game. They'd met last week, but not everyone had, as yet, returned, and the season hadn't truly begun.

Now, finally, everything was back to normal, and it felt so very good, so right.

"Everything all right, Cynthia?" Lady Welles asked, startling Cynthia. She hadn't seen the young woman come in behind her.

"Oh! Yes, Lydia, thank you. It's just so wonderful to have the group back again, that's all," she said.

The girl smiled and looked around the room. "I cannot but agree with you. Is everyone else here?"

Cynthia looked around the room once again. "Everyone but Mrs. Aldridge, er..." She laughed at her mistake. "I mean, Duchess Bolton."

Lydia covered her mouth as she giggled. "It is so difficult when a lady marries, isn't it?"

"Ladies, ladies," Lady Ayres called out. She gave a little clap of her hands to get everyone's attention. "Are we all here? Shall we get started?"

"Oh, I do beg your pardon," Duchess Bolton said, coming in slightly out of breath. "Am I late?"

"You are just on time, Duchess," Lady Ayres said, giving her a smile.

"Goodness, we've got two duchesses!" Diana exclaimed, looking from the new Duchess Bolton to the Duchess of Kendell.

"Well, I shan't be a duchess for very long," the Duchess of Kendell pointed out. "Lord Gorling and I will be marrying on the first of May."

"And you don't need to address me as duchess," the new duchess said. "I was Mrs. Aldridge for nearly forty years! You can't imagine how difficult it is to be addressed by a different name."

"But indeed, Your Grace, it is your name now, and so we must address you as such," Lady

Blakemore pointed. "You'll get used it."

"But where is Duchess, Your Grace?" Lady Moreton asked. "Er... your dog," she added quickly.

The duchess laughed. "She is with her new stepbrothers and sisters. Bolton has four dogs of the same breed, you know. She is so happy being with them. I just didn't have the heart to bring her away."

"Well, there is yet another benefit of your new arrangement," the Duchess of Kendell said with a little chuckle.

"Yes, you won't need to contend with my little pup... at least not today. I'm sure I will be bringing her with me sometimes, however," Duchess Bolton said.

"Ah well..." the Duchess of Kendell said with a little sigh.

"We really should have a party to celebrate all of our new marriages," Lydia said. "We had so many last season."

"Indeed! There are the Kendrick twins, who are now Lady Conway and Lady St. Vincent, our new duchess, Lady Margaret who is now Lady Rossburke, the new Mrs. Aldridge, and soon the Duchess of Kendell who will become Lady Gorling," Lady Ayres said, ticking them off her fingers.

"Six weddings! That's got to be a record!" Diana exclaimed.

"Well, certainly for us," Lydia laughed.

"Oh, and speaking of such things, Lady Sorrell, how is your sister managing with her debut? I know you were worried about her," Duchess Bolton asked.

Cynthia turned and smiled at the kind older lady. She was always thinking of others. "She is doing very well, thank you for asking."

"Does she have any admirers yet?" Lady Ayres asked. "I'm afraid I haven't had a chance to attend very many parties."

"She has two, I'm very happy to say. Two very different gentlemen," Cynthia said, reaching forward to help herself to one of the delicious butter biscuits Lady Ayres always put out.

"Oh?" Diana asked. "Is one of them the tall, blond gentleman I saw her dancing with the other night?"

"Yes. That is Mr. Fitzwalter. He's just returned from India, I understand, where he was working with the East India Company," Cynthia offered.

"A working man?" Lady Blakemore asked sounding slightly horrified.

"Do you know who his family is?" Lady Ayres asked.

"His father is Baron Fitzwalter. That's all I know," Cynthia admitted. "The other gentleman is a Mr. Crome, who is the brother of the Earl of Midton. We met him at a lecture at the Royal Society of Natural Sciences and then again at the Bradmore's ball."

"That's unfortunate," the Duchess of Kendell said quietly.

Cynthia turned toward her. "What's unfortunate, Your Grace?"

"Oh, er, nothing, just that Miss Benton isn't being courted by any titled gentlemen as yet. I'm sure she will, however. She's a very fetching girl," the lady said, giving Cynthia a condescending smile.

"Well, but both are of the nobility," Lydia pointed out.

"Yes, indeed, they are. I would expect nothing less. I simply hope... well, I'm certain that you know best, my lady. She is your sister," the duchess said.

"What is it you're thinking of, Your Grace?" Cynthia asked, becoming more and more worried that she wasn't doing a very good job at being a chaperone to Cassia.

"Well, I do hope they are not fortune hunters, that's all," the woman admitted. "It is so very difficult for a girl from a good family such as yours. You need to be especially vigilant, that's all."

Fortune hunters? Cynthia had never even thought of such a thing! My goodness, she was a terrible chaperone!

"But I'm certain you are doing your due diligence in regards to these gentlemen," the duchess continued.

Cynthia gave her a small smile. "Of course." She was definitely going to have to do something!

"Of course she is!" Diana said, immediately jumping to Cynthia's defense.

"And with that, shall we get started with our game?" Lady Ayes said, redirecting the women to the real reason why they were all there.

~*~

Archer picked up Miss Benton at precisely three o'clock. He helped her up onto her horse and then mounted the one he'd borrowed from Kineton. His friend had always had excellent taste in horseflesh.

He looked over at his companion. She was looking quite stunning in a riding habit of deep green, which brought out the green of her eyes and the pink in her cheeks.

She was eagerly looking all around as they rode toward the park.

"I hear the park is the place to be in the afternoons," she commented after they'd exchanged the ordinary pleasantries.

"It absolutely is the best place to be. You meet everybody," he said, feeling his excitement rise as they entered the park. He loved this more than anything. He loved meeting people, seeing who was with whom, and what everyone was wearing. He loved recognizing those he'd met and being recognized. "There is nothing more thrilling than riding down Rotten Row on a beautiful afternoon. Especially when I have such a beautiful woman by my side," he said, smiling at her.

Miss Benton flushed prettily, and Archer knew his dart had hit its mark. That was one thing about a bluestocking, he thought, they were so easy to charm. Mr. Boring would be a fuzzy memory she would hardly be able to recall by the time he returned her home this afternoon.

"My goodness, look at all the people!" was all Miss Benton could say, clearly amazed at the crowd walking, riding, and in carriages.

"It is wonderful, isn't it?" he asked, looking about.

"You seem to be exceedingly comfortable with people," she said, looking over at him with a critical eye.

"Yes, I am," he acknowledged.

"How do you do it?"

"How do I do what?" he asked. She'd lost him.

"Be comfortable. Know what to say, how to be so charming," she said. "I simply get tongue-tied and wind up staying awkwardly silent. Or I become too overwhelmed by all the people and noise," she said, turning and looking all around them.

For a moment, his heart went out to this poor girl. She truly had no idea how to go on in society, and clearly her sister wasn't assisting her in any significant way.

"I..." he started, but then stopped to think about it. "I wish I knew," he admitted. "I simply say what I think someone might like to hear."

"Even if it's not the truth?" she asked.

"I never lie." He wondered if he should be offended.

"Oh, no! I didn't mean to imply that you did. But perhaps... you exaggerate the truth a little?"

"What do you mean?"

"Well, when you say that I'm beautiful. I know very well that I am not, and yet the words just slip so easily off your tongue," she said, her voice becoming so quiet he could hardly hear her.

"Who said you weren't beautiful?" he demanded.

She gave a little laugh. "My mirror, Mr. Fitzwalter."

"Well, then I believe you need a new one because the one you have clearly isn't showing your true reflection."

Chapter Ten

"Miss Benton! Miss Benton!" a woman's voice called from the walkway.

Archer's companion looked over. "Oh! Bee! Bel!" Miss Benton called out and waved. She seemed extremely relieved at the interruption.

The women she was waving to had Archer taking a second look. They were identical twins, each walking with a gentleman on their arm. He remembered them from Lady Sorrell's home the previous afternoon. Archer hadn't had a chance to be introduced to them then, however.

As they drew up abreast of her friends, they both pulled their mounts to a standstill.

"Good afternoon, Lord Conway, Lord St. Vincent," Miss Benton called out.

Her friends came to the rail to say hello.

"Do you know Mr. Fitzwalter?" Miss Benton said, introducing him.

He doffed his hat. "Good afternoon."

The other gentlemen did the same, and the ladies nodded.

"We won't keep you. People get very unpleasant if you hold up the flow of traffic," one of the women said with a laugh.

"But we did want to say hello," the other said.

"Enjoy your ride," the first said, looking more at Miss Benton than Archer, as if there were some hidden meaning to her words.

They resumed their place in the line of horses and vehicles. "Well, it looks as if your social skills aren't as bad as you feared," he said. "I believe I saw those two ladies at your sister's yesterday."

"But Bee and Bel don't really count. They are my closest friends. Beatrice and Isabel Ken—, I beg your pardon. They were both married last summer," she said with a shake of her head. "They are Lady Conway and Lady St. Vincent. We went to school together."

"Along with Miss Sherman?" he asked, remembering the young lady Miss Benton had introduced him to at Lady Bradmore's ball.

"Yes, that's right. You have an excellent memory," she commented, giving him an approving smile. "I am absolutely horrid with names," she admitted.

~*~

"That can be embarrassing," he said.

"It is! Somehow, I can remember all the Latin names of flowers and all the different breeds of roses, but introduce me to a person and their name escapes me five minutes after I've met them." She gave a rueful shake of her head.

He frowned. "I don't understand. Why would you need to know the Latin names of flowers and, what was it? Breeds of roses?"

She was silent, so he turned and looked at her. She was just staring at him with a confused look on her face. "Do you not know?"

"Know what?"

She gave a little laugh. "I am a botanist. I breed roses."

"Really? I did not know that! Well, that explains a great deal," he said, thinking about it.

"What does it explain?"

"Well, mainly why you were so angry to be forced to leave your garden to meet me last week," he explained, finally beginning to piece things together into a logical whole.

She burst out laughing. "Yes! That's correct. I had just been planting some new specimens in Cynthia's garden when I was called inside."

"Tell me more about the roses you breed," he said, both out of curiosity and because he was certain that it would immediately endear him to her further.

Fifteen minutes later, he almost wished he'd kept his mouth shut. He'd never heard more detail about one subject since he'd been in school. It was the greatest relief when he heard his name being called. He looked around to find Lord Lonsdale waving his hat at him. He pulled his mount up alongside the gentleman's barouche.

"Good afternoon, my lord—" Archer started.

"I have a bone to pick with you, my lad," the man said, feigning anger. It would have been convincing but for the twitching smile. "You said you would pay a call on my MaryAnn, and I have not seen hide nor hair of you these past two weeks."

"May I present Miss Benton?" Archer asked, deftly ignoring the gentleman. "I had the pleasure of Lord Lonsdale's company on the journey from Madras," he told Miss Benton.

"Oh, you were in India as well! Was it as fascinating as Mr. Fitzwalter makes it out to be?" she asked.

"It was indeed, my gel. And if it weren't for the heat and general filth of the place, I would probably still be there," the man said, giving her a warm smile. "All right, Fitzwalter, I can see why you may have been too busy to meet my daughter, but—"

"I assure you, my lord, I shall do my utmost to get there this coming week. I promise," Archer said quickly.

"See that you do!" he said, tapping his driver's back to let him know he could continue onward.

Miss Benton was laughing quietly as the man pulled away. "He seems to be a very determined father."

"He is that," Archer acknowledged. "He is also a very kind gentleman. I will go and meet his MaryAnn. I promised I would."

They'd nearly reached the end of Rotten Row, and Archer was wondering if they should simply turn around or continue on and follow the road which, presumably, led through to another gate.

"What is that?" Miss Benton asked, stopping abruptly and looking off past the end of the road.

Archer looked to see where she was pointing. "It appears to be some sort of ditch and a wall."

"It's a ha-ha, but what is on the other side of it?"

"A ha-ha?" Archer asked.

"Yes, it's sort of a sunken fence," Miss Benton explained.

"Oh. Beyond it, just seems to be more gardens," Archer said, peering ahead.

"Gardens? Do you think they are open to the public?" Miss Benton asked, trying to see. To him, they just looked like a continuation of the park, but perhaps to a botanist it looked a great deal more interesting. And if they were interesting to Miss Benton, he thought they might be quite interesting to him as well.

"I don't see why not. Why, what do you find so interesting over there?"

"I see some roses," she said, sitting up taller in her saddle, trying to get a better view. "They don't look like the ordinary English rose either, but I'm too far away to be able to see properly."

Archer looked in the direction Miss Benton had pointed and could just make out some pale-colored flowers. How could she even tell they were roses from this distance? "Well, there's only one way to see them up close." She turned to look at him, confusion writ across her face.

"How?"

He shrugged. "Go there. Come on!" He spurred his horse and took off at a gallop across the grass. There were a few people walking along the lawn, but he easily rode around them and headed straight for the wall. It would be easy enough to jump. Even the most inexperienced rider wouldn't have trouble with it, he was certain.

He'd just cleared the wall and turned his horse around to see how Miss Benton was coming along, when he discovered that she hadn't even moved from where he'd left her. She was sitting atop her horse with her mouth hanging open. He motioned for her to join him, but she shook her head and indicated that she would be taking the road.

Did the girl have no sense of adventure at all?

~*~

Cassie simply could not believe the temerity of that man! He just jumped the ha-ha that clearly had been built there to keep people—and horses—out. She didn't know if it was a continuation of Hyde Park, Kensington Gardens, or what. But truly, one didn't just jump a fence!

On the other hand, he had done so very handily with no hesitation whatsoever. She'd watched him ride off both shocked and, she hated to admit it, amused. It was exactly the sort of thing Bel and Gwendolyn would have done when they were in school together. She could practically imagine them doing so, leaving her and Bee behind to stare at them in wonder. She practically laughed at the image that came to her mind.

After clearing the wall, Mr. Fitzwalter turned about and motioned for her to join him. She just couldn't. She wondered with a small piece of her heart whether she would ever have the nerve to do so. She shook her head and, instead, took the road leading in the correct direction. She didn't know where it would take her, but she was certain she'd be able to find her way to where Mr. Fitzwalter awaited.

She'd had to leave her horse at a gate, and she had a nagging suspicion that she was on private property. She slipped through, carefully closing the latch behind her, and walked as quickly as she could to where she hoped Mr. Fitzwalter was still waiting.

He was leaning up against a tree when she found him. His horse was grazing nearby. He stood up and started toward her as she approached him.

"Why didn't you follow me?" he asked.

"I... I didn't have the nerve. I'm certain we shouldn't be here. There are fences for a reason, you know," she said, trying not to sound as if she were scolding him.

He gave a little shrug. "So, shall we see the

roses?"

She gave him a guilty little smile and a quick nod.

They walked along the path to where Cassie had seen the flowers. There was a small hedge of them separating a wooded area from the path. They were absolutely lovely. Cassie dropped to her knees next to them and dipped her nose into one perfect, white bloom.

Mr. Fitzwalter bent down next to her and smelled another. "Goodness, they smell nice! They remind me of the roses in India. The flowers there smell heavenly. Much stronger than anything we have here."

Cassie smiled up at him. "Yes, I imagine they do! These aren't English roses. They're Chinese Tea roses, Rosa chinensis of the variety spontanea. They're precisely the sort I'm trying to cross breed with the English roses. I'm attempting to recreate this smell in a pink rose. But even the tea rose I've been working with doesn't smell this good." A terrible, horrible idea slipped unbidden into Cassie's mind. She looked around to see if there was anyone nearby.

Mr. Fitzwalter looked too. "What are you looking for?"

"To see if we've been spotted."

"I don't believe so. I don't see anyone," he said, looking more carefully.

Cassie put a finger to her lips and then fished out the small folding knife she always carried in her reticule. She pulled off her gloves and dug her fingers into the soil at the base of the plant she was kneeling next to. Very carefully, avoiding the thorns, grasped the bottom of a stem and cut downward careful to get down below the soil to obtain bit of the root as well. She shook the dirt off, cut the top so that she only had a few inches of stem, and slipped that, along with her knife, back into her reticule.

She'd just pulled her gloves back on when a voice called out, "Oy! What ye doin' thar?"

Cassie stood up. "Just admiring the roses. I do hope that's all right. They are lovely specimens."

"That they are. But yer not allowed here. The gardens ain't open today. Ye have to come back on Saturday," the man said.

"Oh, dear, I'm terribly sorry. We didn't realize," Cassie said, widening her eyes and trying to look as innocent as possible.

The man noticed Mr. Fitzwalter's horse and turned an infuriated look at them. "Ye didn't jump the fence? You—"

"Oh, er..." Mr. Fitzwalter interrupted. He didn't finish, though, he grabbed Cassie's hand and started running toward his horse. "We're leaving. Thank you," he called back to the man.

As if she weighed nothing, he grabbed Cassie around her waist and tossed her up onto his saddle, jumping up behind. With an arm on either side of her ensuring she didn't fall, he kicked his heels into his horse's flank and took off heading back the way he'd come.

Cassie held on to the horse's mane and pressed back into Mr. Fitzwalter's body to keep from losing her balance. The horse jumped the ha-ha and galloped toward the continuation of Rotten Row but away from the throngs of people still promenading, riding, and driving down the carriageway. Thank goodness, he pulled the animal to a halt before they reached the more crowded area.

Cassie's heart was pounding in her chest, but to her surprise, she burst out laughing as they stopped. "Oh, my word!"

Mr. Fitzwalter gave a little chuckle. "Are you all right?"

"I... I think so."

"Good."

"We need to collect my horse," she reminded him.

He gave a nod and continued at a more sedate pace.

Thank goodness they didn't pass very many people as they rode toward where Cassie had left the animal. She did brave a peek back and found quite a few widened eyes watching them go.

"Don't look back, just ignore them and hopefully they'll ignore you," he said quietly. He held his head up and kept his back straight as if riding this way was the most normal thing in the world.

Cassie couldn't decide if she should do the same or shrink down and try to hide. She opted for sitting straight, looking ahead, and praying very hard.

"Now correct me if I'm wrong, but I would think that taking a cutting would count as even more illegal than jumping the fence," he said with a broad smile as they rode toward her horse which was still tethered where she'd left it.

She gave a little shrug and tried very hard to ignore the fact that doing so rubbed her shoulder against his broad chest. "It might have been. But since you jumped the fence, I figured I could take a cutting. And I do so want to be able to breed roses with that magnificent scent."

"And you always just take what you want?" he asked with a laugh, pulling up to her horse.

She made the mistake of turning toward him. His face was so close to hers, merely inches away. She could see the slight creases radiating from his eyes and on either side of his mouth as he smiled at her. He smelled of sandalwood and sweat—not a bad combination. Somehow, she couldn't remember what he'd asked, so she quickly turned away. "Could you... could you help me down?"

She could feel his warmth disappear as he dismounted, but then his large, strong hands were around her waist, lifting her down. Her hands found their way to his shoulders—for balance plus security, she told herself. Her feet barely felt the ground as she maintained eye contact with him. It was much too soon that he released her and stepped away.

She took a breath, and it felt like the first she'd had in a while. She could feel her heart pounding. "Thank you," she said, her voice barely above a whisper.

"You're welcome." His eyes still hadn't left hers, but she realized she should really move.

With an exhale, she stepped toward her horse and then realized she needed his assistance in mounting. He was right there, lacing his fingers together so she could place her foot into them.

Chapter Eleven

They rode back to Cynthia's home in silence, neither one finding the need to speak. After she'd released her horse into the hands of the groom, she turned back to find Mr. Fitzwalter standing by his horse's head.

"Thank you for a... well, a very diverting afternoon," she said with a slight laugh.

He inclined his head ever so slightly. "It has been entirely my pleasure. I will see you again soon, I expect."

"Yes. I'm certain of it." She took a step back toward the door to the house. "Well, thank you again." Why did she feel as if she didn't want to leave him? It was ridiculous. She quickly turned and went through the door being held open by the footman.

She hadn't even made it to the stair when Sorrell strode from his study. "Oh, Cassia. Good afternoon."

"Good afternoon," she said, pausing.

He frowned at her. "How is it that you are always covered with dirt? Didn't you just come in from riding?"

She looked down at herself. Indeed, there was a smudge of dirt on her riding habit. "Oh, dear. I do seem to attract it somehow. Well, I'm going to change, anyway." She gave a little shrug before turning and going up the stairs, deliberately leaving her brother-in-law without an explanation.

~*~

Cynthia went into her husband's study straight after returning from her Whist Society meeting.

"Oh!" she said, stopping just inside the door when she saw Sorrell sitting at his desk.

He looked up, raising his eyebrows. "Good afternoon. Is there something I can do for you?" he said, rising to his feet.

"Ah... yes, actually." She gave a self-conscious little laugh. "I didn't expect to actually find you here. I was going to write you a note. But, well, since you're here..."

He cocked his head a little at her rambling speech. "What do you need?"

"I, er, I was wondering if you could find out a bit about two gentlemen who have shown a distinct interest in my sister?" she said, coming forward.

"You want me to inquire into two random gentlemen of the ton?"

"Well, they aren't random. They've shown—" She intertwined her fingers in front of her.

"An interest. Yes, I understood that. Where did Cassia meet these gentlemen?" he asked, cutting her off.

"One she met at a ball last week and the other at the Royal Society meeting, and then again at a ball."

"So, she had met them at events that were invitation only, meaning they are accepted members of society, is that correct?" he asked.

"Yes, that's right."

"And has either of them proposed as yet?"

"No, of course not!" she said, feeling a little confused with this intense questioning.

"Then I see no need to investigate them any further. They have already been vetted by society's extremely particular hostesses and found to be acceptable. That's good enough for now. Should either of them come up to scratch, I will, of course, exercise due diligence and find out more about their situations—financial and otherwise. But until that happens, I don't believe anything further is necessary." He sat back down and looked at the paper he'd been working on when she'd come into the room.

When she didn't move, he looked up again. "Is there anything else?"

Cynthia didn't know what to say. She supposed he was right. The gentlemen had been given invitations to society parties, so she supposed they were at least acceptable. Well, they weren't murderers or anything. On the other hand, that didn't answer the question as to whether they were merely fortune hunters, but perhaps it didn't matter if neither was, as yet, asking for Cassie's hand in marriage.

Even if they were... well, it was clear Sorrell didn't have the time to look into the men. It would be all right—she hoped.

~April 15~

Cassie entered the drawing room Friday evening, hoping to see a happy sister and brother-in-law. Oddly, she'd only seen her sister's husband for a few moments here and there since she'd arrived in town two weeks ago. What she saw this evening, sadly, was her sister sitting despondently alone in the drawing room.

After she'd witnessed the fight Cynthia and

Sorrell had had, Cassie had been watching, and she didn't think anything was getting better. Sorrell wasn't spending any amount of time either at home or with his wife. They seemed to live completely separate lives—and Cynthia didn't seem to be happy about it. Honestly, Cassie couldn't blame her. She was sure that if she loved a man enough to marry him, she'd want to spend time with him.

"You look deep in thought," Cynthia said, pulling Cassie from her woolgathering. She must have finally noticed Cassie just standing there.

She started and continued farther into the room. She placed a smile onto her lips. "Oh, nothing. I was wondering if I'd see Sorrell this evening."

"Oh, no. He's gone to his club," Cynthia said, turning away from Cassie.

She didn't like this. Not one little bit. She put a hand on her sister's shoulder. "Cyn, is everything all right... with you and Sorrell?"

Cynthia turned away again, going to the sideboard where she poured out wine for both of them. "Yes, of course! Why wouldn't everything be all right? Sorrell's a busy man, that's all. And he does like spending his evenings at the club. Many men do." She gave a little laugh that sounded forced.

"I've hardly seen him since I arrived," Cassie pointed out.

"I know. It's such a shame. I was hoping you two would get a chance to spend more time together, but... well... these things can't be helped." Cynthia handed Cassie a glass of wine.

"And you're all right with this? Can't you say something to him? Ask him to stay home one evening—not even for the entire evening, just for dinner."

"No. I've tried," Cynthia said. She seemed to suddenly realize the truth she'd revealed and immediately backtracked. "Actually, when he goes to this club, it's not just for pleasure, but for work as well, you know. He goes to speak with other men about bills that are being discussed in Parliament and other such things."

Cassie nodded. "I see."

Cynthia swallowed down half the wine in her glass. "Cassie," she sighed. "Please, leave it alone. This is my marriage, let me handle it."

"I worry, Cyn. I don't want you to be unhappy and... well, it looks as if you are."

Cynthia reached out and pulled Cassie into a one-arm hug. "Thank you for caring, but truly, it's nothing. Everything's fine." She blinked rapidly and then finished her wine. "Oh, but Cassie, I heard the most ridiculous thing!" her sister said, looking like she suddenly remembered something.

"What's that?"

"Lady Haddington said that she saw you—or someone who looked like you—riding up before a gentleman in Hyde Park on Wednesday. I know you said you were going to be riding with Mr. Fitzwalter, but I'm sure you meant on your own horse," Cynthia said with a laugh.

Cassie's mouth dropped open a little, but she closed it again quickly. They had been seen! She forced out a little laugh. "Of course I rode my own horse! But, er, I did ride on Mr. Fitzwalter's for a few minutes. We, er, went to look at some roses, and I left my horse behind, so he needed to give me a ride to retrieve it. It was nothing. Truly, we only rode together for a few minutes. Honestly, I'm surprised anyone noticed at all."

Cynthia narrowed her eyes at Cassie who quickly added, "Is dinner ready, do you think? We should eat and get going. I don't want to be late for the talk tonight at the Royal Society."

"Cassie, you rode on the same horse as Mr. Fitzwalter? In the park? Where anyone and everyone could see you?" Cynthia breathed in horror.

"We were at the very end of Rotten Row—not even on the road! Quite away from it actually. Truly, it was nothing. I'm sure that if we just ignore what anyone says, it will blow over," Cassie said, not waiting for her sister to lead the way to the dining room. She got up and started out the door herself.

"We'll have to deny it," Cynthia said as she followed her down the stairs. "If this were to get around, you'd be ruined."

"I'm certain it will be fine," Cassie said, ignoring the pounding fear in her chest. Ruined? She'd hardly begun the season. She couldn't even imagine what her mother would say if she returned home, her reputation in tatters with no possibility of marriage. No, she had no choice in the matter but to stick to her plan to ignore this and convince Cynthia to do so as well. Her only other option was to somehow convince Mr. Crome to propose to her—quickly.

As Cassie led the way into the dining room, she added, "I wonder if we'll see Mr. Crome again tonight."

"He is a very nice gentleman," Cynthia commented. "He's a younger son, but I don't think that matters over-much." Cynthia seemed as eager as Cassie to put aside the uncomfortable subject of Mr. Fitzwalter and their ride.

"I didn't even think of that. I'm not at all concerned. Do you think Mama wants me to marry someone with a title?" Cassie asked.

"I think she wants you to marry someone who makes you happy—and so do I. I can't imagine that a man who is a scientist wouldn't do so."

"That's my thinking precisely."

"And Mr. Fitzwalter?" Cynthia asked.

"Mr. Crome is a scientist and therefore a much more appropriate husband for me, as you just said," Cassie said.

Happily, Cynthia accepted this statement and moved on to enjoy her dinner. Cassie wished she could get Mr. Fitzwalter and their scandalous ride out of her mind. It had been the most thrilling afternoon she'd ever spent with a gentleman, and her traitorous memory just refused to let it go.

~*~

Cynthia was very grateful to have gotten Cassie off the topic of Sorrell and her marriage. Not only was it none of her sister's business, but there was nothing she could do about how busy her husband was. She was doing all she could to be a patient and understanding wife. Yes, some days it was harder than others, but... well, she didn't have a choice in the matter. Her marriage was what it was, and she supposed she needed to accept and live with it no matter how sad it made her feel.

No, what Cynthia had to focus on now was getting Cassie situated into a loving marriage. To that end, she would both ignore the confusing explanation Cassie had given for having been seen riding in Mr. Fitzwalter's arms, and endure another boring lecture at the Royal Society.

She prayed her sister was right. If they simply denied and then ignored any comments about the ride, it would be quickly forgotten. And at least this evening's talk was going to be on a topic of interest to one of them—botany. Having grown up with a father and sister who were both passionate about the topic, Cynthia knew much more than she would have liked, so at least she would be able to follow the talk without any problem.

The previous week's talk had been rather excruciating. She honestly had no interest in electricity and knew nothing about it. This was all for Cassie, she reminded herself, and she loved her sister very much.

Happily, the talk turned out not to be as boring as Cynthia had feared, and she was able to follow it much more easily than she'd expected. Still, it was with great relief when she stood, along with everyone else in the room, and headed toward the refreshments.

"That was fascinating!" Cassie said with enthusiasm. She had sat enthralled from the moment the speaker was introduced. Cynthia had looked over at her every once in a while, wondering if her sister was even blinking, she was sitting so absolutely still.

"It was. Quite interesting," Cynthia agreed. She was grateful for the glass of lemonade handed to her and started to look around for Mr. Crome. She spotted him speaking with another gentleman not too far away.

After Cassie had gotten herself a drink, she said, "I see Mr. Crome. Shall we go over and say hello?"

"Oh, yes," Cassie said, with nearly as much enthusiasm as she'd had for the lecture.

"Good evening, ladies!" the gentleman said, as they approached. Thankfully, he seemed as happy to see them as they were him.

"Good evening, sir. I do hope you enjoyed the lecture?" Cassie said, giving a small curtsey to both men.

"Indeed! Do you know Lord Orford?" Mr. Crome asked, indicating the other man. He didn't wait for them to deny knowledge of the gentleman. "Orford, may I present Lady Sorrell and her sister, Miss Benton."

The portly gentleman sketched them a slight bow. "A pleasure. Miss Benton, you sound as if you enjoyed this evening's lecture a great deal," he said, giving her a polite smile. "Were you able to follow the complicated theories put forth by the speaker?"

Cynthia didn't think she liked this pompous gentleman very much. Cassie opened her mouth to answer, but Mr. Crome spoke before she could. "Actually, Miss Benton is a botanist herself. She has the most incredible garden and is experimenting with varying breeds of roses. Quite fascinating work, if you ask me."

Cynthia nearly clapped her hands in delight, but it would have been both rude and impossible since she had a glass of lemonade in one hand. Still, she bestowed a very bright smile on the gentleman, letting him know that she approved of his comment.

"Thank you, Mr. Crome," Cassie said. "That is too kind of you. Indeed, I do dabble a touch in breeding roses."

Chapter Twelve

A touch! My goodness, what an understatement," Mr. Crome said with a laugh. "You know, it is the work of young ladies such as Miss Benton that truly gives me hope, Orford."

"Oh? How so?" his friend asked.

"Well, it is my opinion that if one wants to pursue science as we do, it is absolutely necessary for one's household to fully understand the importance of your work. Miss Benton, and other scientifically minded young ladies, are most certainly able to do so."

"I see," the man said, nodding. He turned to Cassie and asked, "And do you understand Mr. Crome's work?"

She blinked for a moment, looking like she couldn't quite believe how the conversation had turned around so quickly. "Er, yes, I do. But don't you think—"

"You see?" Mr. Crome said, interrupting her. "She understands how very important it is that I do my experiments. I can't tell you how difficult it is to conduct my work when no one in my household understands this. Miss Benton certainly would."

"Well, yes, because I have my own—" she started

to say again.

Lord Orford cut her off, however. "I completely understand and sympathize, Crome. Ladies generally don't understand how vital it is that we conduct our experiments. I can't tell you how often my wife has interrupted me with some petty household issue or to invite me out shopping or some other nonsense. She simply cannot comprehend what I do and dismisses it as a silly hobby, if you can believe it."

"Exactly! That is precisely the sort of misunderstanding I'm speaking of," Mr. Crome exclaimed. He turned to Cassie. "You would never do that, I'm certain, now would you Miss Benton?"

"Well, no, not if you were working, naturally," she said, frowning ever so slightly. "And I do hope you would extend to a lady scientist the same courtesy," she added quickly before she could be interrupted once again.

Both men laughed, but Cassie just looked to Cynthia as if she were trying to figure out what they'd found amusing. All Cynthia could do was shrug.

"I'm sorry, but what is funny?" she asked the men.

"You implied that your work might be more important than that of a real scientist," Lord Orford said with a slight chuckle.

"A real scientist? Are you implying..." she started.

Mr. Crome just gave her a condescending little smile. "Miss Benton, I'm certain you don't believe that the breeding of roses can compare to the actual scientific work I am doing with electricity."

"Well..." Cassie began again.

"Of course she doesn't, she's clearly an

intelligent girl," Lord Orford said.

"I believe it's time we left," Cynthia said, interrupting whatever her sister was going to say. "Gentlemen, it's been lovely. Good night." She then grabbed her sister's arm and directed her out of the room, leaving their glasses with a waiting footman on their way out.

~*~

Cassie felt like she was ready to explode. She couldn't believe the nerve of those men! They honestly thought that their work was more important than hers?

"Cynthia! Did you hear what that man said?" Cassie whispered fiercely to her sister as she was dragged from the building.

"Yes, I did. Please hold your temper until we get into our carriage. I do not want you to cause a public scene."

Cassie clamped her mouth shut. Luckily, their carriage didn't take very long to reach them. The door had hardly closed when she burst. "Electricity! Electricity! He thinks that fooling around with sparks and... and... and... making silly dead frogs jump is more important than breeding roses? At least what I do has some practical application!"

"You are right," Cynthia said, settling back against the comfortable seat.

"How dare he imply that my work was insignificant!" Cassie railed.

"It took a lot of nerve to do so to your face," Cynthia said.

"It certainly did! And in front of a stranger, too!"

Cynthia tilted her head a little. "On the other hand, perhaps that's why he said such things. He hasn't implied that your work is insignificant before now, has he?"

"No, he hasn't," Cassie said. The thought made her calm down significantly. "But I don't believe I understand why he would say that tonight."

"Because he is with a friend. Gentlemen can be odd when they're in the presence of other men. They act very differently than when they're alone with you. Perhaps he was... I don't know, showing off for his friend? Pretending that his work was more important so that his friend would think better of him?"

Cassie thought about this. It sounded entirely plausible. In fact, the more she thought about it, it sounded very likely. "You know, I think you're absolutely right. He was very impressed with my roses when I showed them to him earlier in the week."

"I'm certain he was. They are impressive," Cynthia agreed.

"So, yes, maybe he was simply belittling me to puff himself up to his friend."

"It is a thing men do, I'm afraid," Cynthia said.

Cassie felt so much better. Men were so silly sometimes—like little children.

~*~

Lady Kineton had already left to attend some ball or other when Archer and his friend sat back to enjoy a touch of port after their dinner. "Care to join me at Powell's this evening?" Kineton asked.

Archer lowered the glass he'd been about to drink from. "Powell's?"

"Only the newest, most exclusive club in London," his friend explained.

"Oh, er, will they allow me in if I'm not a member?"

"I suppose so. You'll be with me. It would be the perfect place for you to find investors. I tell you, everyone who is anyone is there now."

Archer took a sip of his drink. "Well, in that case, let's go!" he said with a smile, not expecting anything to happen so quickly.

To his surprise, Kineton got right up. "All right," he said, heading out the door.

Archer scrambled to follow, draining his glass quickly, then handing it to the footman standing at the door as he went through.

As expected, Archer was stopped by the man at the door to the club. "Good evening, sir, are you a member of Powell's?" he asked.

"Er, no..." Archer started.

"He's with me," Kineton said loftily.

"That's very good, my lord, but I'm afraid I'll need Lord Wickford's approval before I can allow him entry." He turned and gave a nod to another footman standing nearby. The fellow disappeared into one of the rooms off the foyer.

They waited a few minutes, and then Archer turned to his friend saying, "If you want to go in, I'll explain everything to this fellow."

Kineton looked like he was about to do so when the door opened again, and a man in a very fashionable black suit with a bold, white neckcloth came out. His waistcoat was of a black silk with black flowers embroidered all over it. He was clearly of African descent, making Archer wonder if he was the nobleman he looked to be or simply a very well-dressed servant. The question was answered when he came up and smiled at Kineton. In a voice that could have belonged to any peer in England he said, "Lord Kineton, a pleasure to see you this evening."

~*~

"Ah, Wickford! Good evening," Kineton said, nodding. "This is my very good friend Archibald Fitzwalter, son of Baron Fitzwalter. He's in town for the season—"

"Possibly not even that long," Archer interjected.

"Er, yes. All right, he's in town until he can fund a project he's starting in India."

"Really? What sort of project?" Lord Wickford asked curiously.

"I would be more than happy to tell you all about it, my lord—especially if you might be interested in an excellent investment yourself," Archer said, giving him a bright smile.

Wickford laughed. "I just might be. Can you give me a hint?"

"It's a new company to import spices from India," Archer told him. He paused. "All above board, I can assure you, the East India Company—"

Wickford held up a hand. "I am not involved in the government. Haven't even taken my seat in Parliament as yet."

Archer breathed easier. He had no desire to make a faux pas as he'd done with Lord Sorrell. He gave a nod. "I am hoping to ensure that the suppliers are given a fair price for their goods and aren't forced into doing anything to which they might object. I'm afraid the Company hasn't kept to such practices. They're out to make as much money as possible, regardless of any other considerations."

"Ahhh... I am most definitely intrigued!" He stood back and indicated the door he'd come out of. "Please come in, Mr. Fitzwalter. You can tell me all about it over a glass of my excellent rum."

"Rum? That's unusual, if you don't mind my saying so," Archer commented as he followed the man.

"It is what Powell's has built its name on. I make it myself on my sugar plantation in the West Indies," Lord Wickford said.

He nodded to a few gentlemen as they made their way through a very comfortable, very masculine sitting room. There were carefully arranged seating areas so that groups of gentlemen could sit and chat quietly, interspersed with areas where there was only one or two chairs by a table so that someone might sit comfortably alone.

Wickford led them to a group of chairs toward the back of the room. At some point along the way, he must have given a signal to a footman because a bottle of rum and three glasses were placed on the table nearby. Lord Wickford indicated they have a seat, and he poured them all some rum.

He lifted his glass after handing Kineton and Archer one. "Here's to profitable projects."

Archer lifted his glass and then took a sip. The liquor was delicious, sweet, with a hint of oak and smoke. "Ah, this is excellent!"

"Thank you. You won't find a finer rum in all of England, I can assure you," Lord Wickford said.

"I believe you," Archer said. He then proceeded to sell Lord Wickford on his idea. It was easy to tell the man was very knowledgeable when it came to business. He asked excellent questions, and Archer did all he could to answer them as well as he could.

Archer finished with, "I'm sorry if I can't go into greater detail for you, my lord, we are still in the planning phase of the project."

Lord Wickford smiled. "No worries. It is clearly

a large undertaking. Will you be having others assist you in setting up the details?"

"I have some good friends in important places," Archer said, giving him a wink. In truth, he had a great number of friends just about everywhere one could imagine. He hadn't yet broached any of them to ask for help, but he expected they would still be there when he needed them.

Lord Wickford gave a little chuckle. "Well, I'm afraid, personally, I am not interested just at this moment. However, it is definitely a project which could interest a good number of gentlemen here. You say you're only going to be in town until you are funded?"

"That's right," Archer said.

"Well, then, how about we make an exception for you? Since it wouldn't make sense for you to pay a full membership fee for such a short stay, I'll charge you month by month. Does that work for you? You will then be free to come whenever you want and, potentially, get some excellent business done while enjoying a glass of fine rum, or whatever else you might want," he said, getting up with his glass of rum still in his hand.

"Thank you, my lord. I do greatly appreciate it," Archer said, also standing.

The man smiled. "Always happy to assist a fellow businessman. Good hunting, Mr. Fitzwalter. I'm certain I'll see you around." He sauntered away as Archer turned to his friend.

"Nice fellow," he commented.

"He's a good egg, Wickford," Kineton said, pouring himself some more rum from the bottle Lord Wickford had left with them.

~April 18~

Cassie hoped Wheat & Sons Bookshop had the new book on roses her father had written to tell her about. He was always up on the latest botanical publications and, happily, shared his knowledge with her. He hadn't been able to find a copy in Oxford, but told her he was certain she would be able to locate it in London where absolutely everything was available.

She was browsing through the titles on a table of the latest releases when a voice startled her. "Miss Benton, what a lovely surprise!"

She turned and found Mr. Crome smiling broadly at her.

"Oh, Mr. Crome." For a moment, all she could remember was how furious she'd been after the last time they'd seen each other. If she were completely honest with herself, she would acknowledge she was still rather perturbed.

When she didn't say anything further, he asked, "And how are you on this fine afternoon?"

"I am doing very well, thank you. I'm just looking for a book on roses that has recently been published," she said, turning back to the table.

"Ah, the book by Mr. James Mean?" he asked.

Cassie's mouth dropped open. "Yes! Have you heard of it?"

"Indeed. I am not completely ignorant of horticultural endeavors. Actually the Humes, Mr. Mean's employers and fellow rose enthusiasts, live in the neighborhood of my brother's estate."

"They live..." Cassie nearly exploded. "I can't believe you never mentioned this to me before! They and Mr. Mean lead the entire field of rose breeding and cultivation! They have given their roses to the

Empress Josephine of France!"

"Er, yes, I was aware... I wasn't certain if you'd heard—"

"How could I not hear of them?" Cassie said in a loud whisper, controlling her voice so that she wouldn't shout. "You really do not think very much of me as a botanist, do you?" she asked, feeling tears pricking at her eyes.

"What? Of course I do! How could you even think—"

"Well, based on what you said the other night to your dear friend, Lord Orford, and now this, it is clearly the most obvious conclusion."

Chapter Thirteen

When he didn't say anything immediately, Cassie added, "My sister, always eager to give people the benefit of the doubt, believed that you spoke so disparagingly of me and my work because you were in the company of another man. She thought you might not actually believe my work to be less important. But now... I don't believe she was correct in her hypothesis. It is clear you don't actually believe me a capable and knowledgeable botanist."

The man opened his mouth to say something, but then seemed to change his mind. "I can assure you, I do not think any less of you or your work, Miss Benton. I apologize if I offended you in any way the other evening—or this afternoon."

His words were pretty, but Cassie needed some evidence if she were to let go of her anger and hurt.

"Er, allow me to make it up to you."

She crossed her arms in front of her chest and waited.

"I would be happy to write to Mr. Mean and ask if he might send a signed copy of his latest book. Would that be sufficient? I would invite you to my brother's estate, but I don't think that would be appropriate at all."

Cassie widened her eyes. "No! Indeed, it would not." She softened her stance a little. "But a copy of Mr. Mean's book—"

"Signed," Mr. Crome reminded her.

"Yes, signed, would be very nice."

"Good! I shall write to him immediately." He paused and then added, "And your roses... well, I know that your attempts at breeding flowers is very important work. The Humes and Mr. Mean have devoted their lives to the pursuit."

"It is," she said, just to be certain he understood it to be true. She couldn't possibly tell him how little she thought of his work. That would just be plain rude, especially when he was attempting to be nice.

"Do you possibly think you could forgive my lapse in judgement?" he asked sweetly.

"Well, when you put it that way..."

He took her hand. "Thank you, Miss Benton. You are truly too kind and exceedingly understanding."

She could feel her anger melting away. She lowered her eyes and nodded. When she looked up again at him, she said, "I do hope I'll be seeing you at Lady Emmerton's soirée next week?"

His smile grew. "Yes, indeed! I wouldn't miss another opportunity to spend time with you."

"You are too kind."

"Miss, I think I found the book you were looking for," the shopkeeper said, coming up to her, holding out a volume.

"Oh, thank you," she said. "I will no longer be needing it, however." She turned and gave Mr. Crome a smile.

"Well, I shall let you get back to your shopping. I'll, er, I'll see you at the soirée," Mr. Crome said with a slight bow.

He really was a very kind gentleman, and he was trying. She truly had to allow for that. But strangely enough, thinking of Mr. Crome also led to her thinking of Mr. Fitzwalter. They both seemed to be trying so hard to endear her to them. Never in her life had she ever imagined she'd be in such a situation. She was definitely going to have to do something about this!

~*~

"There's a note for you, Miss," Sally said as she was waiting to take Cassie's gloves after she got home that afternoon.

Cassie looked at the maid. "A note? For me?"

"Yes, Miss," the girl laughed. "It's in the drawing room upstairs. Would you like me to fetch it for you?"

"No, that's all right. I'll go up." Cassie went up as quickly as she could while not looking too eager.

She found it on a salver, on the table just inside the door.

"That came for you a short time ago," Cynthia said, looking up from the book she was reading.

Cassie opened it, reading it as she walked over to sit down across from her sister. "It's from Mr. Fitzwalter. He's inviting me to join him, Lord and Lady Kineton at the theatre tomorrow night." She looked up. "May I go? I've never been to the theatre before." Now that she'd met Philip again, she realized she'd been worried about nothing. She had no feelings for him any longer. She could possibly even imagine becoming friends with him now.

Cynthia gave her a warm smile. "Of course you

may. It sounds as if you'll be properly chaperoned with Lady Kineton there."

"Yes, I imagine so." Cassie didn't really know Lady Kineton, but she supposed she would get to know her the following evening.

~April 19~

When the time came the following evening, Cassie wasn't exactly certain that the lady had any intentions of playing chaperone. She flitted off to visit with friends the very moment they arrived at the theatre and got down from Philip's carriage.

Cassie watched her go and then nearly jumped when a warm hand rested gently on the small of her back.

"Shall we go inside?" Mr. Fitzwalter asked, indicating that they, too, head in the direction the lady had gone.

"Oh, yes, of course." Cassie followed Philip, wondering if he was going to go after his wife or stay with her and Mr. Fitzwalter.

She spotted Lady Kineton talking with great animation to some other ladies near the center of the lobby, but found herself being directed off to the stairs to their left.

"She'll join us later, I'm sure," Philip said, only giving Lady Kineton a quick glance before leading Cassie up the stairs and to his box.

When they were settled in their seats, Cassie looked out at the grand theatre, but even more importantly, at all the other ladies and gentlemen taking their places in their respective boxes. "My sister told me that very few people actually watch the performance but spend the entire evening merely watching each other."

"Your sister is quite correct," Philip agreed.

"But I can watch the play if I want, can I not?" Cassie asked, just to be sure. "I do so like Macbeth."

"You can do whatever you want," Mr. Fitzwalter said with a little laugh. "I happen to be rather fond of the Scottish play myself."

Cassie gave him a grateful smile.

~*~

The play was so much more enjoyable than the rendition Archer had last seen in Madras. But even better than the performance on the stage was watching Miss Benton. She was absolutely lovely and was entirely captivated by the play. Every single emotion showed clearly on her beautiful face.

She clapped enthusiastically when the curtain came down and then turned to him, her eyes shining with excitement. "That was wonderful!"

He laughed. "Indeed, it was, Miss Benton. I am so glad you enjoyed it."

Kineton didn't look nearly as excited as Archer's companion. In fact, he looked downright annoyed. His wife had spent the entire performance in the box of a handsome, young nobleman named Sand-something-or-other. Archer hadn't caught his name and truly didn't care enough to ask.

"I suppose we'll meet Martha someplace on our way to the carriage," Kineton said, standing.

Miss Benton looked around the box as if she were suddenly realizing that Lady Kineton wasn't with them. She'd been so distracted by what was happening on the stage, she hadn't even noticed what was—and wasn't—going on around her. It rather amazed Archer that she had such a strong power of concentration.

They all filed out of the box and joined the throngs of people headed toward the street. Kineton was clearly looking all around for his wife, but neither he nor Archer could see her anywhere. There were simply too many people.

"Perhaps we should wait here," Kineton said, directing them off to one side of the walkway at the bottom of the stairs.

Archer was actually quite happy to stand and watch the people stream by, but after waiting for a few minutes, he felt the slightest tug on his coat. Immediately, his hand shot out and grabbed onto that of a small person. He turned to see who he'd caught.

Large, wide eyes looked up at him from under the brim of an overly large hat. "Lemme go!" the child said, pulling at his hand.

"Oh, my goodness!" Miss Benton exclaimed.

"You think I should let you go when you were trying to pick my pocket?" Archer asked, bending toward the boy while keeping a tight grip on his wrist.

The child merely pouted, but said nothing.

Archer reached into his pocket to retrieve his purse. Luckily, it was still there. "Tell me what you were going to do with my money if you'd gotten it," he demanded of the boy.

Silence.

"Were you going to keep it? Give it to someone? What? Tell me," Archer said, pulling out a ten-pound note. It was what he'd put in there earlier, in anticipation of a jaunt to Powell's after he'd dropped Miss Benton at her home after the theatre.

It hardly seemed possible, but the child's eyes widened even farther at the sight of the note.

He licked his lips as if in anticipation of a delicious treat. "I... I was gonna buy bread an' food for me mum and sister."

"For food? Okay—" Archer started to hand the boy the money, but his hand was grabbed. He swung around to Miss Benton.

"You can't just give a child ten pounds!" she said, clearly shocked.

"Of course I can. He's hungry. His family is hungry. He doesn't mean any harm," Archer said.

The little boy nodded vigorously. "I'm hungry!"

"Then give him a penny, or if you must a sovereign, but you cannot give him ten pounds," she reiterated. "He wouldn't know what to do with so much money. It's entirely likely that his mother would just spend it on gin or something equally inappropriate."

"Hey! My mum don't—" the boy started to object.

Miss Benton turned to him and raised disbelieving eyebrows.

"Well... not much, anyways," the child quickly amended.

"You see," she said. "If you want the child to have money to eat beyond today, give your money to a school where he can learn a trade or to an orphanage where it could buy food for a month or more." When Archer just frowned at her, she added, "If the child learns to work, he'll feed himself and be a productive member of society for the rest of his life, but if he learns to steal, he'll simply end up in gaol. You have to think about this, about the consequences of your actions."

Archer had never actually done that—thought about consequences. He turned back to the child who was looking up at him with such a pleading look on his little face. With a sigh, he put the ten-pound note back into his purse and took out a sovereign. "Do you know where you could learn a trade?" he asked the child.

"I'm certain he doesn't know," Miss Benton said. "But Lord Welles does. He works with the people of the Rookeries."

"Don' know no Lord Welles," the child said.

"Have you heard of Lord Welcome?" Miss Benton asked.

"Ohhh, yeah! 'E comes 'round an' pays fer clothes an' such," the child said, nodding.

"That's the one. Mr. Fitzwalter will give him the ten pounds he was about to give you, so that your mum can buy some clothes or food," Miss Benton told the boy.

"And this is for now so you can go and get some meat pies to take home, all right?" Archer said, giving the child the sovereign in his hand.

"Fank ye!" the child said before running off with the coin clutched to his chest.

"Well, that was a very polite boy," Miss Benton said, giving Archer a satisfied smile. "And you, sir, need to think before handing out an enormous sum of money like that!"

"I don't want to know what you were doing with that filthy urchin," Lord Kineton said, joining them. "But I've found my wife. We can go now."

They all piled into the carriage, but Archer was still thinking about what had just occurred. He was impressed that Miss Benton knew all about how to help the poor—much more, it seemed than he did! He liked that. He liked that a lot.

~April 20~

Cassie slipped her feet out of her shoes and tucked them up next to her on the wide, comfortable chair of Bel's bedchamber. "First, I want to thank you so much for running to my aid."

"Don't be ridiculous!" Bel immediately interrupted her. "You scream for help, we come running!"

Cassie laughed. "I didn't exactly scream for help."

"What do you mean? Of course you did!" Gwendolyn said. "You wrote to all of us and said we needed to meet on an urgent matter. It also just so happens the duchess is not feeling well, so I needed a chaperone for tonight's party, anyway."

"Did I really say urgent?" Cassie asked. At least her call for help had worked out well for Gwendolyn. Now, she had a chaperone for Lady Emmerton's soirée.

"You did. Now out with it, what's the problem?" Bee asked.

"Well, it isn't really urgent..." Cassie hedged.

"Cassia, what is it?" Bel asked.

"It's just... Mr. Fitzwalter is so very sweet and kind, and Mr. Crome is quite fascinating and intelligent and I... I just don't know what to do!" Cassie admitted.

"Ahh... of course," Gwendolyn laughed. "You were never very good at men."

"What do you mean? How can someone be 'good at men'?" Cassie asked with a laugh.

"Well, you could never charm them the way Bel could, or engage with them as well as Bee," Gwendolyn explained.

"And you?" Bee asked with a touch of laughter to her voice.

"Me? Well, men are simply attracted to me because of my wealth, naturally," Gwendolyn said with a shrug.

"You underestimate yourself!" Cassie exclaimed.

"Yes!" Bel agreed. "You are funny and charming and very pretty."

Gwendolyn shook her head, but her cheeks turned pink with embarrassment. "I'm not, but we're not here to discuss my attributes. Now tell us more about Mr. Crome and Mr. Fitzwalter," she said, neatly turning the conversation back to Cassie.

"Wait, is it true that he rode with you up in front of him, on his horse in Hyde Park?" Bel asked.

Bee gasped. "I'd heard that, too, but then someone else said that it wasn't actually you he'd had up before him."

"And you believed them?" Bel asked her sister.

"Knowing Cassia? Yes, I did!" Bee answered.

"Good, you should continue to spread the word—it wasn't me," Cassie interjected.

"But was it you?" Gwendolyn asked.

Cassie could feel her cheeks beginning to burn.

"Oh, my goodness, it was!" Bel squealed.

"It was just for a very short ride to where I'd left my horse," Cassie explained.

"Oh, no you don't! You have to tell us the entire story," Gwendolyn said without hesitation.

Cassie did so because she'd never kept anything from her closest friends, but all of them were gasping by the time she finished.

"I just..." Bee started.

"... can't believe..." Bel continued.

"He's so romantic!" Gwendolyn finished.

Chapter Fourteen

Cassie just laughed. "So what am I going to do? After that incident, I met Mr. Crome, and he was incredibly kind and generous. And... well... I've never had two men court me before. Do I allow them both to do so? Do I need to choose just one? And if so, which one? I just... I don't know what to do!" Cassie said.

Bel shook her head sadly, but with a huge grin on her face. "You poor thing! Two gentlemen!"

"Well, you had two gentlemen vying for your hand last year," her sister pointed out.

"No, I had one gentleman vying for my hand and one for yours," Bel said with a laugh. "It's just that they both thought that we were one person."

"Yes, poor dears," Bee said before chuckling. She clearly remembered the confusion she and Bel had created the previous year when they had taken turns going to parties, allowing everyone to think they were both Bel.

"So, what am I to do?" Cassie asked again.

"Well, which one do you like better?" Gwendolyn asked.

Cassie shook her head. "I don't know. I like them both. They're very different! Mr. Fitzwalter is impetuous, thoughtful, and endearing. Mr. Crome is thoughtful, intelligent, and he respects my work."

"I don't see anything wrong with having two men courting you," Gwendolyn said, giving Cassie a broad smile. "Make them work for your hand!"

"But what if they don't want to? Or if they both do! What if they both offer for me? What do I do?"

"Go with your heart," Bel said.

"Do what you feel is right," her sister said almost at the same time.

"Ah, but there's the problem! My head tells me that Mr. Crome is the right man. He's a scientist, like me! But my heart..." Cassie didn't continue with the thought.

"Are you in love with Mr. Fitzwalter?" Gwendolyn breathed.

"No! I mean... no. I'm not. I couldn't be! Why, we've only known each other a couple of weeks. That's ridiculous. I'm being silly, aren't I?" she asked her friends, looking from one smile to another. "Neither one of them has even made any sort of suggestion that he cares for me beyond enjoying my company. Neither one of them has asked for my hand. I'm jumping to unfounded conclusions!"

"Well, yes," Bee agreed. "But speculation is fun, isn't it?"

Bel giggled, and Gwendolyn nodded vehemently.

~*~

"Now, remember the wallflowers are going to be the most grateful, and there are quite a few of them with dowries that would fund your entire project," Kineton said softly to Archer as they entered Lady Emmerton's soirée that night. "Miss Benton is eating out of your hand, but I don't know that she's right for you—too much of a bluestocking."

Archer turned to his friend. "Listen, Kineton, I appreciate your advice, really I do, but I'm just not—"

"You don't have feelings for the girl?" he asked, stopping mid-stride.

"No!" Archer scoffed immediately, but to be honest, he wasn't sure.

"Well, then... I suppose you'd prefer chasing ugly old men. Or you could spend the evening dancing as you charm some wealthy, shy little thing into falling madly in love with you," his friend said bluntly. "If I were you, I'd pick the girls, but it is up to you." Kineton threw his hands up in surrender and walked away before Archer could even answer him.

He looked over at the girls lining the walls. Some weren't that bad, his stupid brain told him. Could they really have enough to fund his entire project? Just the thought had his feet moving in that direction. Even if one could fund just eighty percent of his project, that would go a long way and get him started on good footing.

Kineton strode with confidence up to one pretty blonde girl. "Miss Cummings, I hope you are doing well this evening?"

She smiled shyly, finding his shoes much more interesting than anything else. "Very well, my lord."

"Excellent. And how is that book you were telling me about the last time we met?" he asked.

Finally, her gaze shot up to his. "Oh, it was excellent! And there's a new one by the same author. This is all about men who breathe under water—" She stopped speaking abruptly, having caught sight of Archer. Her eyes went wide.

"Ah, yes, may I present to you my good friend, Mr. Archer Fitzwalter?" Kineton said, smoothing over her awkwardness.

Archer bowed and gave the terrified girl what he hoped was a friendly smile. "It's a pleasure, Miss Cummings. This book sounds quite fascinating. Men who live under water, you say?"

"Oh, er, yes. It's a novel by Nathan Rice," she said.

"I'll have to look for that one." He paused but with a look from Kineton he quickly added, "Would you care to dance?" He held out a hand.

She didn't say a word, but placed her own gloved hand into his. They took their places on the floor just as the orchestra began to play. Now he only had to think of clever and charming things to say to the girl for the next thirty minutes.

They were only about ten minutes into the dance when he noticed Miss Benton watching him from the side of the room. He turned about and almost missed Miss Cumming's hand, he was so taken with Miss Benton's attention. Quickly, he recalled himself to what he was doing, but a few minutes later, he glanced over at her again. Although it looked like an older woman was trying to speak with her, she was still staring at him.

His heart stuttered and then soared when he decided that she did, indeed, look a trifle jealous. It was the hardest thing to keep the smile from his lips when he realized this. Just for safety's sake, he turned his smile onto his partner who giggled at him for no reason except that he was smiling at her. If only she knew that his grin was not because of her.

Miss Cummings was a rather sweet thing, but he really needed to think of something to say to the chit.

"Er, so, aside from reading is there anything else you enjoy doing, Miss Cummings?"

She started to shake her head, but then said, "Oh, I like to sketch—flowers."

"Really? Perhaps you should meet Miss Benton. She is inordinately fond of her garden."

"Oh, that does sound nice."

And that seemed to be the extent of her conversation. No matter how Archer tried to draw the girl out, her nerves seemed to have gotten the better of her for the remainder of the dance. Well, what she lacked in conversation, she probably made up for in dowry, Archer thought sourly. As Kineton would certainly point out, what difference would it make so long as her purse was full?

That thought made Archer lose his smile altogether. No, he would not be able to marry a girl just for her dowry, no matter what his friend said. Thank goodness, the dance came to an end. He walked Miss Cummings back to her wall, thanked her profusely for her company, and then made a beeline for Miss Benton.

"Did you enjoy the dance, Mr. Fitzwalter?" Miss Benton asked after the usual greetings.

"I did, as a matter of fact. Miss Cummings is a charming young lady. I suggested the two of you should meet. She likes to draw flowers," he said, hoping to arouse that jealousy once again. He was disappointed when she didn't rise to the bait.

"Oh, that is wonderful. I should go over and speak with her later. I'm glad you enjoyed her company," Miss Benton said, looking over his shoulder. "She does look to be a very nice girl."

"Would you care to dance the next set with me?" he asked, hating the fact that he wanted to see that look of longing on her face once again. What was it about this girl that intrigued him so much? He'd done more to win her approval than he'd ever for any other girl, and now he seemed to be after her affections. He truly shouldn't be having such desires.

"I would like that greatly, thank you," she said, turning her gaze back to his.

Perhaps it was just that she was so incredibly lovely. Her deep green eyes glittered with interest and intelligence. Yes, intelligence, he thought, shocked that he found himself as much attracted to her mind as her beauty. The surface was not at all to be discounted, however.

"Do you know the color of your eyes reminds me of the leaves of those roses you were admiring the other day?" he said so softly that only she could hear.

Miss Benton's cheeks flamed pink, and her beautiful full lips parted ever so slightly. "Oh," she breathed.

He put out his hand to lead her onto the dance floor, but as they were making their way in that direction, they started to pass by the French doors leading out into the garden. She suddenly pulled him to stop. "Would you mind very much going for a stroll instead?" she asked. "I'm afraid I get a little overwhelmed with all the noise and people at these parties. A walk in the garden would be most welcome."

"No, I don't mind. I'm actually quite warm after my dance with Miss Cummings and would enjoy the fresh air," he said, leading her outside.

It was rather dark in the garden and giggles—both male and female—could be heard coming from various bushes. Archer avoided them as best as he could and kept to the main pathways.

"Do you think Lady Emmerton has any roses?" he asked as they walked. He'd tucked Miss Benton's hand around his arm and was enjoying the feeling of her being so near.

"I don't know. I suppose we could explore a little and find out," Miss Benton said.

It was exactly what Archer was hoping she'd say. It was an unusually windy evening, but it felt good to his overheated body. "Are you too cold?" he asked, looking down at the tiny little scraps of material he supposed stood in for sleeves. Luckily her gloves reached up past her elbows.

"A little. It is a bracing wind," she admitted. She moved closer to him.

It was all the encouragement he needed. He pulled his arm from between them and wrapped it, instead, around her shoulders. She fit so nicely against his side.

"Oh, look, roses," she said softly.

Indeed, they'd found a few rose bushes amongst all the other flora. None of the buds had yet bloomed, but it was easy to see, even to his untrained eye, that they were indeed roses.

They paused next to the plants so Miss Benton could examine them. She straightened and turned back to him as a cool breeze swirled around them and then moved on. She shivered.

Archer wasn't about to let such an opportunity pass him by. He put arms around her and pulled her closer. She looked up at him with her large, beautiful eyes. She smelled of roses, or was that the plants next to them? He couldn't tell, and he didn't care. All he knew was that a beautiful woman was snuggled up in his arms. He started to lower his head. He had to taste those lips. It was as if they were calling to him, pulling him ever closer.

She was so very lovely. So intelligent. So funny and charming. And so very... off limits.

What was he doing? He was leaving! He was going back to India. He couldn't kiss this girl. He couldn't marry her. What was he even thinking?

Oh, my goodness, he was thinking! Was this girl and her talk of consequences already getting into his head?

He stroked a finger down her soft cheek and looked deeply into her eyes, wanting nothing more than to taste those lips, but... He hated this thinking business. Once he'd started, he didn't think he'd be able to stop.

With a groan, he stepped back away from the siren in his arms.

"What is it?" she asked.

"I'm sorry. I nearly forgot I was a gentleman and you a sweet, refined young lady," he lied. With a heavy sigh, he turned and walked her back to the party. Before he left her with her chaperone, he said, "I do hope you'll forgive my momentary lapse in judgement, Miss Benton."

She looked so incredibly disappointed, his heart filled with joy. "Of course."

~*~

Cassie was attempting to fix her hair in the ladies' retiring room a short time later when Lydia came out from behind one of the screens.

"Cassia," she said, coming up behind her. She smoothed a small bump in Cassie's hair and gave Cassie a smile in the mirror. "There wouldn't possibly be a gentleman responsible for messing up your hair, would there?"

Cassie gave a little laugh. "Only very slightly.

Actually, it was the wind. It's quite breezy this evening, and Mr. Fitzwalter was kind enough to escort me out into the garden, so I could admire Lady Emmerton's roses."

"Uh-huh," Lydia said with a giggle.

"Truly. She's got some lovely classic English roses," Cassie said.

"I'm sure she does."

"And what about you? How are you this evening?" Cassie asked.

Lydia turned slightly pink and whispered, "Having to go to the retiring room a great deal more than usual."

Cassie frowned and turned toward her friend. "Why is that? Is everything all right? I heard Lord Colburne is a wonderful—"

"I've already seen him, and indeed, he is a wonderful physician. But no, there's nothing wrong. I'm, er, enceinte," she said softly.

Cassie widened her eyes but couldn't help her gaze dropping down to Lydia's stomach. "You're going to have a baby?"

Lydia nodded. "I was terrified of when this day would come, but now that it's here, I'm actually rather excited."

"Oh, but that's wonderful! I'm so happy for you!" Cassie gave her friend a quick hug.

"Now, we just have to see you happily married, and then you can start thinking of such joys as well," Lydia said with a giggle.

The thought startled Cassie so much she gave a little yip. "What? No! I mean, I'm sure it will happen, of course, but I'm certain I'm quite a way from such an outcome."

Lydia smiled at her. "You may be a great deal closer than you think—especially if Mr. Fitzwalter is messing up your hair in the garden."

Chapter Fifteen

"Mr. Fitzwalter," Lord Wickford greeted Archer as he came into Powell's.

"Good evening," Archer said, taking the man's outstretched hand.

"Lord Kineton isn't with you this evening?" his lordship asked.

"No. I'm on my own," he said.

The club owner smiled and nodded. "Here to see if you can't find any interested parties for your endeavor?"

Archer returned his smile. "I was rather hoping to blow off some steam, or perhaps lose a few quid. And, I think, another glass of your excellent rum wouldn't go amiss either."

Lord Wickford laughed. "Excellent. That is something every club owner wants to hear. The gaming room is there," he said, indicating the door across from the one Archer knew led to the reading room. "Good luck to you." Lord Wickford gave him a nod and then went into the reading room.

Archer turned and went in the opposite direction. He'd been circumspect and cautious all evening; now it was time to get reckless. Two hours later, his purse was a great deal heavier. He knew when to quit, so he bowed out of the next hand and sauntered over to the reading room to see if there was anything interesting going on there. It was unlikely, but good to check all the same.

The next hour or so was spent casually speaking with a number of men about his project. Some were interested, but not enough to actually ask for more information. It was disappointing and not at all easy work.

Archer rewarded himself, however, with yet another glass of the rum he'd mentioned to Wickford. He'd just sat down with it in an area away from those he'd spoken with earlier when Lord Wickford approached him with another gentleman in tow.

"Mr. Fitzwalter, have you met the Duke of Warwick?" the club owner asked.

Archer jumped to his feet. "Er, ah, no." He bowed low. "It is an honor, Your Grace."

The man looked a little startled, but nodded.

"I, er, I grew up in Warwick," Archer quickly explained. "My father is Baron Fitzwalter."

The duke smiled. "Ah! I was wondering if you were related to the baron." He put out his hand. "I am very happy to meet a neighbor. How is your father doing?"

Archer's heart fell a little as he thought of his father. "Not so well, I'm sorry to say." An idea struck. "But perhaps you might be able to help, if you... you wouldn't mind?"

"Of course!" the duke turned to Lord Wickford. "You were right, I am very happy for this introduction. I don't know how you do it, Wickford, but you always know just the right people to put together."

The gentleman laughed. "Well, I have to say, this is a pleasant surprise. Honestly, I had no idea Mr. Fitzwalter's father lived in your district. I thought you might be interested in a business proposition he's putting together. But I'll leave you two to talk."

The duke looked momentarily intrigued, but he nodded and added, "Do, please, send over a bottle of rum for us to enjoy as we talk business."

"Happy to." Wickford bowed slightly and went off to see to things.

Archer indicated the duke take a seat as he did so himself. Honestly, this couldn't have been more provident.

"Now, tell me what's happening with your father. I'm sorry to hear he's not doing well," the duke said, getting straight down to business.

"Thank you, Your Grace. Physically, my father is fine, it's his estate that is having problems," Archer admitted.

"Correct me if I'm wrong, but your father has always had difficulties there," the duke said.

"You are not wrong. Sadly, from what I understand things have gotten rather worse of late. There has been quite a lot of flooding. Might you have any advice on what to do about it?" Perhaps Archer could do a good turn for the baron. He certainly didn't expect the man to reciprocate, but he wouldn't let that stop him.

The duke sat in silence, sipping at his rum for a minute or more after Archer had finished speaking. He slowly began to nod, despite the frown still furrowing his brow. "It is, indeed, a difficult situation. My own lands are not immune either, naturally. I have managed to find an excellent man who knows just how to handle it. He's done... well, to say that he's performed miracles would not be hyperbole. I'll write and ask him to pay a call on the baron, your father. I'm certain he'll have some ideas on how to improve your father's fields."

"That would be incredible, Your Grace. I can't tell you how much of a relief that would be for me. It's been rather difficult for us since I've been so far away and unable to help out in any way," Archer explained. He failed to say that his father had sent him away because he didn't think Archer had the ability to help, but maybe this might change his mind. Consequences, he thought, as an image of Miss Benton fluttered in his mind's eye, making him smile.

"I understand. Now, do tell me about this new business of yours. Wickford said he was very impressed with your ideas," the duke said, looking relieved to have gotten beyond his ducal business.

Archer spent the next twenty minutes outlining his ideas and answering some very pertinent questions. For a while, he felt as if he were being questioned as closely as any French spy, but he answered all the duke's questions the best he could. By the time he'd finished, the man nodded and smiled.

"It sounds as if you've got a bit more work to do to put it all together, but from what I've heard so far, it sounds quite intriguing."

"Thank you, Your Grace," Archer said, sitting back and taking in a deep breath.

"Come by my house tomorrow, and we will discuss it further. If I'm still in favor after sleeping on the idea, you can count on my participation."

Archer resisted the sudden urge to jump up and

whoop with excitement. "I would be more than happy to do so," he said as calmly as he could.

"Am I your only investor so far?" he asked.

That made Archer's happiness deflate a touch. "At the moment, yes. But I have a number of interested gentlemen."

"Good. I won't be able to contribute enough to fund the entire project, I'm sure, but with enough people, we should be able to ensure that you get it off the ground," the duke said. He lifted his glass. "Here's to a successful business collaboration."

~April 23~

Saturday afternoon Cassie and Cynthia were going over what Cassie would wear that evening to Lady Ayres's soirée. It was going to be a major event—positively everyone who was anyone would be there.

"You absolutely must look your best," Cynthia said, going through Cassie's wardrobe. She shuffled through the gowns there but didn't seem to find what she was looking for.

"Why is this party so important?" Cassie asked, sitting back on her bed, watching her sister.

Cynthia stopped what she was doing and turned to her. "What do you mean 'why is it important'? It's the Ladies' Wagering Whist Society! Ostensibly, the party is to celebrate the nuptials of all the weddings we helped to come about last year. Can you believe we assisted six couples to the alter?" She shook her head in disbelief as she turned back to Cassie's dresses.

"Goodness, that is a lot. I know two of them—Bee and Bel, but who else did you help?" Cassie asked.

Cynthia turned back around and ticked them off on her fingers. "Bee and Lord St. Vincent, Bel and

Lord Conway, Lady Margaret and Lord Rossburke—you'll meet them for the first time tonight, they've been at his estate in Scotland. We also assisted Lady St. Vincent, who was a widow last season, to marry Mr. Aldridge. Also married in this last year was Mr. Aldridge's mother who is now the Duchess of Bolton, and the Duchess of Kendell will soon be married to Lord Gorling."

"That's incredible," Cassie said, impressed despite herself.

"I know!" Cynthia looked so proud as if she had single-handedly assisted all the couples herself. "But even more than that, Cassie, is the reputation the Wagering Whist Society has achieved in the past few years. Everyone, but everyone wants to come to our parties. What started out as a small celebration with just our friends has turned into something so enormous I'm surprised Lady Ayres agreed to host. Her home isn't as large as some, but she insisted that as a founder of the Society, she should host the party."

"So how many people are coming?" Cassie asked, a little afraid to hear the answer. She hated big crowds. She always became too overwhelmed.

"A couple of hundred at least," Cynthia said, returning to her inspection of Cassie's wardrobe. "Why can I not find your new gown with the green ribbons?"

"Oh, er, I might have, um, gotten it dirty," Cassie said, looking down at her much too clean finger-nails.

"What? But it's an evening gown! How could you have?"

"I went into the breakfast room to check on my roses after the ball last week and... well... I don't know, dirt just seems to jump out at me. Sally took it and said she'd do her best to get it out."

Cynthia sighed heavily and shook her head. "You are impossible! Very well, I suppose you should wear this one then," she said, pulling out a white gown with a pale green undress. Cassie liked the double layer, but it was a little more low-cut than most of her other gowns, which made her feel a bit self-conscious.

"Are you sure I should wear—" Cassie started, but then stopped. The look on her sister's face let her know that any arguments would not be entertained.

There was a knock on the door, however, which distracted them both from any potential unpleasantness.

"Come," Cynthia and Cassie called out together.

A footman entered, holding a salver with a rather thick note on it. "This just came for you, Miss Benton," he said, offering it to Cassie.

"Thank you, Frederick," Cassie said, picking up the note.

He bowed and left the room while Cassie opened the seal. A number of slips of paper and coins spilled out. She ignored them and read the note which had her gasping.

"What is it?" Cynthia asked, coming over. She began to pick up the pieces of paper and looking at them. "These are IOUs!" she said, looking through them.

"The note is from Mr. Fitzwalter. He says that this is his winnings from the past two nights at Powell's." She paused and looked up at her sister. "What is Powell's?"

"A gentlemen's club," Cynthia told her.

Cassie nodded and returned her attention to the

note. "He asks that I give the money—four hundred and thirty-six pounds!—to a school for the children of the Rookeries."

"Four hundred... that's a lot of money!" Cynthia exclaimed.

"My goodness!" Cassie sorted through all the IOUs and money, gathering it all back together.

"Why would he send this to you to give to the poor?"

Cassie told her sister about the incident outside the theatre, finishing with, "So, I suppose this is what he earned with those ten pounds he was going to give to that child who tried to pick his pocket."

"That's quite a lot of winnings from ten pounds."

"Yes, it is. I guess I should give this all to Lord Welles. He's the correct person, isn't he?"

"Indeed. I couldn't think of a better person to give it to," Cynthia agreed. "Well, you must have made quite an impression on the gentleman," Cynthia said, handing over the IOUs in her hand and giving her sister a smile. "I'm proud of you. You thought with a clear head and obviously made a compelling argument that impressed the gentleman."

"Yes, I suppose so."

"Now all you need to do is make such an argument for him to propose to you," Cynthia said with a laugh.

"Oh, I don't know about that," Cassie responded even as she felt her cheeks heat with embarrassment.

"No?" her sister asked, narrowing her eyes at her.

"Well, I mean, he's a very nice gentleman, and he's extremely good at making grand gestures. But I want to marry a scientist who would understand me and respect my work. Don't you think?"

"Mr. Crome?" Cynthia asked.

Cassie lifted a shoulder. "I don't know. Perhaps?"

"Well, let's see how things progress, but I don't think you should rule anyone out just yet—especially when he gives you over four hundred pounds to give to the poor," Cynthia said with a laugh.

~*~

"Sorrell, you promised!" Cynthia said, trying both to keep her voice as quiet as possible and the tears from leaking out of her eyes. There were too many ears in the house, and she didn't know which emotion had caused the tears. She was furious. She was going to be horrendously embarrassed. And there was a pain in her heart that hurt so much she almost looked down to see if Sorrell had slipped a knife between her ribs when she wasn't paying attention.

"I know I did and I apologize," her husband said as he tied the laces on his shoes.

"Don't apologize to me, apologize to Lady Ayres! It is her party you won't be attending." Cynthia walked away and then back again. She couldn't keep still; she was so upset.

"You will have to make my apologies to our hostess for me. I simply cannot attend. Lord Dartmouth has requested a meeting, and when the Lord Chamberlain requests a meeting, you show up," he said, straightening up.

"But..." Cynthia paused to walk away again. She could feel the tears trying to escape but she would not—absolutely would not—give Sorrell the satisfaction of seeing just how upset she was. She turned away and blinked furiously. She turned back to say, "All my friends will be there. All the women of the Wagering Whist Society. All the men too! Two dukes!" she added for good measure.

He frowned at her. "A man's rank doesn't always correspond to his position in the government. Neither Warwick nor Bolton are active in Parliament. Lord Gorling, who will also be there is, but the Lord Chamberlain didn't ask to see him. He asked to speak with me, and I am going. I'm sorry. You will make my excuses."

"Well, will your meeting take all night? Perhaps you can join me there later?" Cynthia asked hopefully.

"I don't know how long it's going to take, but if it isn't too late by the time we're finished, then, yes, of course, I will join you at Lady Ayres' soirée," he said as if he were making a great sacrifice.

"Thank you." It was the very least she could get from him, but she would be happy with it. Truthfully, she didn't have a choice in the matter.

Chapter Sixteen

Lady Ayres greeted Cynthia and Cassie the moment they walked in the door. "But where is Lord Sorrell?" she asked immediately.

Cynthia put on her best smile. "He sends his regrets. Apparently, this evening was the only time the Lord Chamberlain could meet with him."

"Oh, I am so sorry," Lady Ayres said, truly looking disappointed.

Cynthia appreciated it a great deal, but she refused to dwell on it. "As am I, however, I am especially excited to be here this evening. It's been too long since we've all been together at once—every member of the Ladies' Wagering Whist Society and their husbands!"

"Yes! Not only that, but Lord and Lady Rossburke have come down from Scotland, the new Mr. and Mrs. Aldridge are here..."

"Have they arrived already?" Cynthia asked, getting excited again.

"The Rossburkes haven't arrived yet, but I expect them any minute. The Aldridges are here already," Lady Ayres said. Her smile just couldn't be wider. She must have been so happy. "And of course, there are so many others as well," she added with a laugh.

"Well, naturally! How could anyone turn down an invitation to what will probably be the event of the season!" Cynthia said.

Lady Ayres laughed. "One can only hope."

Cynthia led Cassie away so their hostess could greet more guests.

~*~

Archer parted ways with the Kinetons almost the moment the three of them had walked through the door of Lady Ayres's soirée. Lady Kineton went off to see her friends, Kineton went in the opposite direction, and Archer paused to look around and see if there was anyone he knew.

Nearby, a slightly gray-haired man in a bottle-green coat with darker green embroidery was laughing loudly at something a beautiful, petite woman with light brown hair was saying. She was pretty—not stunning, but pretty enough. She and the older man she was speaking with seemed to be well made for each other as they were both dressed to the height of fashion. Archer was intrigued.

"She's beautiful, isn't she?" a deep voice said, coming up from behind him.

Archer turned and found the Duke of Warwick looking at the woman with warmth. "Extremely fashionable, is what I was thinking," Archer said with a laugh. "They make a good couple, despite the fact that he's probably twice her age."

Warwick laughed. "He's her father, and she is my wife. Come, I'll introduce you."

Archer followed the duke, trying not to look like a boy heading toward a puppy. He loved fashionable people, and this gentleman and his lovely daughter looked to be precisely his sort of people.

"My sweet, this is Mr. Archibald Fitzwalter. His mother is Lady Fitzwalter. You met her when we were last at Warwick, didn't you?" the duke asked his wife.

"Oh, yes! What a lovely woman. I'm so pleased to meet you, Mr. Fitzwalter. And this is my father, Viscount Ayres," she said, turning a kind smile toward him.

"I'm very pleased to meet you both," Archer said, bowing. He quickly put things together and realized the gentleman was his host. A glance at the sumptuous home in which he was currently standing had him wondering if perhaps Lord Ayres might be persuaded to join his son-in-law in funding his project. He turned to the lady. "I am greatly looking forward to a profitable partnership with your husband, Your Grace."

"Oh?" she turned a quizzical expression on to the duke.

The Duke of Warwick gave a little laugh, clearly understanding immediately what Archer was up to. "Mr. Fitzwalter is looking for investors in a project he's putting together in India. I've agreed to back him if he can get more gentlemen involved. You wouldn't be interested, Ayres, would you?"

Lord Ayres gave an apologetic smile. "I'm afraid not. I've got all my funds tied up in my estate in Ireland. Feel free to ask around, though. You might try the card room. Always a number of gentlemen there with way too much money on their hands," he said with a laugh.

"I imagine that's why they're in the card room, trying to get rid of it, no?" the duchess asked with a laugh.

"One might think so," her husband agreed,

chuckling.

"Thank you, my lord, I think I will follow your suggestion." Archer bowed to them all and headed in the direction the gentlemen indicated.

He paused just inside the door to take in the room. The only people he knew were those who he'd already approached with his proposal. He wondered if he might be able to convince one of them to introduce him to their friends.

~*~

"Lord Welles, would you mind very much if we discussed business for a moment," Cassie asked Lydia's husband the moment she saw him at Lady Ayres's party.

The man smiled broadly at her. "Business, Miss Benton? What sort of business do you have in mind?"

"Your knowledge of the Rookeries," she said, grateful that he hadn't just laughed straight out into her face.

His smile softened. "Ah, that business. Yes, of course."

"A friend of mine—I'm not certain if they want to be named or not—has just given me four hundred and thirty-six pounds. They have requested the money go to funding education. Might you know where to donate it?"

"That's a lot of money!" Lord Welles exclaimed.

"It was their winnings at the card table, I believe."

He nodded. "Of course, that makes sense. Well, the short answer to your question is, yes. I do know where that money could go to very good use."

"Discussing money at a party?" Lord Colburne asked with a slight laugh to his voice as he joined them. He turned and gave Cassie a slight bow. "I can't believe that Lord Welles would be so insufferable as to bore you with such talk, Miss Benton."

Cassie laughed. "I'm afraid I am the insufferable one, my lord."

"No, I do not believe it," he said, clearly teasing her.

"Miss Benton has been given a very nice sum of money which she would like me to turn into education for the children of the Rookeries," Lord Welles informed his friend.

As the two gentlemen bantered back and forth, Cassie's eye was caught by Lord Kineton. He was standing not too far off, staring directly at her. She didn't know why, but there was something in his look that sent a shiver of unease down her spine.

She gave herself a mental shake. How ridiculous! She knew Philip. They were friends now. She'd completely gotten over her girlhood fancy of him. There was no reason to feel at all apprehensive or put out because he was looking at her. She returned her attention to the two gentlemen in front of her.

"Miss Benton?" Lord Colburne said.

"I'm sorry, someone was..." She gave a little laugh. "Never mind. I'm sorry, my lord, I missed what you said."

"I asked whether you knew who the money had come from," his lordship repeated.

"Oh, yes, but I don't know if they want their identity shared," she told him.

"Hmmm, how very curious. Well, if you're sure he wants the money to go for education..." Lord Colburne started.

Lord Welles burst out laughing. "The doctor would like more money given for healthy vegetables and medicines."

"But the health of the people is—"

"Yes, yes, it is vital," Lord Welles answered cutting him off. Clearly, this was an argument the two had on a number of occasions.

"I'm sorry, my lord, but the person specifically requested this money go toward education," Cassie said, jumping in.

"Well," Lord Colburne huffed. He then smiled at her. "I have to agree, education is important too."

~*~

Nearly an hour later, Archer's wallet was a touch lighter, and he'd been turned down by no fewer than twelve gentlemen. This was a disheartening business, he thought as he wandered back out into the main drawing room.

"Good evening, Mr. Fitzwalter," Lady Colburne greeted him from a group of people with two men and an older woman. It took him a moment to remember that she was a friend of Lady Sorrell and Miss Benton's, but he was certain he hadn't met any of the other people she was with.

The older lady looked homely, and one of the men looked to be your typical dandy. He peered at Archer through a ridiculous monocle on a bright red ribbon.

"Good evening, my lady," Archer said, giving her a small bow.

"Oh, put that thing away, Ainsby, you look preposterous," the other gentleman said. He turned back to Archer and then to Lady Colburne, waiting for her introduction.

The man he'd called Ainsby frowned at him. "It

is not preposterous—"

"Yes, it is, my dear. It's a silly affectation, and it doesn't become you at all," the older lady said sweetly. If she had patted his cheek like a little boy, Archer wouldn't have been surprised. It was all he could do not to laugh at the poor fellow.

"Mr. Fitzwalter," Lady Colburne said, clearly trying to hold back her own laughter. "May I make you known to Duchess Bolton, her nephew Lord Ainsby, and her son, Mr. Aldridge?"

He bowed to them all. Oddly, the duchess began to curtsey to him but then stopped herself, ending up with an odd little bob.

She burst out laughing. "I do beg your pardon, Mr. Fitzwalter, I have only just married my dearest Bolton and am still getting used to this duchess business."

He gave her a warm smile. "It must be rather disconcerting."

"Oh, it is! After having spent thirty-five years as the wife of a watchmaker to suddenly find myself a duchess... well, yes, disconcerting is an excellent description," she said with a titter of laughter.

"A watchmaker?" The words burst out of his mouth before he could think. "How fascinating," he said, attempting to redeem himself.

"It actually was quite interesting. My son, of course, has taken over his business," she said, indicating the well-dressed gentleman by her side. Well, that answered that question, Archer thought to himself. Despite his excellent taste in clothing—as compared to his cousin—he clearly would not be in a financial position to invest.

"It's not as interesting as my mother makes it out to be, but I enjoy the occupation," the gentleman said in a friendly way.

"Did I hear right," the dandy said, "that you are looking for investors for a project in India?"

"Yes, that's right," Archer said, not that anyone who spent as much blunt on clothing as this fellow must would have the funds to invest.

"What is the project?" the duchess asked.

"I am setting up a company to import spices from Madras," Archer told her.

"Oh, that sounds interesting," Lord Ainsby said with a slight frown. Perhaps all the pomade in his hair made it difficult for him to understand simple concepts, Archer thought with a little internal laugh.

"Yes, I hope it will be both interesting and profitable. Sadly, I don't have the wherewithal to establish the company myself, so I'm looking for others to buy a share," he explained.

"But you'll do all the work? You're only looking for funding," he clarified.

"Exactly. Are you active in Parliament, my lord?" Archer asked simply to turn the conversation in another direction. He was certain neither of these men were the sort to be able to invest, so he didn't see the point in prolonging the conversation.

At his question, the dandy's aunt burst into giggles, and his cousin smiled broadly in amusement. Lord Ainsby scowled at them both before turning back to Archer. "No, I have very little interest in politics."

~*~

Cassie needed a break. She was feeling overwhelmed, which wasn't at all surprising, considering the number of people packed into Lady Ayres's drawing rooms. It was nearly impossible to move!

Too many people. Too much noise. Her head was spinning.

Usually she was able to go for a walk with someone outside. She distinctly remembered a very nice walk with Mr. Fitzwalter not too long ago.

But this evening neither he nor Mr. Crome were nearby. She gave a shrug and decided to go alone.

She leaned toward her sister who was standing next to her, watching the dancers or perhaps just staring off at nothing. Cynthia seemed particularly distracted this evening. "I'm going to look at Lady Ayres' roses. Do you want to join me?"

It took a moment, but finally her sister blinked and turned to her. "No, you go on."

"Are you all right?" Cassie asked.

Cynthia gave a little smile. "Yes, thank you. You go and admire the roses, just don't be too long."

Cassie gave a nod and found her way through the crowd to the French doors and into the garden. It was a lovely evening. A little chill, but not so cold that Cassie felt the need to go back in for her shawl. The garden turned out to be bigger than she expected. It was a simple, but elegant design—a large circle with a fountain in the center, a path running around the circumference, and others going toward the center. Each quadrant was filled with larger bushes toward the center, tapering down to the shorter spring flowers at the edges. And yes, they included some lovely roses which were just beginning to bloom.

Cassie wandered around the perimeter, admiring the flowers. She'd just reached one side and the path leading toward the center when Lord Kineton stepped out from behind an evergreen.

"Oh! Lord Kineton, I didn't see you," Cassie

said, startled by his sudden appearance.

"The bushes do an excellent job of hiding people, don't they?" he asked.

Cassie looked toward them. "Yes, I suppose they do. Despite that, it's a very pleasing design." When she turned back to him, he'd come closer—much closer. Cassie took a step back. There wasn't a lot of room between the path leading toward the center and the outer flower bed that lined the wall separating the Ayres's garden from the neighbor's.

Her heart began to beat faster as he came even closer. She was trapped, and they both knew it.

Chapter Seventeen

"You're looking particularly lovely tonight, Cassia," Lord Kineton said.

"Er, thank you. Is Lady Kineton with you?" Cassie asked, looking behind him pointedly.

A harsh laugh burst out of him. "Martha? God, no! She doesn't want anything to do with me when we're out in public. No, no, she's got her swains who dote on her. I'm only good to satisfy her need for attention at home when there's no one else."

"Oh." Cassie didn't know what else to say. It sounded like a horrific marriage.

"Indeed. You, however, are beautiful. Why did I not marry you? Do you remember?"

"You married money," Cassie reminded him.

"Ah, right," he nodded, taking yet another step forward. "And I had no idea that dear professor, Lord Benton, was rich as Croesus."

"I don't know about that, but I do know my parents knew you needed to marry for money," Cassie told him honestly.

"Hah!" he laughed again. "And they didn't want a gold-digger for a son-in-law, is that it?"

Cassie just shrugged, but it was the truth. She

wouldn't have cared. She was in love with him, then. But no longer, she realized. Goodness, she'd been so afraid of coming to London for fear of meeting this man. Now that she had, repeatedly, she realized he no longer held that special place in her heart. He no longer affected her in the least—except now when she felt trapped by his attention. She tried to side step away from him, but he simply moved with her.

"It is just as well. Martha and her father are more than rich enough for my taste. You, on the other hand..." He reached out and ran a finger down her cheek. "Are much more beautiful than my dear, wealthy wife." He leaned in toward her, and Cassie tried to retreat, but she had nowhere to go. If she stepped backwards, she would be trampling on flowers, and she couldn't do that.

"Lord Kineton," Cassie started. She put her hands on his chest to push him away, but he was too strong and determined. "No—" she started just before his lips landed on hers.

She tried to shake him off, catching sight of some movement out of the corner of her eye. Mr. Crome! He would save her. Oh, thank goodness!

She pushed at Lord Kineton's chest and tried to move her face away to show Mr. Crome that she was not a willing participant. But the man just stopped where he was and watched them!

She tried to scream at him, but Lord Kineton grabbed the back of her head and pressed his lips even harder against hers. It was impossible to scream with a man's lips pressed against hers, but she had to do something. Surely Mr. Crome—

"What the hell?!"

Her would-be savior was shoved out of the way, and Mr. Fitzwalter strode forward. He grabbed Lord

Kineton's coat, pulled him off her, and then, without warning, planted his fist in the man's face. Lord Kineton went flying backward into the nearest bush. He stumbled, trying to regain his balance.

"What the... Fitz!" Lord Kineton objected.

"Are you foxed?" Mr. Fitzwalter demanded. He didn't wait for an answer, but instead turned back to her. "Are you all right, Miss Benton?"

"Yes, thank you," Cassie said, wiping the back of her hand across her lips. "I tried to push him off, but..."

"But he's an imbecile who doesn't know when to back off, apparently," Mr. Fitzwalter said angrily, shifting his eyes toward his friend.

"She—" Lord Kineton started.

"Don't even think of saying that she wanted you kissing her. It was clear as day she didn't!" Mr. Fitzwalter snapped.

"Thank you, sir, for saving me," Cassie said. Her heart was still beating wildly, but now she thought it might be more because of the gentleman's heroics than Lord Kineton's inappropriate behavior.

"Anytime," he said with a slight bow. His hand shot out and grabbed Lord Kineton who looked like he was trying to sneak off. He turned back toward her with a little half smile on his lips. "Would you care to have a go at him? I'll be more than happy to hold him steady."

Cassie just looked from Mr. Fitzwalter to Lord Kineton and back again. "I... I don't know what you mean."

"I think he was offering you a chance to scold or hit me," Lord Kineton said with a little laugh at Cassie's confusion. He turned to his friend. "She doesn't exhibit such behavior. She is much too even-tempered."

"I believe logical is what you mean, perhaps even analytical," Cassie supplied. She was beginning to calm, especially with the absurdity of the situation. "I'm a scientist."

"Are you really so cool that you don't feel any anger toward this imbecile?" Mr. Fitzwalter asked in disbelief.

"No! I am angry," Cassie said, feeling a little shocked and hurt at the accusation. "I don't know if it would do any good for me to…"

"Hit him? I think it would do you both a lot of good, actually. You'll feel better, and he'll feel worse," Mr. Fitzwalter said with a laugh.

Cassie thought about it for a moment.

"No! Don't think! Just act!" the man snapped.

And before she even realized what she was doing, she'd pulled her arm back, and her hand shot out and punched Lord Kineton in the nose. "That's for tonight," she said with enthusiasm. And then with only the most minute pause to consider, she did it again. "And that's for three summers ago."

There was a horrifying crunch and Cassie's hand hurt like the dickens. Lord Kineton yelped, but she was too busy shaking out her hand and inspecting her knuckles to pay him any attention. If it hadn't hurt so much, that would have felt really good. She practically laughed out loud at the absurdity of it.

"Well done! I think you broke his nose!" Mr. Fitzwalter said, standing back.

Lord Kineton was pressing a handkerchief to his face. "I can'b believe you bunched me! Dwice!" he said, sounding congested.

"Well, you deserved it," Cassie argued. She looked a little more closely at him, noticing that his pristine white handkerchief was beginning to turn red with blood. "Is it actually broken?"

"It feelds like id. Ow!" the man said, staggering backwards a step.

"I should get Lord Colburne." She took a step sideways toward the house.

Mr. Fitzwalter grabbed her arm. He was smiling broadly now. "That was brilliant," he told her. "Absolutely brilliant—and you acted without thought. I am proud of you," he added with a laugh.

Cassie could only giggle, she felt so... elated! It was definitely the oddest thing and would take some thinking to understand it. But no, perhaps she shouldn't think. Perhaps sometimes, it was simply better to just act. Never in her life had she even considered such a thing. And just now, she most definitely shouldn't be thinking, but acting on bringing a doctor to attend to Lord Kineton.

She turned and ran back into the house.

~*~

"Well, dat was a brilliand idea," Kineton said as soon as Miss Benton had gone. He tilted his head back to try to stem the flow of blood.

"Yes, actually, I think it was," Archer agreed with a chuckle. "Of course, I didn't expect her to break your nose. But I'm not going to say that you didn't deserve it."

"All I did was—"

"Kiss her against her will," Archer replied, his own anger spiking again. "Just what the hell were you thinking?"

"Just havin' a lidle fun, dat's all," his erstwhile friend said with a shrug.

"Fun! Fun? You call attacking a girl, forcing your attentions on her fun?" Nope, he was not angry, not any more. Now he was simply disgusted. "Have you no morals?"

"I hab morals! I aldso hab a wibe who is out carousing all she dikes, so I didn't see any reason—"

"If your wife is carousing, first of all, it is not with unwilling participants, and secondly, it is your own fault for allowing her to do so!"

"Id's not dike I can condrol her! She's her own berson. She makes her own decisionds. And she holds the burse strinks," he added much more softly.

Archer could only shake his head. "You're bloody lucky it wasn't me who punched you. I can guarantee you I would have done a lot more than break your nose," he said.

"So, you breally like her?" Kineton said.

"What? I saved her from your beastly paws, that's all," Archer said, not even bothering to look his way.

"Yes, but you wouldn' habe done so if you didn' dike her," his friend pressed.

Archer had nothing to say to that. Did he like her?

No, you idiot, you love her. The words came completely unbidden into his mind, but once they were there, he simply could not shake them out again. No matter that he well knew how wrong it was.

He couldn't love her. He was leaving, he reminded himself. He was moving back to India, and he couldn't take a sweet, innocent like Miss Benton with him.

Why not? his traitorous mind asked.

"She's got her roses. Her botany," he said out loud.

"Whad?" Kineton looked over at him.

"Nothing. I'm just being a fool, don't mind me."

Kineton nodded as if there was nothing unusual in that, which just made Archer question why he was friends with this man.

~*~

Inside Lady Ayres's drawing room, Cassie looked about frantically.

"Is everything all right, Miss Benton?" Duchess Bolton asked, coming up to her.

"Oh, er, yes. I'm looking for Lord Colburne. You wouldn't happen to know where he is, would you?"

"Yes, I saw him a few moments ago... yes, there he is, speaking with the Duke of Warwick." She indicated the men standing off near a wall.

"Thank you." Cassie rushed off toward them.

She approached cautiously, not wanting to be rude. "I do beg your pardon, Lord Colburne?"

He turned to her and gave her a smile. It quickly disappeared, however, when he saw her right hand cradled in her left. "Is everything all right, Miss Benton?" he asked, reaching out and taking her hand and opening it flat. "Have you hurt your hand?" he asked when she winced.

"Only slightly. I'm afraid Lord Kineton is in much worse shape. Would you mind coming and taking a look?" she asked.

Lord Colburne exchanged a look with the duke, and both men indicated she should lead the way.

When they reached the garden, Mr. Fitzwalter was looking oddly confused at the ground, his arms crossed in front of his chest. Lord Kineton was still standing with his now bright red handkerchief pressed to his nose, his head tilted back.

"My goodness!" Lord Colburne said, moving forward to the injured man more quickly. He pulled Lord Kineton's handkerchief away and gently inspected his face.

"Ow! Dat hurds!" the man said.

"I am so sorry, but I need to see if it's broken," his lordship said.

"Ib is!" Lord Kineton said, nearly incomprehensibly.

The duke turned to Cassie, trying very hard to contain a smile. "Can you tell me what inspired you to, er, I assume, punch Lord Kineton, Miss Benton?"

"He kissed—"

"He attacked her," Mr. Fitzwalter interrupted her. "I put a stop to it and then held him while Miss Benton delivered the well-deserved blow."

The duke's mouth dropped open.

Voices behind her made Cassie turn around. She was horrified to see the Duchess of Bolton, Cynthia, Lady Ayres, Lydia, and Diana all approaching with avid curiosity.

The duke also saw the ladies and strode forward to meet them. "Ladies, I don't think we want an audience, nor for this little incident to get around."

"What happened?" Lady Ayres asked.

"Miss Benton exacted a little retribution when Lord Kineton made an unwelcome advance. Everything is fine. Colburne is taking care of Kineton, and Miss Benton, er, I think is fine as well." He turned to get her confirmation on that.

She nodded. "I may have bruised my hand, that's all," she said with an apologetic smile.

"Cassie?" Cynthia came forward, even as the other women turned around giggling but returning to the party as requested.

"It was Mr. Fitzwalter's idea. Perhaps he isn't such a good influence..."

"I think it was brilliant," the man said, coming up from behind her. "She's got a mean right hook," he told her sister.

"But you're all right?" Cynthia asked, tucking a strand of hair back up into Cassie's chignon.

"Yes, I'm fine."

"All right. Perhaps... perhaps we should leave," Cynthia said.

"If you do, there is sure to be talk," the duke pointed out. "I think it would be best if the four of us returned—"

"I should probably stay with Kineton and see him home," Mr. Fitzwalter said.

"Oh, yes. Yes, of course," the duke said.

"You're a very good friend," Cynthia agreed.

"Not really. I did hold him while your sister hit him," he said, giving Cassie a wink.

She couldn't help the giggle that gurgled up her throat. She couldn't believe she had punched a man—no more than she could understand the strange feelings of warmth and joy she was feeling as she remembered how Mr. Fitzwalter had shoved Mr. Crome aside and come to her rescue.

Chapter Eighteen

~April 24~

"Cynthia, what are your plans for this afternoon?" Sorrell asked that morning at breakfast, not even looking up from his paper.

"Nothing significant, why?" Cynthia asked, curious.

"I thought we might go for a ride in the park," he said, finally raising his eyes.

Cynthia nearly started out of her chair. Sorrell wanted to go riding in the park? With her?

"If you don't want to—" he started when she didn't say anything.

"No! No, I'd be more than happy to do so," she said quickly.

"Good. Cassia will join us, naturally," he said, returning his attention to whatever it was he was reading.

"Of course," she replied. And he wanted to spend time with her sister? What had gotten into the man? Could he possibly be trying to make up for all the times he'd spurned them both in order to go out on his own?

No, it couldn't be that—could it?

The question nagged at Cynthia all morning until, finally at three, he sent the footman up to see whether they were ready to leave. Cynthia had just finished dressing, so she went in to check on her sister.

"Are you ready?" she asked Cassie.

"Yes," her sister said, standing. She'd been sitting on the chair in her room, reading, looking as if she'd been ready for some time. That was the nice thing about Cassie; she was always on time.

They went down and met Sorrell in the foyer. He gave them both a warm smile. "Don't you both look lovely this afternoon? Every man in the park will envy me."

Cynthia couldn't stop the giggle. "Oh, Sorrell," she said, walking past him and out the door to where their horses were being held for them. She hoped he didn't see how very pleased she was at his comment. The man certainly could be extremely charming when he wanted—it was how she'd fallen in love with him in the first place. Sadly, it didn't seem as if the feeling had been mutual. But, no, she refused to think of that now. They were going for a ride in the park at the height of the afternoon when everyone, but everyone, would be out. She was going to enjoy herself.

It had been so long since Cynthia had been to the park at the height of the promenade that she'd almost forgotten how very crowded it could be. There was a steady stream of traffic moving in both directions, as well as a number of people walking along the pathway next to Rotten Row.

"Oh, Lady Sorrell!" a voice called out to them soon after they'd joined the crowds.

Cynthia looked to see who it was and found

Lydia waving at her from a phaeton coming toward them. Diana was at the reins, and the two looked wonderfully fashionable perched up high. She laughed and waved. She turned and caught Cassie's attention and motioned to their friends.

Cassie waved. "You look very grand!" she called out as they passed by.

The girls laughed and continued on.

Cynthia, Cassie, and Sorrell rode in silence, each one looking around as they moved ever so slowly forward. Sorrell spotted someone he knew, walking along the path, and they paused for a moment while he greeted them. As they did so, a carriage came up behind them.

"Blocking the way, ladies," a friendly voice called out from the carriage.

Cynthia turned and found the Duke and Duchess of Bolton smiling at them.

"We don't mean to be rude," the duchess said with a little laugh, "but you are holding up everyone behind you."

"Sorrell," Cassie called out after giving their friends a wave.

"Yes, yes, we're moving on," Sorrell said, giving a nod to Lord Stenford and Miss Cummings, who he'd been speaking with.

Cynthia maneuvered her horse so that she could ride next to her friends for a moment as they all got moving again. "Good afternoon, Duke, Duchess. How are you on this very fine afternoon?"

"Very well, Lady Sorrell, and you?" the duke asked, looking quite jovial next to his lady and two of their dogs.

"Also well, thank you. Is that Duchess up next to you?" she asked, smiling at the pups who were both looking so entirely comfortable on the seat.

"Yes, and Fluff, who has taken Duchess under her wing, so to speak." The duchess gave the all-black spaniel a fond caress. "Did you enjoy the party last night?" she asked.

"Immensely," Cynthia answered. "I have to say, Lady Ayres and Lady Blakemore do an excellent job arranging parties. I think everyone who was anyone was in attendance."

"I do believe you're right. Or if they weren't there, I'm certain today they are wishing they had been," the duchess said with a laugh.

"Cynthia!" Sorrell called out. "Care to join us?" He sounded a bit annoyed, so she gave her friends a happy wave and rode forward to rejoin him and Cassie.

"Sorry, I just wanted to greet my friends," she said, taking her place beside him.

"I appreciate that, but you'd just forced me to move on, so—"

"Yes, fair's fair," she interrupted.

They rode on for some time, nearly reaching the end of the road when Sorrell suddenly said, "Ah-ha! I knew it!" He directed his horse off to the side and actually dismounted. "Bunbury, old man." He reached a hand out and shook the shorter gentleman's hand.

"Sorrell! Surprised to see you out here today," Lord Bunbury said. He glanced up and saw Cynthia and Cassie doing their best to hold their mounts steady as a barouche passed them by. "And Lady Sorrell, what a treat to see you again."

"And you, my lord. Have you met my sister, Miss Benton?" Cynthia asked, giving a nod toward Cassie.

"No, I have not had the pleasure," he nodded

toward her sister.

"Been out of town, Bunbury? I've been trying to set up a meeting, but your man has been fobbing me off," Sorrell said, reclaiming the man's attention.

"Eh? Yes. We were in the country visiting the children. You know, a little rest, relaxation, family time," the man said, smiling up at Cynthia and Cassie.

No, he didn't know about that, Cynthia thought. She desperately wished he did, but never since they'd been married had he simply gone to their country estate to relax and spend time with her. And now it was painfully obvious to Cynthia why Sorrell had been so eager to go out this afternoon.

Clearly, he'd been looking for this man.

"Well, I'm glad you're back. I need to discuss this bill with you. It comes up for a vote next week," Sorrell said, losing the smile from his face.

"Does it? Next week? Well, then, yes, we definitely do need to discuss it and at length," Lord Bunbury agreed.

"Do you have some time to spare tomorrow?" Sorrell asked.

"Er... no..." the fellow said, thinking about it. "Unless..." he turned to his wife. "Would you mind terribly if I joined you a little late at the Martenson's?"

"Yes, I would," Lady Bunbury said unequivocally. Cynthia was impressed.

"Ah, er, it'll have to be the day after, then," he said, returning his attention to Sorrell. He gave a little shrug and a smile. "Previous engagement. You understand."

Sorrell looked at Lady Bunbury. "I promise I wouldn't keep him very long..." he started.

"We have a commitment, Lord Sorrell. It can wait another day," the lady told him.

Lord Bunbury gave a little laugh. "Truly, it can. I'll see you on Saturday."

Cynthia's mouth must have been open or her eyes overly wide because Lady Bunbury just laughed and addressed her. "You simply cannot let these men run roughshod over your plans, can you?"

Cynthia could only shake her head in amazement. Her husband didn't run over her plans, he completely ignored them and her! She wondered whether she could ever be as brave and strong as this lady—and whether Sorrell would fold like Lord Bunbury if she did.

~*~

Cassie could see the wheels turning inside of her sister's head as she watched Lady Bunbury insist that her husband attend to her rather than his own business. If only Cynthia was able to convince Sorrell to do that! Cassie figured it had to be a combination of love and commitment that had the gentleman dancing to his wife's tune. Sadly, Cassie truly wondered whether her brother-in-law felt either for Cynthia.

They were all silent on their ride back to the gate, each one of them lost in their own thoughts.

"Miss Benton, Lady Sorrell!" a gentleman called to them just after they'd left the park. They paused as Mr. Crome turned his horse around and rode over to them.

"Good afternoon, Mr. Crome," Cynthia said as he pulled up beside them. "Lord Sorrell, this is the gentleman we met at the Royal Society, Mr. Crome."

Sorrell nodded but didn't smile, which Cassie thought odd.

"How do you do?" Mr. Crome said amicably. At least he was being polite, even if her brother-in-law wasn't. "And how are you on this lovely afternoon, Miss Benton?" he asked, giving her a slightly tentative smile.

"I am very well, thank you," she answered coolly. In her mind's eye, she could see him standing in Lady Ayres's garden stock still, not moving an inch to come to her assistance.

"Excellent! I, er, I wanted to apologize again—" he started.

"There is no need, Mr. Crome. You behaved as you deemed appropriate," Cassie said, not wanting to rehash the whole thing. Certainly not in front of her brother-in-law and sister, who she hadn't even informed of Mr. Crome's part in the incident at Lady Ayres's party.

"Er, yes, well. I thought I could make it up to you by inviting you—and your lovely sister, naturally—to view my laboratory," he said, as if he were bestowing a fantastic gift upon them.

Cassie thought about this for a moment. Did she really want to see Mr. Crome's laboratory?

"It is full of wonders which I'm certain will fascinate you," he added when she didn't say anything.

"That is very kind of you, Mr. Crome," Cynthia said after giving Cassie a side-long look. "We would be delighted."

"Excellent! Shall we say tomorrow afternoon around three?" the man asked.

"We shall be there," Cynthia said. "We look forward to it, don't we, Cassia?"

Cassie relented. He was clearly trying very hard to apologize in the only way he knew how. Maybe he had been frozen in shock, which was why he hadn't moved to help her. Maybe he didn't know whether she was kissing Lord Kineton back, or possibly even desiring the man's advances. She really should give Mr. Crome the benefit of the doubt. He was trying. She gave a little sigh and then smiled at the gentleman. "Yes, of course. Thank you."

Cynthia and Sorrel both gave the man a nod, and they continued on their way.

"This isn't the same incident from Lady Ayres's party, is it?" Cynthia asked as they rode away.

Cassie gave a short nod.

"You didn't tell me he was involved."

Cassie looked over at her brother-in-law, riding on Cynthia's other side. Cynthia got the hint, merely saying quietly, "You will tell me about it as soon as we get home, Cassia." It wasn't a question. It was a statement and not one with which Cassie could argue, that was certainly clear.

"So that is the Mr. Crome you wanted me to look into?" Sorrell asked.

"Yes, although it may not be necessary after all," Cynthia commented.

"Just as well I didn't waste my time, then, isn't it?" he said, frowning at her. She hardly needed to look his way; his voice held as much frown as his face.

Watching her sister and her husband interact only reinforced the idea in Cassie's mind that it was much better to marry for love and respect.

~*~

"He didn't move? He didn't come to your assistance at all?" Cynthia asked after Cassie had told her the entire story of the incident from the night before. She'd been grateful that Cynthia hadn't asked about it last night, but she supposed her grace period had come to an end.

"No. Mr. Fitzwalter had to shove him aside to come to my aide," Cassie said.

"Well, thank God for Mr. Fitzwalter!"

"Indeed. I don't know what I would have done if he hadn't come along just when he did," Cassie agreed.

"But why didn't you tell me any of this last evening?" Cynthia asked.

Cassie gave a little shrug. "I didn't want to upset you. And truly, there was nothing you could have done. It's over, and I'm certain Lord Kineton will never try anything like that again."

Cynthia gave a snort of laughter. "That's for certain. You had a thing for him a few years ago, didn't you?"

"Yes. We had a wonderful summer together. He took me punting on the river, on picnics, and all sorts of fun outings," Cassie said, remembering the time fondly. "And then I learned that he was looking for a rich wife. I think Papa said something to him, but I'm not sure. All I know is when I came back from school for the Christmas holidays, he was gone to London and soon thereafter married."

"Just as well," Cynthia said with a nod. She was quiet for a moment and then said, "And now I've accepted Mr. Crome's invitation when you probably want nothing more to do with the man."

"No, it's all right. I'm certain he'll have some very good excuse why he was unable to come to my aid. And his laboratory may be very interesting to visit too. I've never actually seen electricity. I suppose he has a machine or something he uses to generate it."

"Most likely. I've been to a demonstration once. It was quite fascinating."

With a burst of laughter, Cynthia added, "I still can't believe you broke Lord Kineton's nose!"

Cassie couldn't help her own giggles. "I know! I... I've never punched anyone before."

"What made you do it? It's so unlike you to simply act out that way."

Cassie shook her head. "Mr. Fitzwalter was holding him. He urged me to do it. He said..." She paused to think about it. "He said I shouldn't think. I should just act. So I did." She finished with a shrug.

"And how did that feel?" Cynthia asked, still smiling.

It was odd, but Cassie hadn't thought about it at all. Now, however, she realized... "It felt good. It felt really good." Her hand flew to her mouth. "I can't believe it. Just acting on impulse, giving that man what he deserved..."

"Oh, I can believe it," Cynthia said with another laugh. "And you know what?"

Cassie looked over at her older sister.

"I'm proud of you."

Chapter Nineteen

~April 25~

The following afternoon Cassie and her sister were in the odd position of knocking on a gentleman's door. Cynthia kept looking around uncomfortably as they waited. Ladies did not call upon gentlemen, it simply wasn't done! But there they were, and it was unsurprisingly awkward.

They were shown into a very fashionably decorated drawing room. Cassie was pleasantly surprised, and by Cynthia's expression, she was as well. She supposed they'd both been expecting something much more masculine or sparse. Even more surprising was the lady who stood to greet them along with Mr. Crome.

He strode forward, stopping only a few feet short of where they stood to bow. "Lady Sorrell, Miss Benton, thank you so very much for coming."

Cassie curtsied. "Thank you for inviting us. I am greatly looking forward to seeing your work."

"Yes, yes, er, first, er, may I make you known to my sister-in-law, Lady Midton?" he said, indicating the lady.

"I believe we've met before," Cynthia said, moving forward.

"I'm certain we have," she said kindly. "But I don't believe I've had the pleasure of meeting your sister. You are making your debut, Miss Benton?"

"Yes, my lady," Cassie said, curtseying to the lady. She was a little older than Cynthia, but seemed to be a very warm and welcoming lady. "Will you be visiting Mr. Crome's laboratory as well?"

The lady burst out laughing. "Oh no! No, I am here for propriety's sake much like your sister." She turned to Cynthia. "When Humphrey came home yesterday and told us that he'd invited two ladies over I just laughed. He knows that ladies do not visit gentlemen, and yet, it had completely slipped his mind in his excitement to show you his work."

Cynthia gave a polite laugh and looked to Mr. Crome before turning back to Lady Midton. "Thank you for taking the time out of your day, my lady, to join us. I have to say I did feel distinctly uncomfortable coming over here today. But now that you are here, everything is all right."

"Good. Now, I know Humphrey is quite eager to show you his work. I shall stay here and await your reactions when you are finished," the lady said kindly.

Mr. Crome gave her a slight bow and then directed Cassie and Cynthia to the back of the house.

The laboratory looked to have once been the library of the house but now was filled with tables covered with machines, spools of wire, and other debris of his work. Cassie was relieved there weren't any frog legs that she could see.

"You will excuse the mess. I'm in the process of attempting to create a battery much like Mr. Volta's. I am experimenting with different types of conductive materials," he said, walking over to one table where there were stacks of metal discs and various bits of wire.

"What type of metal are you using?" Cassie asked as she examined the materials on the table.

"These are copper and zinc with an electrolyte layer in between, naturally," he explained.

"Yes, and the wire?" Cassie asked.

"It is copper," he answered.

Cassie and Cynthia spent a moment examining the pile and looking over the various implements, discs, and what-not scattered over the table.

"And this pile over here?" Cynthia asked, pointing to a second stack of discs on another table as she walked over to take a look at it.

"That is the dry pile," he answered. "This is the wet—although it is not actually wet at the moment," he explained. "I'm running some experiments to see... well, you probably wouldn't understand..."

Cassie narrowed her eyes at him. Did he think them stupid?

"Why don't you explain?" Cynthia said, probably noticing Cassie's expression. Neither one of them liked to think they were incapable of understanding a scientific principle if it were adequately explained.

"Oh, er, of course. Mr. Volta's battery works when the electrolyte material between each disc is wet. But it has also been discovered that it can work equally as well when dry."

"Yes, I've read of Mr. Ritter's discoveries a few years ago," Cassie commented.

"Have you?" Mr. Crome said, looking rather surprised. "Well, then, what I am doing is testing to see if the dry pile reacts differently to various types of conductive material than the wet battery."

"How fascinating," Cynthia said, nodding her understanding.

"And what have you discovered so far?" Cassie asked.

Mr. Crome opened his mouth to answer but then closed it again and, instead, smiled at her. "I'm certain this is all quite boring for you and your sister, Miss Benton. Perhaps we should return to the drawing room. I wouldn't want to keep my sister-in-law waiting for too long."

Cassie was about to open her mouth to tell him that she was finding his work quite fascinating and encourage him to expand on his explanation when Cynthia said, "I'm certain you're right, Mr. Crome. We shouldn't keep the countess waiting." Without waiting for Cassie to agree, she turned and walked out the door, leading the way back to the drawing room.

"I do hope Humphrey didn't bore you both to tears with his long-winded explanations," Lady Midton said soon after they were seated.

"Oh no," Cassie said quickly. "In fact, I wish he'd explained more. I find his work quite fascinating."

"Really," the lady said, putting down the tea pot she was about to pour from. She picked it back up and returned to the task at hand with a small smile on her face. "How very wonderful that you think so, Miss Benton."

"My sister is also a natural scientist," Cynthia explained. "Although her area of expertise lies in the garden rather than in a laboratory."

"Oh? Do tell," the lady said, handing Cynthia a cup of tea and then returning to the pot to pour out a cup for Cassie.

"I am a botanist," Cassie explained.

"She has the most incredible roses, Dorothea," Mr. Crome commented. "I was honored to have them shown to me when I visited a few weeks ago.

"Oh, I do love roses," Lady Midton sighed, handing Cassie her cup.

"I am attempting to breed a pink tea rose. They are among the strongest smelling roses," Cassie explained.

"Really? I'm afraid I don't know one rose from another, but I do love the smell."

~April 28~

Archer sat back with a glass of whisky in his hand. He'd decided not to take his chances in Powell's card room this evening. He didn't have a great deal of funds to risk, and he was, after all, trying to raise money for his new company. It wouldn't look good to be wagering too much.

Kineton had refused to come out with him tonight. He was steadfastly refusing to even leave the house until the swelling of his nose went down.

Archer laughed to himself. When he'd offered to hold Kineton still for Miss Benton to get her retribution, he certainly hadn't anticipated that she'd be strong enough or have good enough aim to actually break the man's nose.

"You seem to be in a good mood this evening," Lord Wickford said, coming around his chair.

"Good evening, my lord," Archer said, sitting up a little and reaching his hand out to the man.

"You seemed to have an exciting time at the Ladies' Wagering Whist Society party earlier this week."

"The what society?" Archer asked, indicating

Wickford take the chair on the other side of the small table next to him.

"The Ladies' Wagering Whist Society. You must have heard of it since you were invited to the party," the man said with a little laugh.

"I was invited to Lady Ayres's soirée—or so I thought," Archer responded.

"Lady Ayres is the founder of the society. They're notorious throughout the haute ton. They have arranged about a dozen marriages in the past two years, including those of half their own members."

"Ah, so they arrange marriages? Then where does the wagering and whist come in?"

Wickford laughed. "That's when they do their arranging, while they play whist."

"That is most unusual."

"It is, but clearly, it works."

"And have you gotten caught by their marriage-making gambles?" Archer asked.

"Me? No, I leave that for others. The Duke of Warwick, Lord Gorling, Lord Colburne, Lord Welles. As I say, they're very good at what they do. "He finished with a laugh.

"Warwick, huh? Well, that's impressive."

"He was their first from what I understand. By the way, you are still looking for investors, aren't you?"

Archer stopped tilting his glass as he was about to take a sip of his drink. "I am. You wouldn't happen to know of someone who might be interested, would you?"

Wickford smiled. "As a matter of fact, I do."

Archer followed him to the back corner of the

reading room. Oddly, the candles seemed to have been doused as they moved to the back of the room.

Archer peered through the dark and was just able to make out a man sitting in the corner.

"Lord Pennyston, I do hope you'll forgive the intrusion," Wickford said to the man. "But I'd like to introduce Mr. Archer Fitzwalter to you. He's the fellow with the business you said you were interested in."

A large man stood up and came forward just enough so Archer could make out his profile. "How do you do, Mr. Fitzwalter? I'm Christopher Pennyston. Lord Colburne and Lord Wickford have both told me a little about this new business you're putting together. I'd like to hear more about it from you if you don't mind."

"I'd be honored my lord. But, er, it's odd that this corner is so dark..." Archer started.

"No. It is at my request," Lord Pennyston said briefly. "Please, have a seat. Would you care for a drink? I've got a bottle of brandy."

"Well, I'll leave you two gentlemen," Lord Wickford said.

"Yes, thank you, Wickford," Pennyston said as he took his seat again. He indicated that Archer take the chair opposite.

"Thank you. I've actually got a glass of my own." Archer held up his glass but wasn't sure the gentleman could see it in the dark.

"Ah, yes, very good. Now, tell me about this idea of yours. Colburne gave me only the barest sketch of it when he told me about it, merely whetting my curiosity, and Wickford wasn't any more forthcoming."

Archer gave a polite little laugh. "Of course. Let

me start by telling you about what I've been doing for the past few years, if you don't mind. It will make the rest more understandable."

"Very well."

Archer peered into the darkness, trying to see him, but the lack of light was making it impossible. "I've been in the East India Company army, fighting around the area of Madras," he explained.

"Really? I've heard some about the army in India, but not very much. Is it similar to being in the British Army? I've been fighting for our country in Spain and Portugal for the past three years."

"You're a lucky man. I only wish my father had bought me a commission in the British Army."

"Any idea why he may not have?" Pennyston asked.

"Honestly? I have a feeling he wanted me as far away as possible. Can't get much farther than India," Archer said with a laugh that held no amusement.

"Or perhaps he hoped to keep you safe? My father had me sent to Malta when I first joined. Not a lick of fighting to be seen there," Pennyston offered.

"No. We saw a good bit of action in Madras. Your father sounds like a clever man. Mine just wanted to be rid of me. Not terribly pleased I'm back either. But I'll be gone just as soon as I round up the funding I need, and he'll be happy again."

Pennyston shake his head. "Fathers!"

"Difficult, aren't they?" Archer punctuated his words with a long drink from his glass.

Pennyston reached forward and refilled it.

"Thank you. So, the thing is, while I was in India, I couldn't help but become aware that the East

India Company was working hard to squeeze every penny from the local farmers. They would buy their goods—spices, cotton, and so on—ship it back here to England and make a very nice profit off of it. With more and more of their efforts going toward empire building, they have slowly moved away from exporting some items. My idea is to fill the gap they have created but pay the farmers a more reasonable amount for their goods. It will make the price higher when it's resold here, but I think if we ensure the quality is good people will pay."

"That sounds remarkably fair," Pennyston commented.

"Unusual, I know," Archer said with a true laugh.

"What are you thinking of importing?"

"Spices. There are a great number of spices English households have come to rely upon that are grown in Madras. I think we could do very well with them," Archer said.

"And how much are you looking for a share?"

They discussed particulars. By the time the bottle of brandy was finished, Archer was pretty sure he had his newest investor. The man was making all the right noises, much to Archer's delight.

"I like your ideas, Archer," Pennyston said as he emptied the bottle into Archer's glass. "And I want to buy in to your company. I don't have the ready just now. When would you need a firm commitment?"

Archer gave a silent sigh of relief. "Whenever you can—preferably before the season is over. I don't have a firm date as to when I'm going to be returning to India, but it will most likely be early in summer."

"Excellent. I will get back to you as soon as I can. Naturally, I've got to speak with my solicitor and see what I can do."

"Of course. Take your time."

Pennyston gave a nod of acknowledgement. "We seem to be quite alike, you and I."

Chapter Twenty

"Oh?" Archer looked at the man sitting across from him and wondered what they could possibly have in common.

"Tell me if I'm wrong, but you seem to have loved the adventure of army life."

"I did. I have to admit the fighting was not at all appealing, though. I resigned my commission as quickly as I could. Did you do the same?"

"No. I didn't mind the fighting. I liked the glory of it," Pennyston admitted. "I deliberately petitioned for a transfer to where I knew I'd see some action."

"And did you?"

"I have the scar to prove it," Pennyston said dryly.

"So what made you return?" Archer asked. "Or are you simply here for a short time and then going back?"

"I am here for good. I was injured and sent home." Pennyston leaned forward into the light.

"I'm sorry to hear—" Archer started, but then his gaze caught the left side of the man's face. His words dried on his tongue. He'd seen a number of war injuries in his time. This was a particularly nasty one—poor bugger. It wouldn't do to make anything of it; he knew that much. He quickly cleared his throat and started again. "Er, was it a saber?"

"Yes." Pennyston leaned back again.

"You're lucky to be alive, I imagine," Archer commented.

"I am. Very. A little lower, and it would have sliced open my neck. A little to the left, and I would be missing an eye. And if I hadn't had immediate medical attention, I would have bled out on the spot."

Archer shook his head. "Adventure is fun. Exploring new places, meeting different people—all good. A swipe with a saber or a bullet aimed just right can ruin a man's life."

"I knew you'd understand. So, you'll forgive me if I sit in the dark." Pennyston gave a dry chuckle.

"Not at all! Not at all."

~May 1~

"Wasn't that just the most wonderful wedding?" Cynthia gushed for the seventh time.

Cassie just looked at her sister, trying her hardest to keep from laughing.

"What? You don't agree? It's only because you don't know the duchess—I mean, Lady Gorling," her sister said.

"No, I do agree. And I agreed the six other times you said so," Cassie said, no longer attempting to contain her laughter.

"Oh." Cynthia turned and looked at the other members of the wedding party. They were enjoying a Champagne toast before the wedding breakfast was served. "But it was just so very special. If you knew..."

"Cynthia, you've told me. The duchess came from a difficult background and was happily married to her duke for many years," Cassie recited.

"Yes. Much like the Duchess of Bolton," Cynthia agreed. "Do you know she was married to a watchmaker for over thirty years before she met and fell in love with the Duke of Bolton?"

"Yes, you told me all about it last year in your letters to me."

"Oh."

"Why are you not chatting with Lydia or Diana or one of your other Society friends? You don't have to stay with me, you know," Cassie said.

"But I do. I'm chaperoning you. I'm supposed to stay—"

"Ladies and gentlemen, luncheon is served," the footman called out above the noise of so many people talking.

"Ah, lunch," Cynthia said, sounding rather relieved.

Cassie had no idea what was going on with her today. She seemed quite distracted. Sorrell hadn't joined them, but that was normal. She would have to quiz her sister later. For now, she needed to find where she'd been seated at the extremely long table in Lord Gorling's formal dining room.

She was following along with the others, searching for her name among the place cards when she heard a gentleman call out from the other side of the table, "Miss Benton, oh, Miss Benton! You are here. We are to be dining companions."

She looked across and saw Mr. Hershawn smiling and waving at her. He indicated the chair next to where he was standing. "Oh! Thank you!"

She made her way around through the crowded

room and the people who were still looking for where they'd been placed. When she reached his side, a footman was right there to pull out her chair and seat her at the table. She looked around to see who else was nearby and where Cynthia had been seated as Mr. Hershawn settled himself next to her.

"Are you looking for someone in particular?" he asked.

"What? Oh, no," she said with a slightly embarrassed laugh. "I was just seeing where my sister was. But she's there," Cassie said, indicating across the table and down a little farther. "I'm sure I've never sat at a table with so many people before—well, not since school, anyway."

He smiled at her. "I have to say, I don't usually attend such large dinner parties myself."

"But this is a wonderful occasion—er, you are happy with your father's choice of bride, are you not? Otherwise, my condolences."

Mr. Hershawn burst out laughing, making a few heads turn their way. "No, no, I am quite happy, thank you."

"Oh, good! That does make things easier, I imagine," Cassie said with a little giggle.

"It does. We don't get together as a family very often, but considering that both I and my father live in town and, therefore see each other rather frequently, it is a good thing that I like his new wife," Mr. Hershawn said. "The duchess, er, Lady Gorling, is a very nice person and, truly, I don't believe I've ever seen my father so happy."

"That is quite amazing to find love twice in one's life," Cassie agreed as she picked up her spoon to dip into the soup course placed before them.

"Twice? Oh, my parents certainly were not in

love. No, that's why this marriage is so very nice," Mr. Hershawn commented.

"Oh, dear, I do hope they got along, then."

Mr. Hershawn smiled reassuringly at her. "They did. For a marriage based entirely on position and wealth, as so many are, I think they were reasonably happy."

Cassie hadn't thought about her own parent's marriage, but she figured they had been paired for much the same reasons. They certainly weren't in love, and sadly, Sorrell wasn't either. She wondered whether Cynthia was. She thought so, which was why her sister was so upset that Sorrell paid her so little attention—aside from the fact that it was rather embarrassing for her to go about unaccompanied. "I imagine it's easier when one knows what to expect," she said idly.

"To expect?"

"Yes. Whether to expect the other person to love you or hold you in esteem. Or... or not."

"Are you looking for a love-match, Miss Benton?" Mr. Hershawn asked, a small smile playing on his lips.

"It's an excellent question and I... I don't know that I have an answer."

"Really? That's unusual. Most people know, I would imagine," he said, returning to his soup.

"Yes. Well, I thought I knew exactly what I wanted from a husband, but now... now I'm not so sure," she admitted.

"What did you think you wanted?" he asked, clearly fascinated by this conversation.

"I thought I wanted to marry a scientist who would value and respect my scientific endeavors—I'm a botanist," she told him.

"I believe I might have heard something about that. You grow roses, is that right?" he asked.

"Yes! Precisely," she said, giving him a smile.

"So, marrying another scientist makes perfect sense," he agreed.

"Yes."

"But…" he prompted.

Cassie played with her soup for a moment, scooping it up and then dipping her spoon back into the liquid. "But then I met a gentleman who is not a scientist."

"Ah, and he has captured your heart?"

"Well, I certainly like him a great deal." She wasn't actually certain that she was in love with Mr. Fitzwalter, but she was definitely willing to entertain the hypothesis.

"And is there a gentleman scientist who has captured your attention, or is that spot still vacant?" Mr. Hershawn asked.

"There is," she said, not certain she wanted to name him just in case Mr. Hershawn was friends with Mr. Crome. Although, she seriously doubted the man had any friends among the ton.

"And are your feelings for him as strong as those for the other gentleman?"

"I don't believe I have feelings for the scientific gentleman. I mean, I like him well enough, but it's more that he'll understand the importance of my work if we marry."

"I see. So, it's a matter of your heart versus your head. You like the scientist well enough to marry him, but you would do so only because it's the logical thing to do. Whereas the other fellow has captured your heart, but you're not entirely certain he would fulfil the needs of your head. You don't know whether he would be respectful of your work."

"What an extraordinarily apt summation of the situation!" she said, putting down her fork which she'd just laden with the fish he'd helped her to as he spoke.

"Why, thank you," he said, giving her a smile before taking a bit of his own food.

The more she thought about it, that was precisely what she was grappling with—her heart versus her head. Mr. Fitzwalter versus Mr. Crome. Did she marry someone who made her feel cherished, who was charming, and sweet, and kind. Or did she marry a man who, while he was very nice and certainly extremely intelligent, would respect her own intellect and her work. "Now, I only wish you could tell me which I should follow—my head or my heart."

He chuckled. "I would if I could, but sadly it is not for me to decide."

"It is very sad indeed, Mr. Hershawn, for you are clearly a very astute gentleman. I believe you would make an excellent decision for me."

"No, no, flattery will not get me to tell you what you should do. You must decide that entirely on your own."

She could only laugh and secretly wish that someone else could make that decision for her.

~May 4~

Cynthia entered Lady Ayres's drawing room the following Wednesday for the weekly meeting of the Wagering Whist Society and looked around for a moment. "Ah! Right," she said to herself.

"Good afternoon, Lady Sorrell," Lady Blakemore said, turning toward her with a welcoming smile.

"Good afternoon, my lady. I was looking forward to congratulating Lady Gorling, once again, but she is off on her honeymoon, isn't she?" Cynthia said, coming farther into the room.

The lady's smile grew broader. "Indeed, she is."

"Where did they say they were going?" Lydia asked as she helped herself to a piece of cake.

"To Canterbury and then along the coastline south to Dover," Lady Ayres answered.

"Oh, that's right. I remember hearing Lord Gorling saying something about pirates," Lydia said, nodding.

Cynthia could only laugh. "Could you imagine the Duchess of Kendell looking forward to visiting pirate coves?"

"Lady Gorling now," Lady Ayres reminded her.

"Yes, that's my point. The Duchess of Kendell would have looked down her nose at such common and nefarious activities, but Lady Gorling just laughs and is amused by it all," Cynthia said.

Lydia and Diana both burst out laughing. "You are absolutely right, Cynthia! My word, but she has changed ever since she met Lord Gorling."

"It is amazing what love will do," Lady Ayres agreed.

"What will love do?" Lady Moreton asked, coming into the room behind Cynthia.

"We were just discussing the difference between the Duchess of Kendell and Lady Gorling," Cynthia explained.

Lady Moreton looked confused. "But they are the same person."

"No, they're really not—which is what Lady

Sorrell's point was," Lydia explained.

"Oh, I see. She's changed thanks to falling in love with Lord Gorling and isn't the same as when she was the duchess," Lady Moreton said, nodding her understanding. She smiled at Cynthia. "It is truly wonderful, I have to agree."

Cynthia wondered if there was something—or someone—Lady Moreton wasn't telling them about.

"Well, do come in and sit down, everyone," Lady Ayres said. With Lady Moreton's arrival they were all present, aside from Lady Gorling.

"How are we going to play this afternoon with one too few?" Diana asked.

"I was thinking that we wouldn't actually play cards today," Lady Ayres said. "The thing is, we have completed another game and have, I'm sorry to say, another loser who must confess something to us all."

"Without Lady Gorling here?" Duchess Bolton asked.

"I'm afraid so. She can be filled in on what she missed when she returns," Lady Ayres said.

"I'm surprised it wasn't Lady Gorling who lost again this time," Lydia said with a giggle.

"She came very close, but sadly, it was Lady Sorrell who came in last place," Lady Ayres said.

Cynthia started. "What? Me?"

"I'm afraid so," Lady Ayres said, looking down at the open book in her lap where she kept tally of their points.

"Oh, I suppose I've been so distracted with my sister and her debut that I haven't been paying much attention to my card playing," Cynthia said. Goodness! Now she had to think of a secret to tell. But what... She was rather unhappy to realize immediately what her secret was, but she wondered whether her friends could do anything about it. She wondered whether they could actually help her. Knowing them, she had a strong feeling they could. They were truly wonderful and clever women in that way.

"Well then, if I am to divulge a secret, you all must promise to help me out with it," she said, settling herself on the sofa next to the Duchess of Bolton.

Chapter Twenty-One

"Help you?" Lady Blakemore asked.

"How can we help? You know we're always very happy to do so," Lydia said, almost at the same time.

Cynthia gave her a grateful smile. "I know, that's why I have absolutely no qualms about asking." She got lots of nods all around. Taking in a deep breath, she said, "My secret is this—I..." She paused. Goodness, this was harder than she had imagined. But no, she would persevere. It would help in so many ways; she was certain of it. "My secret is that I don't believe my husband loves me, and I don't know what to do about it. I love him, but the feeling does not seem to be reciprocated."

"Oh, dear," Diana sighed.

"Why do you think that is so?" the duchess asked.

"Because he never wants to spend time with me. Whenever I ask him to go someplace with me, he always has someplace else to go. I have only seen him very briefly, in passing, a few times in the past few months," she explained. "He always comes up with some excuse, usually pertaining to his work in Parliament. I've asked him repeatedly to go with me to this party or that, or even to simply have dinner, but he is too busy, always." She could feel her throat grow tighter, but she absolutely would not cry. She simply would not.

"That is a difficult situation," Lady Blakemore said.

"And you are certain this isn't simply a temporary thing that will pass...?" Lady Ayres asked.

"It's been going on for over a year. The only time I can be certain he'll join me is at our annual soirée. Even then, I wasn't absolutely certain of it this year, which is why we haven't even arranged a date for it yet."

"Oh, yes," Lady Colburne said. "That's right. You usually have it by this point in the season."

"I do. But Sorrell has simply been too busy," Cynthia said. She looked around at her friends all frowning as they thought this problem through. "So, what should I do? Should I ask for a divorce? Smother him with a pillow as he sleeps? Simply ignore it and... I don't know. I don't think it's ever going to go away."

"I think the first would be prohibitively difficult..." Lady Blakemore started.

"And you say that you love him, so I can't imagine you want to divorce him," Lydia said, jumping in.

"And the second would most likely land you in jail," Lady Blakemore continued.

"You most certainly don't want to do that—be in jail. I don't know how strongly you feel about murdering your husband," the duchess amended.

Nearly all the ladies laughed at that.

"Truthfully, the thought has only passed through my mind a few times," Cynthia admitted.

"And that was usually when he promised to go someplace with me and then cancelled at the last minute."

They all nodded, understanding immediately, which was precisely why Cynthia loved these women so very much.

"It sounds like what you need to do is somehow get his attention," Lady Colburne said as if she were thinking aloud.

"Or become more important than his work," Lady Ayres added.

"Or you could simply forget about him," Lady Moreton said.

Everyone turned toward her.

"Forget about him?" Cynthia asked.

"Yes. Oh, I don't mean literally, but you could simply stop trying to win his love and attention and go about your life as if you weren't married." She paused and looked around the room wide-eyed. "Is that too scandalous?"

"No, I think you're on to something," Lydia said.

"And I'm proud of you for even thinking of such a thing," the duchess said, giving her an approving nod.

Lady Moreton gave a little shake of her head. "My continuing efforts at living large."

"You're doing a fantastic job," Cynthia said. "And I don't wonder if you aren't right."

"I think she is absolutely right," Lydia said. "You should simply go about your life as if he weren't in it. Dance. Go to parties."

"Laugh and have fun, and don't give him a second thought," Diana agreed.

"It's true. You've been living a very demure,

quiet life," Lady Blakemore agreed.

"Well, I do go to parties," Cynthia pointed out.

"Yes, to chaperone your sister. But I don't believe I've ever seen you dance," Lady Ayres said.

"No, I don't. I haven't since Sorrell and I got married. I thought that maybe I shouldn't without him," Cynthia admitted.

"I don't see any reason for you not to. Many married women dance with gentlemen other than their husbands," Lady Moreton pointed out.

"That's true," Cynthia said, thinking about it. "And you say I should just forget about him?"

"You could even have an affair—if you're discreet, of course," the duchess said with a little titter.

Cynthia's jaw dropped open. "I don't..."

"You don't need to go quite that far," Lady Blakemore said quickly.

"But it couldn't hurt to make the man jealous," Lydia pointed out.

"It's true. Maybe he'll pay more attention to you if he thinks you might be having an affair," Diana said.

"It's not a bad idea—to make him jealous," Cynthia said, thinking it through. "Very well, I'll give it a try."

"The affair?" the duchess asked.

"Not that, but dancing certainly. And... and having more fun!"

~May 5~

Archer wandered through the card room at Powell's. Somehow he simply could not find the enthusiasm to actually sit down and play a hand. He knew he needed to speak with people about funding his project, but as he looked about the room, he couldn't see a man who he hadn't already spoken to.

He could hardly believe how many people he'd met and told about this project in a little over a month. He loved meeting people. He loved speaking with them. But right now he just felt like he needed a night off. On the other hand, he was almost there. He just needed one big investor—or two small ones—to get his project moving forward.

He took another look around the room. Surely, he couldn't have spoken with everyone here. There had to be at least forty or fifty people in this room.

Archer had moved to return to the front of the room when someone tapped on his shoulder. "Mr. Fitzwalter, you wouldn't still be looking for investors in your business venture, would you?"

Archer turned and found Lord Pennyston there smiling at him. "I'm afraid so," Archer admitted, slightly embarrassed to be discovered searching for investors.

"Well, look no more." Pennyston held out his hand.

Archer took it. As realization dawned on him, excitement grew. "You? You were able to dispose of your building?"

"I was. My solicitor informed me this very afternoon. He has a buyer."

"Well, this calls for a celebration!" Archer said, pumping Pennyston's hand a little harder. He indicated a couple of empty chairs, pausing to order a bottle of Champagne from a footman.

They moved in that direction, but Archer could hardly sit still. He was so thrilled that maybe, just possibly, this would be done, and he'd be able to move on and get his business started. He perched at the very edge of the chair. "Tell me about it! Did you get the price you were expecting?"

"The details aren't hashed out yet," Pennyston admitted. "But there's a buyer and he's very interested. My man said the deal was as good as done."

"All right, then! We'll count it as done."

The footman delivered their Champagne, and Lord Wickford came along with it. "Is this a celebration? Good news?" he asked.

"I have my last investor," Archer told him.

"Congratulations! Lord Pennyston, is it you?" Lord Wickford asked.

"Yes. I managed to sell a building I inherited years ago. I'll be investing in Fitzwalter's brilliant idea as soon as I get the funds," Pennyston said. He lifted his glass. "To Fitzwalter's spice business."

Archer lifted his glass as well. "Thank you. And to you, for choosing to invest so wisely." He took a sip, enjoying the sharp, bubbly wine.

"Now, I suppose, you'll be able to return to India and get this idea off the ground," Wickford said, still smiling at Archer.

"Yes." That was right. Now Archer had no reason to stay here in London any longer. In fact, just the opposite. He would need to book a ticket on a ship back to Madras as soon as possible, so he could get started on putting the business together and earning back his investor's money.

But what about Miss Benton? That would mean leaving her. Archer looked at the glass in his hand. There must be something off about this wine. It was causing a sharp pain in his chest. His throat felt tight as well. He put down the glass.

"Everything all right?" Wickford asked, looking

a little concerned.

"Yes, yes, of course," Archer said quickly.

"There was some talk about you and Miss Benton," Wickford started. "But I suppose you were just enjoying yourself while trying to find your funding. She does know you'll be leaving, doesn't she?"

"Er..." Archer really wasn't feeling well.

"Don't tell me you didn't tell her that you were only here for a short time?" Wickford asked, beginning to look serious.

"I... er... I shall do so. I'm certain she'll understand. I, um, I believe she was most interested in that natural scientist, er, Crome I think his name is," Archer said. He was beginning to feel over-warm and yet seemed to have the chills at the same time. He stood up. "I'm terribly sorry, I seem to be feeling a little unwell. Please, do excuse me." He paused and turned to Lord Pennyston. "We shall meet very soon to discuss particulars."

"Very good. I hope you feel better," the man said, looking concerned.

Archer forced a smile onto his lips. "I'm sure I will. Thank you. Good evening."

He got out of there as quickly as he could, feeling the eyes of the two men on his back the whole way to the door.

~*~

Cassie was jolted awake by someone banging very loudly on the front door of the house. Always a light sleeper, she sat up wondering who could possibly be making so much noise this late at night. It couldn't have been Sorrell. He never made much noise when he came in, and besides, she was certain she'd heard him hardly an hour earlier.

As she sat there wondering about this, there was definitely a commotion downstairs. Not only that, but she was pretty certain she heard her own name being called.

She quickly got up and pulled on her wrapper. She'd just gotten to the bottom of one flight of stairs when her sister came out of her own room on the first floor.

"What is going on?" Cynthia asked, turning to look up at Cassie.

"I was just coming down to see." She turned and looked down the hall toward Sorrell's room, wondering if her brother-in-law would be joining them.

"He sleeps like the dead," Cynthia said, following Cassie's line of sight. "We won't be seeing him."

"Cassia! Miss Benton!" a man's voice called from the base of the stairs on the ground floor.

"Shhhh! Sir, please!" Another man could be heard.

Cassie rushed down, followed by her sister.

Mr. Fitzwalter was standing in the foyer trying to get farther into the house but was blocked by the footman. "Miss Ben—oh! There you are!" he said, smiling up at her as she came down the stairs. "My God, but you're beautiful in your night clothes."

Cassie could feel the heat rush through her face. "Mr. Fitzwalter, what are you doing here at this time of night?"

"I needed to see you. And yes, it is of the utmost urgency," he said, looking toward the footman.

"What is it?" Cynthia asked, coming down behind Cassie.

"May I have a word? In private?" he asked, looking from the footman to Cynthia before finally letting his gaze land on Cassie.

"Why? What is so important?" Cassie asked.

"Yes. If it is so very urgent you can say it right here," Cynthia said, crossing her arms.

"I... er..." He cleared his throat. "Really? In public, Miss Benton? We can't have a moment of privacy?"

"Mr. Fitzwalter anything you want to say to me, you can say in front of my sister," Cassie said, beginning to seriously wonder about the state of this man's mind.

"Fine! Marry me! Come and live with me in Madras. I love you, and I want to spend the rest of my days with you," he declared.

"Are you drunk?" Cassie asked. He had to be. No man in his right mind would come to propose to a woman past midnight. What she couldn't understand was why her heart was suddenly pounding in her chest so hard and so fast. Surely, he couldn't mean what he'd just said. No, no, it was ridiculous. He didn't know what he was saying.

"I am not! I've had two, maybe three glasses of brandy. Oh, and a bit of Champagne, but very little," he admitted.

"He's got to be drunk," Cynthia said quietly from behind her.

Cassie turned and nodded.

"I am not! I love your sister, and I want to marry her!" he protested.

"I see. And will your love for her not last until morning? Is that why you absolutely had to get us all out of bed so that you could profess this to everyone and ask her immediately—urgently—to marry you?"

Cynthia asked dryly.

Cassie resisted the urge to giggle.

Mr. Fitzwalter didn't seem to have an answer to that one.

"Right. This can all wait until after you have slept off the alcohol currently befuddling your mind. Good night, Mr. Fitzwalter." Cynthia then turned and strode back up the stairs.

Cassie's giggles could no longer be withheld.

"Come along, Cassia," Cynthia snapped from the top of the stairs.

"Good night, Mr. Fitzwalter," Cassie said, running after her sister.

Chapter Twenty-Two

~May 6~

Archer dropped his head into his hands, but it was all he could do to keep from bashing it against the dining table again and again.

"Rough night?" Kineton asked, coming into the room.

Straightening himself, he said, "One which I wish I couldn't remember with such clarity."

"Drunk?" his friend asked, taking his place at the head of the table.

"Sadly, no. I was completely sober, and that is precisely the problem. If I had been properly drunk, I would not have the events of the evening going through my mind now. No, I would be blissfully ignorant of my own stupidity. Instead, I remember everything, every single last detail down to the color of the ribbons on Miss Benton's nightgown."

Kineton started, nearly jumping from his chair. "I beg your pardon?" he nearly shouted. "You did not just say Miss Benton's nightgown. I must have misheard you, for how would you ever be in a position to see such an item, whether adorned by the young lady or otherwise?"

"I saw it. On her. And she looked incredibly

adorable," Archer moaned.

"Oh, now you have to explain it all to me in minute detail, and I will need much, much more coffee," he added, looking at the footman. "Bring the pot."

"Yes, my lord," the fellow said, looking particularly reluctant to leave the room lest he miss any of Archer's explanation.

Half an hour later, Archer had given his friend—and the footman—a blow-by-blow description of exactly what happened from the moment Lord Pennyston had come into Powell's to inform Archer he would be funding his project, to the moment Sorrell's footman threw him out of the house.

"Oh. My. God." It was all Kineton could say. And he said it again until he said, "I simply cannot believe... you're going to have to pay her a call this morning. Perhaps you can tell her you were drunk. She already believes it to be true."

"But I wasn't," Archer said.

"Whether you actually were or not makes no difference. You can claim that you were."

Archer nodded. It wasn't a bad idea, actually. He certainly wished he'd been. He considered exactly what he was going to do, what he was going to say to Miss Benton later this afternoon when he went to call on her.

He did, in fact, want to marry her. He truly did love her. But because he loved her, he absolutely could not bring her to India.

He'd seen how the ladies there suffered with so few female companions. How could he even consider doing that to Miss Benton? And not only that, but there was her garden to consider. Her roses. He doubted very much she would be able to bring them—and have them survive—the arduous journey to Madras. No, it was impossible.

"I beg your pardon, sir, but the Duke of Warwick is here to see you. Are you at home?" a footman asked after coming into the dining room.

"Me? He's come to see me?" Kineton asked, looking very confused.

"No, I beg your pardon, my lord, he's here to see Mr. Fitzwalter," the man clarified.

"Of course I'm at home to the duke!" Archer said, standing up. He couldn't have stomached any breakfast, anyway. He looked down at the table. He hadn't even drunk his coffee. Well, it didn't matter now, there was a duke waiting for him.

He followed the footman out to the formal drawing room where the duke was standing admiring the painting above the fireplace.

"Your Grace, what a pleasant surprise," Archer said, coming into the room. He paused to bow.

Warwick nodded in return and said, "I'm afraid you will not think so in a moment."

"Oh? Is there something wrong?"

"I'm afraid I came to inform you that I cannot, after all, invest in your project," the duke said.

"Oh."

"I am terribly sorry about this. I do feel that it is a very worthy business proposition..."

"But?"

"But..." He paused, frowning. "There was a fire at one of my estates. Two of my tenants have lost their homes."

"Oh, I am sorry," Archer said, trying his best to keep his voice polite, despite that inside it felt like his stomach was turning into a rock.

"Thank you, that is very gracious of you. I understand your disappointment. I just wish I could think of someone else who you might ask to take my place. I assume you asked the Duke of Bolton? Or Lord Gorling? I would imagine Lord Gorling would be particularly interested. He lived in India for a time."

"Yes, he did," Archer said. "I've spoken with him about his time there. He doesn't see the benefit of trying to do better than the East India Company with regards to the native population."

"Really? I'd have thought he would be the sort to go for such a scheme," the duke said, surprised. "He believes very strongly in democracy."

"Yes, but democracy for the educated. He also believes that the poorer people should work and get ahead if they want to be paid a living wage or a respectable price for the fruits of their labor." Archer distinctly remembered having a strongly worded argument with the earl over the matter. He'd had the hardest time not calling the man out for being such a bloody moron.

"Ah, yes. I imagine there are a great many gentlemen like him," Warwick said.

"Too many in my opinion," Archer said dryly.

"Well, I wish you the best of luck." The duke came forward, his hand outstretched.

It was tempting to ignore it and send the man on his way, but Archer was a bigger man than that. Besides, the duke was helping Archer's father with his drainage problem. So Archer took his hand and gave it a slight squeeze. "Thank you for coming over and giving me the news in person, Your Grace. That was very considerate of you."

Archer returned to the dining room where

Kineton was finishing his breakfast. He looked up when Archer came back into the room. "What did the duke want?"

"To tell me he was backing out of my project," Archer said, dropping down into his chair. His cup of now cold coffee was still sitting there, so he downed it in two big gulps. It was disgusting. "I'm now back to where I was last night with one investor and not another in sight."

"Well, now you have your fiancée whose father is as rich as Croesus," he pointed out happily.

"Miss Benton is not my fiancée—she has not actually accepted my proposal. And I told you, I'm not marrying for money."

"Uh-huh..." Kineton said, returning his attention to the newspaper.

Archer wasn't going to have this argument with him. Not now. He needed to think about what he was going to say to Miss Benton when he finally got up the nerve to go and see her. It had to be today, but surely it would could wait until later—much later.

~*~

Cassie looked up from the book she hadn't been reading as her sister entered the drawing room. "Oh."

"Oh?"

"You're not the footman," Cassie explained.

Cynthia smiled. "No, I'm not. I take it Mr. Fitzwalter hasn't made an appearance yet?"

"No. I was sure he'd be here, if not this morning, then at least by two."

"It is extremely disappointing that he's not," Cynthia agreed, taking a seat and pulling out her stitching.

"Do you think he might be speaking with Sorrell? He couldn't have gone to Oxford to speak with Papa, could he?"

Cynthia considered it for a moment and then shook her head. "No, I can't imagine he would have gone that—"

A knock on the door interrupted her.

"Ah! Maybe this is him," she said, giving Cassie a broad smile.

"There is a gentleman to see you, Miss Benton," Frederick said.

"Finally!" Cassie said. "Yes, do show him up."

She stood and smoothed the gown she had taken nearly fifteen minutes to choose that morning. She'd finally settled on a pale green dress that brought out the green in her eyes. It only had a slight soil stain her maid hadn't been able to scrub out, but it was lower down on her skirt and could easily be mistaken for a shadow. Although she tried very hard to contain the smile on her face, she was certain she wasn't doing a very good job of it.

And then Mr. Crome walked in.

"Mr. Humphrey Crome," Frederick announced.

"Oh." The disappointment in Cassie's voice couldn't have been any clearer. Even Mr. Crome noticed it.

"Er, good afternoon, Lady Sorrell, Miss Benton," he said, clearly wondering why they were both looking so upset.

"I'm sorry, Mr. Crome, it is lovely to see you again," Cassie said, determined to be polite, despite her disappointment. "Please come in."

"Thank you. I came by to, er, give you this book I promised." He came forward and handed her the large book in his hand.

She took it and gasped. It was the book on roses he'd promised her at the book store.

"Open the cover," he prompted with a smile.

She did so and inside on the front page was written, "For Miss Cassia Benton. James Mean."

"Oh, how wonderful! You did manage to get it signed by the author." She smiled up at him. "Thank you so very much!"

"You are very welcome," he said, giving her a slight bow. "I do always try to keep my word."

"Of course you do. I never doubted you for a moment," she said, giving him a smile. "Please, do come and sit down."

"I shall order some tea," Cynthia said, standing.

"Actually, my lady, I was wondering if I might be able to have a word in private with Miss Benton," he said, awkwardly.

"Oh, er... Cassia?" Cynthia asked, looking toward her.

Cassie didn't know what to do, so she gave a slight lift of her shoulders.

"Very well, then. I'll return in a quarter of an hour." She left the room but, notably, left the door wide open.

She hadn't been gone a full minute before Mr. Crome was on one knee in front of Cassie. "Miss Benton, would you do me the great honor of becoming my wife?"

"Oh, Mr. Crome! I cannot imagine what has prompted you to ask me such a question, and in particular today of all days."

"I... I ask because I believe us to be quite compatible. We are both scientists, are we not? We are both dedicated to our work. I am certain I could not find another who would understand the necessity of my spending long hours in my lab. I... I admit I am quite the bane of my sister-in-law's existence. She does not and cannot comprehend the importance of what I do. She insists that I join her and my brother for dinner every single night. You, I am certain would not do so. I am sure you would understand that genius cannot be paused simply to fill one's stomach."

"Ah, yes, of course," Cassie said. She did understand. She understood completely. She, herself, had felt that frustration of being in the midst of some important work only to have it interrupted by some silly, ordinary task such as eating a meal. "I understand completely, and, well, to be completely honest if you had asked me this even so much as two weeks ago, I'm certain my answer would have been an enthusiastic 'yes'."

"Two weeks ago?"

"Yes. Before a certain incident in Lady Ayres's garden?"

"I thought I'd adequately explained why I was unable to come to your aid that evening," he said, sounding ever so petulant.

"You did. But then last night the gentleman who did come to my aid asked me very much the same question you just asked me," she admitted.

"He did?"

"Yes."

"And you have said...?"

"Well, I... I haven't said anything yet, but I plan on accepting his proposal," she admitted.

"That idiot? You plan on marrying a stupid fellow because of what? His looks? A handsome face? For there is certainly very little intelligence behind it," Mr. Crome snapped.

Cassie's mouth fell open. "I beg your pardon?"

The man stood up. "I had thought you more intelligent, but clearly you are very much like the rest of your sex—silly when it comes to men. Well, let me tell you that you have lost out on an excellent match with me. I am absolutely brilliant, and with your dowry, I could have done incredible things."

"I'm sorry? What did you just say?"

"You heard me. I said I was brilliant. I am a genius, and you have lost out on being associated with my excellent name," he said, lifting his nose into the air.

"I couldn't care less about that. You said that with my dowry you could have done great things? My dowry? You were just marrying me for my money!"

"Oh, well, yes. Why else? Aside from the fact that you are one of the very few women in this city—perhaps the country—who might not expect me to go trotting after them to all sorts of ridiculous functions and wouldn't harangue me for working instead."

"Get out."

Chapter Twenty-Three

"I... what?" Mr. Crome stopped and stared at her.

"You heard me. Get out. You are not only not a genius, Mr. Crome, you are incredibly stupid. Much more so than Mr. Fitzwalter who, I'll have you know, is quite intelligent. He may not have a scientific mind, but he's got an excellent one. He can see things and understand human behavior a great deal better than you," Cassie said, slowly advancing on the man. "For example, only a blinding idiot would tell a woman he was only asking her to marry him for her dowry. Many of us are aware of this sad truth, but I can tell you we do not like being reminded that our best quality comes from our father's purse."

As she moved forward, he had the wherewithal to retreat. He was nearly to the door when she stopped speaking.

"Well, I..." he started.

"You are leaving," Cassie finished for him.

"Yes, indeed, I am. Good day to you. You shall be sorry for this ill-considered decision, you mark my words!" And with that, he turned and left.

Cassie suddenly found her heart was racing, but she felt unusually light and content. She was very well rid of that man.

Cynthia came into the room a moment later. "I ordered tea," she announced to Cassie who was still standing where she'd been when Mr. Crome had turned and left. "I thought you might need some considering how quickly Mr. Crome left the house."

Cassie released her breath and gave her sister a little smile. "Thank you. Do you know he had the nerve to tell me that I was going to be sorry I didn't agree to marry his brilliance? And he said that with my dowry he could have done great things! With my dowry! That was all he was interested in."

Cynthia snorted a laugh. "Some men's minds are so full of hot air they don't even realize when they're being idiots."

Cassie laughed at that. She was about to turn and return to the sofa when Frederick was back.

"I beg your pardon, Miss Benton, but Mr. Fitzwalter is here, asking to have a word with you."

"Finally!" Cynthia cried.

"I think I'll take him for a walk through the garden, if you don't mind, Cynthia," Cassie said, looking to her sister. "I need a breath of fresh air after the stink of Mr. Crome and his 'honesty'."

"An excellent idea."

Cassie truly had the most wonderful sister. She gave her an impulsive hug and went down to greet Mr. Fitzwalter.

He was standing in the foyer, very much in the same spot where he'd been last night when he'd come to declare his love for her. Cassie couldn't help the smile that came to her face when she thought of that moment.

"Mr. Fitzwalter, you are here at a much more reasonable hour this time. Would you care to join me for a walk in the garden?" Cassie asked, coming down the stairs.

He looked up at her and smiled. "Thank you, Miss Benton, I would love to go for a walk... and apologize for my behavior last night."

She paused. "Apologize or retract what you said?" she asked, tilting her head with her query.

One side of his lips quirked up into a half smile. "Apologize only."

Her heart, and indeed all of her, warmed. "Well, then, shall we go for our walk and you can do so appropriately?"

He gave her a slight bow and strolled with her to the back garden.

~*~

Once they were outside and had gone a little way from the house, Archer turned to Miss Benton and said, "I'm afraid I have no excuse for my behavior last night. I was not, in fact, drunk. I was..." He paused and thought about how honest he should be. Should he put his heart out there where she might step on it? Or should he be more circumspect?

Considering his behavior from the night before, he figured it was already too late to protect that most tender organ within his chest. With a slight shrug, he said, "I was simply following my heart. I suppose I should have learned by now to stop and think before doing so. You have certainly done your best to impress this upon me. And yet, I still find myself jumping into things and then realizing the consequences of them later." He paused and turned to her, taking her hands in his. "Can you ever forgive me, Miss Benton? Can you forgive a headstrong, incorrigible man?"

"Of course, I forgive you. How could I not, when

you were acting upon your desire to tell me something that could only make me the happiest woman in the world," she said, smiling up at him.

"Really?" he asked hopefully. Did she... could she possibly love him as much as he loved her? Could the world be that wonderful and that cruel at the same time?

"Truly. Knowing that you love me is... unquantifiably wonderful," she said with a little laugh. But then she turned her gaze downward as she added, "And I love you."

"Knowing that makes me immeasurably happy," he said with a little laugh. He looked down at her hands in his. It wasn't enough. He wanted more. He needed to do more. Yes, he admitted, he wanted this woman who stood before him. He wanted her like he'd never wanted anyone or anything in his life.

She was looking up at him questioningly.

"I want you," he told her, sharing what was going through his mind. "I want to be with you, to listen to you speak about your roses, or anything else, for that matter. I want to share my life with you, my hopes, and dreams. I want..." He swallowed. "I want to have a family with you of beautiful, intelligent children who will dig in the garden and watch things grow with a patience I will never understand."

She giggled, and Archer just couldn't control himself. He put a hand to her beautiful cheek, caressing the softness of it. His lips found hers, and he tasted her sweetness, her joy, her essence. Pulling her close, he wanted to press himself to her, but he was also so very aware of her innocence. He would never do anything to scare her or make her feel uncomfortable, and yet at the same time, he wanted so much to be with her. He would know the carnal pleasures of this woman—

And that was when reality slammed back into him, nearly sending him staggering backwards.

He pulled away.

Apparently, life could be both glorious and distressing. What could he do? What could he tell this beautiful, intelligent woman? Dare he tell her the truth that he had absolutely no right to propose marriage to her because he couldn't follow through on it? Dare he ask her to come with him to India? No! That one was absolutely out of the question. He'd already come to that conclusion.

"What? What is it? Mr. Fitzwalter, I... I wish I knew what was going through your mind," Miss Benton said, looking up at him with such concern in her eyes. "You look like you are waging a fantastic battle inside."

"After a kiss like that, I think you should call me Archer."

She laughed. "Archer, then. And you must call me Cassia—or Cassie—if you prefer."

"I like Cassie. It's rather adorable." He paused and then said, "And I suppose there is a war, of sorts, going through my mind. The problem is... the problem is that I love you so very much."

"I don't see what the problem with that might be, especially considering that I love you too," she said.

He brushed a finger down her face. "The problem, you see, is that I actually have no right to ask you to marry me. I... I don't know if you've heard, but I'm putting together a business. It's a spice importing proposition. I'm going to be working with farmers in Madras to sell their spices here in

England. I still need to work out the fine details, but... but it's work that needs to be done in India."

A frown marred her lovely forehead. "I see."

"I couldn't, and wouldn't, ask you to move to India. It's a horrid place to live. It's too hot. Too humid. Too filthy for a gently bred young lady." But I love you, he wanted to say. Instead, he bit back the words not wanting to make this any harder than it was.

"So your marriage proposal..."

"Was made out of line. As I said, I was speaking from my heart, not my head."

She turned and looked away. Archer worried that there might be tears, but oddly enough, she seemed quite stoic. When she turned back to him, she said, "So, in fact, you have come to rescind your proposal."

"I don't want to."

"That doesn't change the fact, now, does it?"

Archer sighed, hating every minute of this conversation. "No, it doesn't."

"What if I said that I didn't care about heat and humidity and filth? What if I loved you enough to happily put up with all of that just so that I could be with you?" she asked, looking up at him.

His throat tightened. "I would say that you were... not thinking rationally."

"Sometimes, perhaps, it's better to think with your heart rather than your head. It's a lesson a wise man taught me—just before I punched his best friend in the nose." She gave him a sly little smile.

Archer couldn't help but laugh.

"Mr. Fitzwalter—"

"Archer," he reminded her.

She nodded. "Archer, I love you. I think you have the biggest heart of anyone I've ever met. All you do is think of others, their happiness and their comfort. It's the most wonderful thing, even if it does lead to doing some particularly silly things like try to give a child a ten-pound note." She laughed again, clearly remembering their night at the theatre. "But sometimes you need to let others make their own decisions."

"Like now?" he asked, appreciating where this was going.

She nodded. "Like now."

"How about..." He paused. His conscience still was uncomfortable at the idea of displacing her from all she'd ever known, no matter how much she thought she wouldn't mind. "How if you think about it? I believe you might like to have some time to really think this through, examine all the consequences of making a move like this. Consider all you would be leaving and all you would be gaining if you accepted my rash proposal."

"Use my head rather than my heart?" she asked, smiling broadly at him.

He laughed. "Yes. In this instance, I think using your head is the best thing."

She nodded. "You may very well be right."

This was the right thing, he realized. Giving her the choice rather than making it for her. He hated knowing that he was going to have to wait for her decision, but at least now there was the possibility that he could become the happiest man and return to India with a bride on his arm.

~*~

"Ladies St. Vincent and Conway are in the drawing room with Lady Sorrell, Miss Benton," the footman informed Cassie after he closed the door behind Archer.

"Oh! Thank you." She ran lightly up the stairs, excited to see her friends, although the thought of telling them everything that had just occurred did make her slow ever so slightly. She'd wanted a little time to think about it herself, but she supposed Cynthia wouldn't have given her that opportunity any way. She was surely eagerly waiting to hear what happened.

The three women were laughing over tea when Cassie came into the room. Bel jumped up nearly upsetting her tea cup. "Tell us everything!" she demanded.

Cassie just laughed and came farther into the room. "You don't mind if I help myself to some refreshments first, do you?"

Her friend sat back down, deflated. "No, I suppose not."

"At least inform us if you are engaged," Bee said hopefully.

"No, I am not," Cassie said. She couldn't be that cruel to her friends as to withhold that information. "At least... not yet," she added with a little smile.

They all gasped.

"Well, now you've got to tell us everything," Cynthia said.

"Cynthia has filled us in on last night's excitement," Bee started.

"I didn't think you'd mind," Cassie's sister said quickly.

"No, of course not."

"And on your falling out with Mr. Crome," Bel added.

"Good," Cassie said, taking a sip of tea.

"It sounds as if he was a complete idiot," Bee commented while Cassie took a bite of seed cake.

She could only nod her agreement since her mouth was full.

"But we are, naturally, dying to hear what Mr. Fitzwalter said," Cynthia finished.

Cassie nodded and took another drink of her tea to clear her mouth. Cynthia's cook's seed cake was not nearly as moist as her mother's. She then told them everything, leaving out only their kiss because they didn't need to hear about that. Although she didn't doubt for one minute that they would be most interested.

What was incredible was that all three stayed absolutely spell-bound silent throughout her recitation and, in fact, stayed that way for a full minute after she was done.

"So he's left the decision up to you. His offer still stands, though..." Bee summarized.

"Yes," Cassie said with a shrug. "I simply need to decide whether to accept."

"That's a big decision," Bel breathed.

"A very big one. Going to India! Could you do that?" Cynthia asked.

"I honestly don't know. It would mean leaving everything I know and everyone I love—the three of you," Cassie said, feeling her throat tighten at the thought. Could she actually do that? Did she love him enough?

"Well, you'd be back! You wouldn't be moving there forever, I presume," Bee said.

"Yes, I'm certain we would return, but after how many years? How long would it take to get his business started? And then he'd need someone in India to run it if he were to return to England," Cassie said.

"At some point, he'll be inheriting his father's title. I imagine he'd be back then whether his business continues or not," Cynthia pointed out.

"That's true! I hadn't remembered that," Cassie said, feeling better again.

"Well, it's still a big decision, Cassia. I suggest you take your time making it." Bee reached out and took Cassie's hand. "But know that whatever you decide, we'll be behind you."

"Yes! And if it is to go to India, we will write faithfully," Bel agreed.

"Thank you. You are definitely the very best friends a girl could have," Cassie said. This time actual tears pricked at her eyes, but she was not going to cry. She would not.

CHAPTER TWENTY-FOUR

~May 14~

"I wonder what this evening will be like," Cassie commented to her sister as they drove to Lady Rexford's ball.

Cynthia gave her an odd little smile that made Cassie wonder what was on her mind. "I don't know about you, but I'm determined to have a wonderful time."

"Really?" Cassie asked, wondering what her sister was up to. "I was thinking about Mr. Crome and Mr. Fitzwalter. I haven't seen or spoken to either one since they both proposed."

"Ahh," Cynthia said with an understanding nod. "Well, I imagine Mr. Crome won't be in attendance, considering that the only reason he came to any parties at all was to woo you. Now that he's gotten his answer on that head, I don't expect we'll be seeing him again."

"Unless he tries to go after some other poor, unsuspecting girl," Cassie pointed out.

"True. He may still be licking his wounds, however. And as for Mr. Fitzwalter, I would imagine that we'll be seeing him, and things will be awkward until you make up your mind," Cynthia said, astute as ever. "Have you come to any conclusions, by the way?"

"No. If I had, you would be the first to know, I assure you," Cassie said.

"I appreciate that. And you will tell me if I can do anything to help?"

"Thank you, I will. I'm just trying to figure things out. It's not easy with so many unknowns, but I'm doing my best to weigh the pros and cons and try to think it out logically."

Cynthia laughed. "Of course you are."

As they arrived that moment at the ball, Cassie did not have time to give an appropriate retort to her sister's comment.

They happily greeted those of their friends who'd already arrived.

"Have you made a decision yet, Miss Benton," Lady Blakemore asked Cassie quietly.

"A decision, my lady?" Cassie asked. She knew what the lady was asking about but wondered how she knew of Mr. Fitzwalter's proposal.

"My nieces tell me everything, but I assure you the information stops with me," the lady said.

"Oh, er, thank you, and no, I haven't. I'm still going through the pros and cons and trying to consider all the variables," Cassie said.

"Are you discussing one of your experiments with your roses?" Lydia asked, joining them.

"Er, no," Cassie started.

Lady Blakemore laughed. "It does sound as if she is, doesn't it? Are you currently working on any experiments, Miss Benton?"

"I am attempting to grow a new plant from a cutting I received not too long ago," Cassie answered, grateful for the change in subject. "Hopefully, next year I'll be able to breed it with the roses I've already been working with."

"What sort of rose is it?" Lydia asked.

"A Chinese tea rose. They have a very strong, very lovely fragrance—exactly the sort of thing I've been searching for. I'm quite excited by it, actually," Cassie answered.

"Is that Lady Sorrell dancing?" Gwendolyn asked, interrupting their conversation.

"Good evening, Gwendolyn," Cassie said, giving her friend a smile.

"Oh, good evening. I do beg your pardon," Cassie's friend said, giving everyone a small curtsey.

Duchess Bolton, as always, was just behind Cassie's friend. She greeted everyone with a broad smile and then asked the very same question.

"Yes, I do believe it is," Lydia answered with a giggle. They all turned toward the dance floor to see Cynthia laughing as she executed a very pretty turn-about with a gentleman.

"I didn't even see her go," Cassie commented.

"I don't believe I've ever seen her dance," the duchess said.

"Neither have I," Lydia agreed.

"Well, she does so very prettily," Lady Blakemore said, also watching.

"We shouldn't all stare," Cassie said with a laugh, turning back to her friends.

"No, we should not. You are absolutely correct, Miss Benton," Lady Blakemore agreed.

"It's just so nice to see her having fun," the duchess said, finally turning back to the group.

"It is. And you are right, it's unusual," Cassie

agreed. In fact, now that she thought about it, she didn't believe she'd seen her sister dance once this entire season. "I wonder what made her dance this evening—or why she hasn't done so before this? I do hope it wasn't because of me!"

"No, I'm sure it wasn't. As I said, I've known her for three years, and I don't think I've ever seen her do so," Lydia said.

"Oh, well, that's good," Cassie said, a bit relieved. She would hate to think that she was making it so Cynthia felt she couldn't enjoy herself. She stole a look back at her sister, and it truly did look like she was having fun.

A few minutes later, Cassie was surprised by the sweet baritone of Mr. Fitzwalter's voice. "Good evening, Miss Benton," he said, joining them.

"Oh, good evening, Mr. Fitzwalter," Cassie said. She had no idea why her face suddenly decided to heat, but she hoped desperately she wasn't turning too pink.

He smiled down at her. "May I have the next dance?"

"I would like that," Cassie said. She caught Lady Blakemore's smile out of the corner of her eye but studiously ignored it.

Archer was polite to the other ladies until it was time for them to take to the floor. Strangely enough, Cynthia didn't leave it but, instead, simply exchanged one partner for another.

"I assume you don't have an answer for me as yet?" he asked hopefully.

"I'm sorry. I do not. You will be the first to know, I assure you," Cassie said.

"Well, goodness, I should hope so!" he said with a laugh.

Cassie giggled. "Well, my sister also wants to be one of the first to know. She's been asking me about it almost every day."

"Ah, I see." He took the hand of the lady to Cassie's right and turned about with her. When he returned to Cassie, he said, "Is that your sister there, dancing?"

"Yes. It seems she's decided to dance this evening. It isn't like her at all, but I can't fault her for wanting to have some fun."

"No, indeed. She deserves to do so as much as anyone," he agreed.

After the dance finished, Cassie looked about for Cynthia, wanting to ask her about this sudden desire to dance, but she was nowhere to be found.

"Would you care for a refreshment?" Archer asked.

"Oh, yes. That sounds lovely, thank you," Cassie said.

They made their way to the dining room and found Cynthia surrounded by at least three gentlemen, all looking as if they were trying to ply her with Champagne.

"Oh, my word!" Cassie exclaimed involuntarily.

Archer just laughed. "Well, it looks like she is, indeed, having a good time."

"Too much of one. Is that possible?" Cassie asked.

Her companion just lifted and then dropped one of his broad shoulders.

"Well, I suppose I'm happy she's enjoying herself."

Cassie didn't actually see Cynthia again until her sister approached her and asked whether she was ready to leave. "Actually, about half an hour ago, but you were having so much fun I didn't want to disturb you," Cassie admitted.

"Oh, I'm sorry! You most definitely could have interrupted me," Cynthia said.

"I don't believe I've ever seen you dance and enjoy yourself like you did tonight," Cassie commented as they made their way to their carriage.

"That's because I haven't done so," Cynthia answered.

"Why? Or rather, why haven't you?"

"I thought I was being faithful to Sorrell, but with the sage advice of the Ladies' Wagering Whist Society, I've realized that I don't need to be," Cynthia said with a nonchalant shrug.

"You don't?"

"Not when he's not with me, and honestly, he's never with me, so why not?"

Cassie didn't have a response to that. Her sister was right. He was never with them when they went out and was almost never even at home. Well, it served him right if other gentlemen got to enjoy Cynthia's company when he'd chosen not to.

~May 15~

"Cynthia, we need to talk," Sorrell said, walking into Cynthia's bed chamber while she was still waking up with her morning chocolate and toast.

She scrambled to sit up farther and nearly spilled her chocolate all over her pristine white blankets. "What is it?" She put her cup down on the tray next to her.

"I beg your pardon, I don't mean to disturb your morning routine, but I do wish to speak with you."

"No, it's fine." she said, settling herself again.

He sat gingerly on the side of the bed close to her knees. "I, er... There was talk. At the club," he began hesitantly.

She waited for more information.

"It seems you had quite an evening last night," he began again.

"Are you speaking of my behavior at Lady Rexford's ball? I assure you, it was entirely proper. I did nothing but dance. And, well, have supper with my friends, naturally."

"You were the talk of the ball," Sorrell said with a straight face. Cynthia was trying to figure out if he was angry or what, but she simply could not read his expression. She didn't think it was one she'd ever seen before. His brow was knotted, as if he were thinking about something very seriously, but the line of his mouth was... not angry, but clearly not happy either.

"Only because it's been so long since I've danced at a ball," Cynthia explained. "I did nothing improper, I assure you."

"No, I know that. No one ever said you did. It's... it's that you danced and apparently enjoyed yourself a great deal. People commented that they hadn't seen you so happy and animated since... well, since we were married."

"Oh." Indeed, what could she say to that? It was the truth.

He placed a hand on the bed and leaned toward her. "Have you been unhappy?"

If Cynthia didn't know better, she would think he was truly concerned. She also didn't know what to say. Telling him the truth would sound so callous. On the other hand, she certainly couldn't lie. "Do you care?" she finally asked.

"What does that mean?" he asked, sitting up again. "Of course I care! What a question."

"It's an honest question. You've never shown that you do."

He opened his mouth, perhaps to refute the statement, but then closed it again. "Have I not?"

"When was the last time you spent any time with me, Francis?"

He started at the use of his given name. In truth, Cynthia had only ever called him that on one occasion—the day they were married. "We went out for a ride in Hyde Park just two weeks ago."

"Yes, so that you could meet someone you hadn't been able to get a hold of. You paid absolutely no attention to either me or Cassie because you were so busy looking for this man," she said.

"That's unfair! Of course I paid attention to you."

"What color was my habit? Did I wear feathers in my hat? Did we converse about anything interesting?"

He frowned, trying to think of the answers to her questions but clearly could come up with none.

"You didn't even see me. You only asked me to go to the park to use me as a tool, an excuse while you were looking for Lord Bunbury," Cynthia said. "And before that outing? When have you seen me before that?"

He thought about it, but Cynthia had an answer before he could even try to come up with one. "Months, Sorrell. It's been months. You have not attended one party, one dinner, nothing! I haven't seen you since... since Christmas! Truly, I don't think we've spent any time together since the new year, and now you're asking me if I'm unhappy? What do you think?"

"You have your sister here," he said, as if that were an excuse.

"Yes, I do, and it would have been nice if you'd spent a little time with her as well. Did you know she's planted an entire rose garden in the back?"

"She has?"

"Did you know we've converted the breakfast parlor into a makeshift hot house for her roses?"

"I was wondering why I've been served breakfast in the dining room," he said, turning his gaze away.

"You know nothing of what's going on under your own roof. You have taken no interest in her or me or our household. You refused to even ask around when she had two suitors!"

"One of them we met on the street after our ride in Hyde Park. You said at that time it would be unnecessary for me to look into him. Cassia wasn't interested or some such thing," he said defensively.

"Cassie was attacked during Lady Ayres's party as Mr. Crome stood by and watched. Mr. Fitzwalter came to her aid. Mr. Crome attempted to make it up to her by allowing us to visit his laboratory, but it turned out he was simply interested in Cassie's dowry. She declined the honor of funding his work through marriage."

"Cassia was attacked?"

"Yes. At the party you said you were too busy to attend—but then you've said that with every party I've asked you to attend this entire season." Cynthia could feel herself getting more and more annoyed the longer this discussion went on. "Sorrell, was there a reason you wanted to talk or was it simply to remind me of all of your failings this year? Oh, yes, I remember now, you were upset because I danced at a ball. Well, that's too bad!

"I'm tired of waiting for you. I'm tired of standing by the wall, watching other people enjoy themselves. I want to have fun. I want to dance, and laugh. I'm not going to stand by because I'm worried you might not approve or it might, in some way, harm your precious career. I'm done, Sorrell!" She threw back the covers and climbed out of bed, ready to head to her dressing room.

She didn't take two steps away before Sorrell caught her arm.

"Wait."

She looked up at him. Why was he so annoyingly handsome! He stood there looking down at her with pale blue eyes filled with such concern as if... as if he actually cared for her. It hurt more than anything.

It was those eyes, those high cheekbones, strong jaw, and those broad shoulders that had lured her into this marriage. He'd been so clever and intelligent. He'd tickled her mind and teased her senses with his humor and charm. If only she'd known his attention wouldn't even last through the day of their wedding. It had been four years, but finally Cynthia, with the help of the Ladies' Wagering Whist Society, had realized it was time for her stop waiting for him. It was time she moved on with her life.

"I'm sorry," he said simply. "I don't think I've treated you very well."

She lifted her chin but said nothing.

Chapter Twenty-Five

"I'm trying to make a name for myself in Parliament. It takes a very long time and a lot of work," Sorrell explained.

Still she said nothing.

"But that's no excuse," he said, finally letting go of her arm. "I haven't been here for you. I haven't paid any attention to either you or your sister and that... that was wrong of me."

She waited, feeling her heart begin to pound a little harder in her chest.

"That's going to change, Cynthia."

She swallowed as her throat tightened.

"I am going to do my best. It's not easy... but I'm going to try," he continued. He ran a hand through his always perfect, pale blond hair. For the first time ever, a clump of it flipped the wrong way and stuck up awkwardly. It was perfect.

"Will you join me for dinner every so often? I don't even need you there every night—just, just once in a while."

"I will, I promise!" he said, leaning ever so slightly toward her.

"And might you attend a party with me and

Cassie?" she asked, seeing how far she could push her luck.

"Yes, absolutely!"

She looked down for a moment and then gave him a slightly coquettish smile. "Will you dance with me?"

He laughed. "I would be honored."

He ran his thumb down her cheek, brushing away a tear she hadn't even realized was there. "I love you, Cynthia. I don't deserve a wife as brilliant and thoughtful as you. But you're mine, and I'm not ready to give you up just yet. I do need you to be patient with me, though. And remind me of what I should be doing—I know, I know," he said quickly, throwing his hands up. "You are always asking me to attend some event with you, and I always have an excuse, but just... be patient, and I promise to do my best. If I don't... If I go back to my old ways, you absolutely have my permission to dance and flirt and... and enjoy yourself because I deserve it. No, because you deserve it. You deserve to be happy, and I am very sorry I have not made you so for far too long."

~May 18~

Archer was in a foul mood. He was back yet again at Powell's, searching for another open-hearted gentleman with an open wallet to give him the financial backing he needed to start his company. He'd been there already! He'd had all the funding he needed—and then the Duke of Warwick had backed out because he needed his funds for his tenants.

Honestly! He could have rebuilt those homes, even added a stable and a gazebo once Archer's business became profitable. He was certain the man had funds enough to build those houses and fund Archer. He was trying to be understanding of

Warwick's decision but... he took in a deep breath. He needed to calm himself and set his mind to this task. He wasn't being practical or thoughtful.

"Archer!" Kineton's voice penetrated Archer's thoughts. "You walked right past me," his friend said, sounding slightly annoyed.

"Oh, sorry. I didn't see you," Archer said as he sat down in the chair by Kineton's side. He didn't know why he'd left the chair opposite him empty—wishful thinking, perhaps.

"You seemed to be deep in thought," his friend commented.

"I was just thinking about how annoying it is that I'm still trying to find funding for my company. If Warwick only had the intelligence to realize—"

"What do you mean? Did Cassia turn you down?" Kineton asked, interrupting him.

"Cassia? What has she got to do with this?"

"You proposed to her. Did she turn you down?"

"No. She hasn't turned me down. She still hasn't given me any answer, which is another thing that's rocking my boat tonight, I can tell you!" Archer said, accepting the glass from the footman, who'd come over after Archer had signaled to him. Archer filled it from the bottle by Kineton's side.

"Of course, help yourself," his friend said, watching him.

"Thank you, I will. You can afford it much more easily than I can."

"You will be able to afford it—and fully fund your company once Cassia accepts your proposal," Kineton pointed out.

"If she accepts it," Archer said. "But even if she does, I told you, I'm not going to use her money to fund my project. That's not why I proposed to her."

"Hmm-hmmm," Kineton said with a leering smile.

"I told you, I am not marrying anyone for their money. I will find financial backers for my company," Archer growled. Kineton was really pushing him tonight.

"Don't be daft—"

"Look, just because you sold yourself to the highest bidder doesn't mean that I'm going to do the same. I am not for sale. I am not going to debase myself to some father-in-law in the hopes that he throws me a sovereign every now and then. I'm not doing it. I am also not going to marry a girl and leave her high-and-dry here in London while I return to India. It's not happening. If I marry Miss Benton, it will be because she loves me as much as I love her. It will be because she is willing to give up everything she cares for to join me in India, and I will be forever grateful to her for doing so because it won't be easy. But I will not and am not marrying her for her dowry." By the time Archer finished speaking, his voice was practically down to a whisper, he was so furious.

He placed his glass down on the table with barely a sound and strode off. He needed to get away from Kineton. The man was driving him to distraction, and Archer was trying really hard to remember why he ever liked him in the first place.

Hours later, Archer was tired, but the thought of going back to Kineton's left a sour taste in his mouth. He needed to find an alternative living arrangement.

He called a footman over. "Another whisky." He held up his empty glass. "And is Lord Wickford here this evening?" Wickford had done well by him, introducing him to both Warwick and Lord Pennyston. Perhaps he could help once again.

"I'm terribly sorry, sir. We do not expect his lordship this evening."

Archer nodded as the man bowed and went off to fetch Archer's drink.

He had given up his search for the evening and was reading a paper someone had left on a nearby chair when he was interrupted by a gentleman.

"Ah! Fitzwalter! I've been looking for you," Lord Pennyston said, approaching him after he'd just ordered his third—and, he promised himself, his last—glass.

Archer stood to shake his investor's hand. He swayed for a moment but pulled himself together. "Good evening, my lord. What can I do for you?" Archer asked, giving him a smile.

"Er... I'm afraid we need to talk," he said.

"Care to join me? I'm enjoying a rather fine whisky," Archer said.

"Oh, er, no, thank you. I, er, won't be long. It's getting late."

Archer nodded and indicated that Pennyston take the other chair.

He sat at the very edge, his hands clasped tightly between his knees. "I'm afraid I have bad news. I, er, I won't be able to invest in your company after all. I just learned that the building I was planning to sell is being used as a hospital for wounded veterans." He gave Archer an apologetic smile. "Can't kick them out, you know."

Archer felt his throat tighten. "No, of course not," he managed.

"No. So, I, er, I had to cancel the sale. The fellow

wanted to tear the building down and build some new, grand house on the site," Pennyston explained.

"I see."

"Yes, I knew you would." Lord Pennyston gave him a hesitant smile. "I'm truly very sorry. I truly wanted to be a part of this project. It sounds excellent and as if it will be an excellent investment. I'm sure you'll have no trouble finding others—"

"Actually, while there were a number of people who were interested, no one actually wanted to support their words of encouragement with the financial backing."

"Oh. I'm sorry. Well, I'm sure..."

"My other investor backed out as well," Archer told him. For some reason—perhaps it was the liquor, he didn't know—he started to laugh. Suddenly, it was all very funny.

Lord Pennyston smiled but looked confused. "What... what's so funny?"

Archer just shook his head, almost unable to speak, he was laughing so hard. "This! Me! This entire situation! I came back to England, certain I would have no trouble finding the investors for this incredible idea I had. Do right by the people. Do some good and earn money at the same time. But no. It isn't that easy. Once again I followed my heart instead of my head, and once again it is coming back to bite me..." He paused. "I think my father was right. I will never amount to anything. Cassie—Miss Benton—was right too. I don't consider the consequences before I act. I thought I'd do something good, but instead, I'm sitting here with nothing and no prospects."

He looked over at Pennyston who was watching him with concern. "I proposed to her, you know."

"No! Congratulations are in order, then?" he asked with a smile.

Archer just shook his head. "I proposed to her in the middle of the night—the same evening you said you would be able to fund my business. The very next morning, Warwick pulled his investment. I proposed to Miss Benton and was told she needed to think on it. I don't blame her, but I can tell you that patience has never been my strong suite."

"I am so—" Pennyston started.

Archer waved his words away. "I deserve it. I must, right? I leap and don't consider where I'll land. I try to help people, to care, to love, and it all gets thrown back into my face. Every. Single. Time! I think I must be incredibly stupid or something because I never learn."

"Fitzwalter..."

"No. No. I'm sorry. I apologize. I've had too much to drink," Archer said, dropping his empty glass onto the floor and his head into his hands. The glass bounced on the soft carpet even as his head felt like it was shattering into a million pieces.

~May 20~

"Cynthia, you were incredible the other night!" Lydia said the moment she walked into the Sorrell drawing room. Cynthia was hosting her weekly at-home. There were only a few women and gentlemen scattered about the blue brocade sofas and chairs of the drawing room, but it was still early yet.

"Was I?" Cynthia asked, laughing. "How so?"

"What do you mean? You danced almost every single dance! You laughed and flirted and... and... I don't know what! I can tell you, I just came from Lady Smithton's, and you are the talk of the ton!"

"Oh dear! I didn't mean for that to happen,"

Cynthia said, beginning to look a little worried.

"Is it good talk or cruel talk?" Cassie asked.

"Good! All good, I assure you," Lydia said.

"All right," Cynthia said, still sounding unsure. "What are people saying, then?"

"Only that you looked fabulous. And people were wondering what brought about the change, but everyone—and I mean everyone—applauded it. They all agreed that you have been meek as a kitten these last few years, and they've been worried for you. I didn't know that you had cut quite a figure upon your coming out," she said with a little twinkle in her eye. She clearly wanted to know much more.

"I don't know I did that, precisely. I certainly enjoyed myself," Cynthia said with a little laugh.

"Well, everyone agreed you were the most intelligent, most fun girl to make her come out in years," Lydia said. "And they were so happy to see you back."

"I have to admit, I had fun. It did feel like the old me," Cynthia said with a sigh.

"I don't understand why you stopped behaving that way," Cassie said.

"Because I thought it was inappropriate behavior for the wife of an active member of Parliament. I've tried to be more staid, more circumspect," Cynthia explained.

"And you see what that got you?" Lydia asked.

Cynthia looked at her in curiosity.

"Nothing! Your husband is too busy paying attention to his own affairs, and you were left high and dry standing on the outskirts of the fun," Lydia said.

"Oh, yes. But no more!" Cynthia said. "From

now on I am going to dance. I truly enjoyed myself at the Rexford's ball. And you—" Cynthia pointed at Cassie. "You need to have fun like that too!"

"But I'm not like you. I'm not..." Cassie started, but just then the footman came in and announced, "Lord Kineton."

"What is he doing here?" Cynthia asked, looking over toward her newest guest.

"I don't know. I can't say I'm thrilled," Cassie commented.

"Why? I thought he was a nice man," Lydia said, looking over at him.

"No, he's not." Cassie wouldn't say any more than that because she didn't want to cause a stir, but she wished he'd not come. And even worse, he was headed right their way. Oh, but he was probably just coming to greet the hostess. Still, she couldn't help but feel all her muscles tense.

"Good afternoon, Lord Kineton," Cynthia said in the coldest voice Cassie had ever heard her use.

"Good afternoon, Lady Sorrell. I do beg your pardon, but may I have a word with Miss Benton?" he asked, looking at Cassie.

"I don't know that's a good idea," Cynthia said honestly.

"I assure you, I only want to have a word. We will not leave the room. Perhaps, I might prevail upon the young lady to take a turn-about with me?" he asked, giving Cassie a small bow.

Cassie looked at her sister who just gave the most minute shrug.

"And may I remind you that I was the one who walked away from our last encounter physically injured?" he added.

That did make Cassie feel slightly better. "Very well." She turned and started toward the edge of the room, so they could walk around the perimeter. Lord Kineton fell into step next to her.

Chapter Twenty-Six

"I hope you are doing well," Lord Kineton began.

"Yes, thank you. What did you want to say to me?" Cassie answered. She didn't particularly want to spend much time in this man's presence, and she saw no reason to engage in polite chatter.

He seemed put off for a moment, but then collected himself and got right to the point. "Have you given your answer to Fitzwalter yet regarding his proposal?"

"No, I haven't. Why?"

"Because it might interest you to know that since he proposed he's stopped searching for another investor in his company," Lord Kineton said, sounding ever so slightly pleased to be imparting this information.

Cassie thought about that for a moment and then said, "Are you implying that he believes he can use my dowry to fund his company?"

"That is precisely what I'm saying—always knew you were a clever girl."

"But that's not why he proposed. He loves me," she pointed out.

"He told you that after returning from Powell's

after a frustrating evening of not being able to find the second investor he needs," Lord Kineton said.

Cassie stopped walking. "Are you saying he lied? Why should I believe you?" she asked, turning to him.

"Because he's been playing me too. He's been staying in my home, eating my food, and using my connections to find his investors and giving me what in return? Nothing. Not a thing but a huge headache and an earful of malice when I told him that you weren't a girl to be taken lightly. I suggested he find himself a wealthy girl to marry, but when he showed a marked interest in you, I tried to warn him away. All I got was a sharp warning to leave him be to do what he thought best. So now I am here to warn you to be on your guard. He wants only one thing from you, and it's not your intelligent mind and lovely face."

With that, Lord Kineton bowed and strode out of the room.

Cassie couldn't believe it. Would Archer really do that? Would he truly use her to fund his business? He'd said he'd loved her, but... how could she know that empirically? How could she know if he was just telling her that so she would marry him?

Someone who might know the answers to her questions walked into the room. Lord Wickford was extremely well-informed. He knew everything that went on in society. It was probably why he was here—to find out why Cynthia had been having so much fun at the Rexford's ball. Surely, he was here to hear the latest gossip.

She walked over to the gentleman, curtseying to him. "Good afternoon, my lord."

"Good afternoon. Miss Benton, is it not? I don't

believe we've officially met," Lord Wickford said.

"Haven't we? I feel as if we have," Cassie said, taken off guard. He'd certainly been pointed out to her a number of times. She heard talk of him. Surely they'd met.

"I know precisely what you mean, but no, I don't believe we have." He gave her a warm smile and a bow. "I am delighted to finally make your acquaintance."

She gave a little laugh. "And I you." She lost her smile quickly, though. "I'm afraid I need to ask you an odd question, if I may."

He raised his eyebrows over his deep-set, gold-colored eyes. Gwendolyn had been right, they were beautiful, especially fringed as they were by the longest lashes a man could have. But she was getting distracted.

"I was wondering if you knew if Mr. Fitzwalter was still looking for investors for his new business. I understand he was in search of some. Perhaps even spending a great deal of time at Powell's for that reason?" she asked.

His eyes widened ever so slightly. "Yes, he has been looking for investors there, why?"

"Recently? Say, within the past week? Has he continued his search?"

"As far as I know he's found all the funding he needed. I could be wrong, however. I haven't seen him in some time."

"Oh, but the last time you saw him, he was no longer looking for investors," Cassie confirmed.

"Yes. He was quite happy about it too," he said, smiling at her.

She did her best to return the smile. "I see. Thank you. If you'll excuse me, I see someone else I need to speak with."

He bowed and she walked off to the other side of the room, not so much to talk to someone as to specifically talk to no one. She needed to think. And perhaps to calm down because all of a sudden she felt her heart pounding inside her chest.

Lord Kineton had been right. Archer had stopped looking for funding because he'd found it—in her dowry! How dare he? He lied to her! He'd told her he loved her, but clearly it was a lie!

No, Cassie was not going to speak to anyone. She couldn't. She needed her garden. Roses never lied. Roses never told you something they thought you wanted to hear just so they could get a hold of your money.

She made her way out of the room as quickly and politely as she could. It wasn't easy with the huge crowd of people that had suddenly appeared. Yes, everyone wanted to know about Cynthia. Well, that was wonderful because it meant that Cassie could escape without being noticed.

~*~

Archer made his way out to the garden, certain that it was where he'd find Cassie. He'd come into Lady Sorrell's drawing room a mere quarter of an hour ago, but it felt more like a life-time.

Of course, he'd seen her speaking with Kineton the moment he'd walked in. Somehow, his eyes always found Cassie the moment he came into a room. She hadn't looked happy. Her eyes were narrowed and her mouth pinched as she questioned Kineton. His friend had been shifty-eyed but somehow had missed seeing Archer. Or if he had seen him, he pretended as if he hadn't.

Archer didn't like the look on either of their

faces, and he didn't like the fact that Kineton was speaking with Cassie privately. He became even more concerned when she obviously had told him to leave, and he did so with a much too-determined air—as if he'd come to say something, and now he'd said it.

What could Kineton have wanted to tell Cassie? That was the question. Whatever it was, she'd immediately gone to Lord Wickford for confirmation and had received it.

Archer followed the path as it led around some bushes and down toward a section of roses. They were tiny plants, looking like they'd just been planted this year. Cassie was kneeling down in the dirt, tending to them and... was she simply digging her hands in the dirt? He couldn't quite make out what she was doing.

"Cassie? Is everything all right?" he asked, approaching her.

She jumped to her feet, wiping her dirty hands down her pale green gown, leaving streaks of dirt. "Archer! What are you doing here?"

"I came to your sister's drawing room in the hopes of seeing you," he said. "Instead, I saw Kineton speaking with you and then you confirming something with Lord Wickford. May I ask what that was about?"

Cassie's beautiful mouth pinched together again, as if she were holding back her words, but then in a rush she let them all out. Archer almost wished she hadn't.

"What was it about?" she repeated. "It was about you, Archer. Lord Kineton told me that you proposed to me simply for my dowry because you needed the money to start your business. Is that true? Because if it is, I'll have you know I do not appreciate being lied to. I do not like it when a man tells me he loves me when what he means is he loves my father's money. At least when Mr. Crome proposed to me, he was—mostly—honest and forthright telling me he was doing so for my dowry. He didn't try to hide his intentions behind false declarations of love. That's what it was about. Now, I'd appreciate it if you'd leave me be. And by that, I mean forever." With that, she turned and strode away.

"Cassie!" Archer called after her, but short of running and physically restraining her, there was nothing he could do. It was the oddest thing, though. As he watched her walk away, all he could think was that he hoped she wasn't going back into her sister's drawing room with dirt smudged down her gown.

~*~

One might have thought that turning down a proposal of marriage would lead to tears, but strangely, Cassie had none. No, she wasn't sad. She was angry. Angry at Archer. Angry at herself for having been so taken in by him.

She'd truly thought he cared.

With a shake of her head, she started toward the drawing room but simply could not stomach being social right now. She was standing outside of the drawing-room door when Cynthia came out, followed by Bel.

"Oh, there you are! I was beginning to worry," Cynthia said. "I didn't want to send someone to find you..."

"I offered," Bel said, jumping into Cynthia's pause.

"But I thought you might need... someone,"

Cynthia finished hesitantly.

"I don't need anyone, thank you." Cassie didn't know why, but she had absolutely no desire to share with her sister the fact that yet another man only wanted her for her dowry. It was too humiliating! She looked at Bel and inspiration struck. "Bel, I promised you some roses for your garden, didn't I?"

"Did you?" her friend asked with a slight frown.

"Yes, I'm certain that I did. If you wait for just a moment, I'll go up and change into a morning gown I can garden in."

"You already seem to have dirt on your dress," Bel said.

Cassie looked down. "Oh, dear!"

"Yes, and I rather liked this dress on you," Cynthia said sadly.

"Well, maybe it can be cleaned. I'll change and be right with you, Bel. In the meantime, why don't you go down to the breakfast parlor and pick out some roses you'd like to have."

"Um... all right," Bel said, turning to look at Cynthia for some reason. Cassie wondered what they were silently communicating to each other. She didn't have time to ask about it; she needed to change.

A mere ten minutes later, she met her friend staring out the large windows of the breakfast parlor.

"Did you find any you liked?" Cassie asked, making Bel jump a little.

"Oh, I, er, I didn't know which ones you could spare," Bel said.

"Ah, true. Let's see..." Cassie had set aside the ones she was experimenting with to one side, to catch the most light. There were three others she'd simply given up on because they didn't seem to be exhibiting the traits she'd wanted. "These. They're very pretty—two are red and one is white. They aren't as fragrant as I'd hoped. Is that all right?"

"Yes! Of course. I'm sure they'll be very pretty."

"Most definitely," Cassie said. "Do you have your carriage here? We could take them over now, and I'll plant them for you."

"Are you sure you want to do that now?" Bel asked. She was looking a little concerned.

"Absolutely! Come, you take that one—be careful of the thorns—and I'll take these two." Cassie picked up the two red English roses and led the way out.

Bel didn't live far, and it wasn't long before Cassie was happily examining the layout of Bel's garden and deciding where to put the roses. A maid approached with a spade for her.

"Thank you," Cassie said, taking it. "What do you think about over here?" she asked, pointing to an area where there would be full sun light.

"That looks fine to me," Bel agreed.

"Excellent. It's a good spot for both the sun and in conjunction with the other plants you already have," Cassie said, dropping down onto her knees just in front of the garden. She would need to reach around the low flowers already there, to plant the roses behind them. They would eventually grow taller, but happily there was plenty of space for them.

Bel placed the two plants she was holding onto the ground and looked down to examine her dress to be sure it hadn't gotten dirty while she'd carried them.

Cassie laughed at her. "You're perfect, as always."

"No, I got a little smudge. It's all right. I'm sure it will come out," Bel said, giving a little wipe to her gown.

Cassie got to work digging into the soil. It felt good. She dug deep, using all of her muscles to drive the spade into the ground. She dropped the pile of dirt next to the hole and dug in again, and again, faster and faster. And suddenly, she didn't know why, but she found that tears were streaming down her face. A sob broke from her, but she just kept digging.

A warm hand on Cassie's shoulder made her pause.

"Cassia, tell me," Bel's soft voice implored.

Cassie closed her eyes for a moment but then went back to digging. It just felt so good. She shook her head, unable to speak with her throat so tight as she tried to hold back her tears.

"Did Mr. Fitzwalter... did he do something? Say something?" Bel asked.

Cassie paused to wipe her face with her arm—her hands were covered in dirt. Bel reached over and wiped away her tears with a handkerchief. Cassie gave a little laugh; of course Bel had one. Cassie never did.

"I'm sorry. No, Mr. Fitzwalter didn't say something. Lord Kineton did. He told me Archer was only marrying me for my dowry," Cassie told her. She then told her everything Lord Kineton had said and how she'd confirmed it with Lord Wickford.

"What did Mr. Fitzwalter say when you told him you knew this?" Bel asked.

"Nothing. He said absolutely noth—" Sobs interrupted her words.

Bel folded her into her arms and just held her

while she cried.

"I'm... I'm sorry," she managed to say, finally. "I don't know why I'm being so stupid."

"You're not being stupid, you're being sad—which you have every right to be. You love him," Bel said.

"I do. But he doesn't love me," Cassie said with a hiccough.

"Do you know that for certain? Did he say so?"

"No, but..."

"Then you are jumping to conclusions," her sweet friend said.

Cassie stopped to think about that.

"Lord Kineton told you that Mr. Fitzwalter needed your dowry to fund his company, but he didn't say the gentleman didn't love you," Bel pointed out.

"No... No, he didn't!" Cassie thought about it for another moment. "Do you think it's possible that he does?"

"He told you so, didn't he?"

"Well, yes, but—"

"No," Bel said, interrupting her. "He told you he loved you. I'm certain a gentleman would not lie about that."

"So, if he loves me..."

"He's been searching for investors for his company for a while now. Maybe he just hasn't been successful at getting all the money he needs. Perhaps he has some, but since he loves you and thinks you love him—perhaps he thought it wouldn't be a problem to use some of your dowry to complete the funding he needs."

"You think he didn't propose only for my

money?" Cassie said, feeling her throat tighten once more. She swallowed hard, trying to push it away.

"I don't think he would do that."

"But if that's the case..." Cassie paused to think this through. While she did so, she turned back to the garden, digging her hand into the dirt, loving the feel and the smell of the fresh earth. She turned and scooped out more soil from the hole she'd been digging. It was big enough now to put in the rose bush, so she did that too while allowing her mind to wander through pathways, thinking of Archer.

She sat back on her heels after properly heaping the soil around the bottom of the plant. "It will need fertilization, but your gardener can do that," she commented.

"What were you thinking?" Bel asked.

Cassie exhaled. "I was thinking about Archer, and I believe I know what to do."

"What?"

"I need to see Gwendolyn. She'll be able to help me and then... then I'll speak with Archer."

Chapter Twenty-Seven

Powell's was nearly empty, but then Archer supposed everyone was at home preparing for the evening. It was still too early for even the most determined of men to be out at a club. But not Archer. No, he wanted to start drinking early and not stop until they had to carry him out.

"A glass of whisky—no, make it a bottle," he told the footman as he walked into the reading room.

He was well into his second glass when Lord Wickford came over. "Dinner is now being served in the dining room, Mr. Fitzwalter."

"Thank you. I'm not interested," Archer told him.

"Are you certain? We've got a lovely roast—"

"What did she ask you?" Archer asked, interrupting the man.

"I beg your pardon?"

"What did Miss Benton ask you this afternoon?" he repeated.

His lordship had the grace to look uncomfortable for a moment. "She asked whether you were still looking for investors for your new company."

"And you told her… what precisely?"

He looked away temporarily. "I told her you had been, but I hadn't seen you do so recently. I did assure her that I wasn't entirely certain since I've been rather busy of late."

"Yes, you have been, clearly, because I've lost all of my funding. Warwick pulled out two weeks ago and Pennyston last week. I've got nothing. No funding and now, thanks to you, no beautiful woman at my side."

"I am very sorry, Fitzwalter. I had no way of knowing…" He sighed. "I simply answered her question."

"Perhaps not. Perhaps I've had too much to drink. My apologies." He swiped a hand down his face. "It's just… she now thinks I proposed merely to get her dowry to fund my project," Archer added quietly, turning his glass so the liquid rolled around the sides.

"But you proposed when you were fully funded," Lord Wickford said.

"She doesn't know that."

"Why didn't you tell her—"

Archer just shook his head and poured himself another drink.

"You can do something about this, you know," Wickford said.

Archer sat back in his chair and looked up at the man. "Yes? I can go back to India. Rejoin the bloody East India Company army and go back to murdering people because they aren't English and won't follow our ways. Yes, I could do that, my lord."

"No. That's not what I meant," Lord Wickford said, frowning at him.

"Then what did you mean?" Archer mumbled, draining his glass once again.

"You could ask for help from the Ladies' Wagering Whist Society," he said, refilling Archer's glass again. "I've heard they perform miracles when it comes to matters of the heart."

"The Ladies'... Oh yes, I've heard of them." Archer took a sip, trying to get his brain to work again. With the burn of the alcohol on his tongue, he realized he didn't actually want any more to drink. He placed the glass on the table next to the mostly empty bottle.

"They are only the most influential group of women in the ton, and your Miss Benton's sister, Lady Sorrell, is a member," Lord Wickford informed him. "But don't let that stop you. If you truly love Miss Benton, Mr. Fitzwalter, you will go and seek counsel from the Ladies' Wagering Whist Society. They'll tell you what you need to do to make things right. If you do that, I can almost guarantee you will marry Miss Cassia Benton."

~May 25~

Cassie had tried. She'd tried very, very hard at the Lady Ashton's ball two nights ago. She'd tried to speak with other men. To dance with them. To flirt and be "interesting," but it had been too hard. Too much effort. And then the moment she'd seen Archer simply leaning against the wall watching her, her intentions simply crumbled to dust like a garden in a drought.

Nothing could possibly grow inside of her. There was no interest. No enthusiasm. All she wanted was to be with Archer, but her mind kept telling her that he only wanted her for her money.

She'd thought she'd figured out the answer to her problems when she'd been in Bel's garden, but her mind kept telling her she was wrong. She shouldn't do anything, her logical brain said. It was over and done. He didn't love her and had only proposed for her dowry.

But now, every time she closed her eyes at night, she could see him watching her.

She knew precisely what she needed to do. She simply needed to stop listening to her head and start following her heart.

She knocked with determination on Gwendolyn's door.

"Miss Cassia Benton to see Miss Sherman," she informed the footman who answered the door.

He bowed her into the house. "This way, Miss," he said, leading her straight upstairs.

"Miss Benton," he announced as he walked into the drawing room.

Gwendolyn stood up and came forward to greet Cassie. "I was wondering how long it would take you to get here," her friend said with a broad smile. She then looked behind Cassie. "What? Are Bel and Bee not with you? I was sure you'd bring them along, or will they be joining us soon?"

Cassie laughed. "You are too clever for words, Gwendolyn. But not clever enough. I did not ask the twins to join us. I need to speak with you alone. I need your keen business sense and knowledge."

"Really? Oh, now this sounds very intriguing. Do come in." Gwendolyn led the way to the sofa and sat down so Cassie could sit next to her.

"I'm certain you've heard that I turned down Mr. Fitzwalter," Cassie said.

"Please! Old news," Gwendolyn said with a wave of her hand.

"I did so because I was informed he only wanted to marry me for my money," Cassie told her.

"Oh-ho! This is becoming more interesting."

"I have decided I'd rather be with him than without—money or no. If he doesn't actually love me, surely he will after some time, don't you think?" Cassie asked.

"I'm sure he loves you now! How could anyone not love you?" Gwendolyn exclaimed.

Cassie laughed and gave her friend's hand a squeeze. "Well, whether that is true or not, I've decided to follow my heart and not my head. However, in order to do so, I need your head."

"Go on."

"Archer needs my money to start his company. From what I understand, it's an import-export company—"

"I happen to know something about them," Gwendolyn said with a little laugh.

"I know. You've been managing the export of your father's cotton cloth for years," Cassie said, giving her friend a big grin. "That's why I came to you. Archer's not going to be exporting anything from England, but rather importing spices from India. We need to find out how much money he'd need to actually start such a business."

"Why don't you ask him?" Gwendolyn asked with a tilt of her head.

Cassie just smiled at her. "Because I know Archer. He probably has no idea how he's even going to start the business, let alone how much financing it's actually going to need. He's probably just made up a number in his head and is attempting to get that much money to start the company, but I seriously doubt it's an accurate number. It's quite likely he doesn't even know how he's going to organize what he wants to do."

"I can't believe—"

"He tried to give a street urchin ten pounds when the child attempted to steal his purse. He's got a big heart but doesn't think things through," Cassie told her.

Gwendolyn's mouth dropped open. She then stood and started out the door. "All right, then. Let's go look at the books, timetables, and get some shipping information. I should be able to find out all we'll need to know in a few hours," she said on her way down to her study.

Cassie followed saying, "I knew I could count on you."

Gwendolyn paused half-way down the stairs and turned around. "Of course you can! Always."

Gwendolyn set Cassie to work looking through ledgers to gather information while she wrote to people she knew to find out more specifically about shipping from Madras. Her father's company only shipped to the continent and sometimes to America, so she didn't have any direct knowledge of shipping from the subcontinent, but she knew people who did. As notes came back filled with information, she compiled the numbers and calculated costs. By the end of the afternoon, she had a rough estimate of how much such a business would need in start-up funds and a list of interested ship owners willing to do business with an associate of David and Gwendolyn Sherman.

"Thank you, thank you!" Cassie said, giving Gwendolyn a huge hug.

Gwendolyn just laughed. "Actually, that was a lot fun!"

Cassie giggled. "Only you would think so."

"You'll let me know when he's ready to get serious about this?" she asked.

"Absolutely! You'll be the first to know." Cassie went home happier than she'd been in days.

~*~

Cynthia walked into Lady Ayres's drawing room the following Wednesday to find many of the ladies already present.

"Lady Sorrell, I'm certain you've heard this a hundred times already, but I was so happy to see you dancing last week," Lady Ayres said soon after she'd greeted everyone.

"Thank you, my lady, but I have even better news," Cynthia said, hardly able to contain her happiness.

"Oh?" Lady Ayres asked.

"Has your sister become engaged?" Duchess Bolton asked.

"Sadly, no. I do not have good news on that topic. But after hearing of my behavior last week at Lady Rexford's ball, Sorrell has promised to be more attentive and to join me more often when I go out."

"But that's wonderful!" Lady Blakemore exclaimed.

"And so quick!" Lady Ayres agreed.

"I certainly didn't expect just one evening's entertainment to change his mind," the duchess commented.

Diana and Lydia, the last to arrive, came in just then.

"Ladies, have you heard Lady Sorrell's good news?" Lady Gorling asked. She'd returned from her honeymoon happier and more at ease than any of them had ever seen the lady.

"No!" Diana said, turning to Cynthia.

"You must tell us!" Lydia said.

"Our evil plan worked," Cynthia said with a laugh. "Sorrell has promised to be more attentive from now on."

"But that's wonderful!" Lydia gushed. She gave Cynthia a quick hug. "Oh, I am so happy for you."

"Indeed, congratulations, Cynthia!" Diana said.

"You must be thrilled," Lady Moreton said, piping in.

"Now, let's just hope that he keeps true to his good intentions," Cynthia said, voicing her worries.

"I beg your pardon, ladies, a gentleman wishes an audience," the footman intoned from the door.

"Who is it, Michael?" Lady Ayres asked.

"A Mr. Fitzwalter, my lady."

"Oh! Do show him up," the lady responded, turning back to Cynthia.

She could only shrug. "I only know Cassie said she'd refused his suit. She didn't specify why."

"I suppose we're about to learn the answer," Lady Gorling said just as the gentleman walked in and bowed to them all.

"My ladies," Mr. Fitzwalter said as he straightened. "I do beg your pardon for the interruption, but I was told you were who I needed to see for advice."

"Who told you this?" Lady Gorling asked, looking down her nose at the gentleman, returning to her normal condescending self in the blink of an eye.

"Lord Wickford, my lady," the gentleman said,

beginning to look concerned.

"He does know—" Lady Blakemore started.

"And as I imagine this concerns Lady Sorrell's sister—" Lady Gorling interrupted.

"Yes," Lady Blakemore agreed, "Since this involves the sister of a member, you are most welcome to seek out our advice," Lady Blakemore said. "Ladies?" she asked, turning to look at them all for confirmation. There was a general consensus of nodding heads.

"What is the problem, Mr. Fitzwalter?" Lady Moreton asked.

"It is a delicate matter," he admitted, deliberately not looking at Cynthia.

"Perhaps you would care to share with us why Miss Benton turned down your proposal of marriage?" the duchess asked.

His gaze flew to Cynthia. "Did she not tell you?"

"No. She only said that she refused your offer," Cynthia told him, beginning to feel for the man.

He took in a deep breath. "Lord Kineton told her that I only proposed because I wanted her dowry to fund my new company, but it's untrue, my lady. In fact, the first night I proposed—"

"At two in the morning?" Lady Moreton clarified.

"Er, yes. I had just come from Powell's where Lord Pennyston had told me he would provide the rest of the funding I needed. At that moment, when I proposed, I didn't need any more money. That's why I felt comfortable proposing," he explained.

Cynthia nodded.

"But then what happened?" Lady Blakemore asked.

"The following morning the Duke of Warwick rescinded his pledge because he needs to assist his tenants rebuild their homes after a fire," Mr. Fitzwalter explained.

"Oh, that *is* disappointing!" Diana said with feeling.

"But even then, you proposed to Cassie a second time knowing you no longer had your full funding," Cynthia said, bringing the conversation back.

"Yes, my lady. But then Lord Pennyston pulled his funding too. He had been planning on giving me money he would earn from selling a building he owns, but the sale has fallen through."

Many of the ladies nodded. They'd learned this the previous week from Mr. Sherman.

"But you still want to marry my sister?" Cynthia confirmed.

"Yes, my lady. I love her. I promise I will not use her dowry to fund my project. I can have it specifically written into the marriage agreement," he said.

There was silence for a moment as all the ladies thought about this.

"So what you need is a way to convince Miss Benton that your intentions are pure, and you don't simply want to marry her for her money, is that right?" Diana asked.

"Yes, precisely," the gentleman said with a nod.

"What if Lord Pennyston was able to invest?" Lady Moreton asked.

"Lady Moreton?" Cynthia asked, curious as to what she knew.

"I don't know. Perhaps I can speak with him," she suggested.

"That would be incredible, my lady, and go a long way to solving my financial problems," Mr. Fitzwalter said, bowing to her slightly.

"If Lord Pennyston can invest in your scheme, would that be enough for you not to have to use Miss Benton's dowry?" Lady Gorling asked.

"It's a company, my lady, not a scheme. I assure you, every part of it is above board," Mr. Fitzwalter said. "But yes, if Lord Pennyston can give me some financial backing then I should be able to find the rest. It's the prospect of having to find at least two or three more—considering how much each man would be willing to invest—that would be overwhelming."

"Would it be impossible?" the duchess asked.

"At this moment, yes, I believe so," he agreed. "It's easier to find additional investors, more difficult to find people willing to risk their money when I have none."

"Very well, we'll see what we can do for you," Lady Ayres said with a decisive nod.

"And then you'll propose once again to Cassie," Cynthia confirmed. "And tell her the entire truth?"

"Absolutely!" he agreed readily.

Cynthia just hoped that Cassie would be happy with this. She was nearly positive she would be, but sadly, she couldn't really ask her. If she did, she would have to admit the gentleman came to her and the Wagering Whist Society for help and that wouldn't do. What happened at the Ladies' Wagering Whist Society stayed there.

Chapter Twenty-Eight

~May 28~

Archer had been sitting on his hands for two days. He'd tried going to Powell's to search for another investor, but his heart hadn't been in it. He was at a loss. He was beginning to wonder if his appeal to the ladies of the Wagering Whist Society had been for nothing.

The only thing he had managed to do was to get himself out of Kineton's house. He'd done that pretty much as soon as he'd sobered himself up after Cassie had turned him down and Wickford had told him to seek out the Ladies' Wagering Whist Society. He should have done it a month ago. No, he shouldn't have ever gone there in the first place.

He'd thought Kineton had been a friend. How he had been mistaken!

A knock on Archer's door forced him out of his reverie. He had no man servant. No footman. No one to answer the door. His purse was getting much too close to empty to afford any luxuries whatsoever, and he would occupy a shallow grave before he applied to his father for funds.

He'd never lived entirely on his own before, but now that he'd experienced it, he was certain he never wanted to do so again. He'd already burned his hand twice while simply attempting to make tea.

He was shocked to find Lord Pennyston standing on the other side of his door. "My lord, what a pleasant surprise," he forced himself to say. He might have even managed to turn up the corners of his mouth into something resembling a welcoming smile.

"Fitzwalter, you're not an easy man to find," Pennyston said, walking in. "I searched for you at Powell's and then at Lord Kineton's home. I was informed there that you'd moved, but it took a good deal of searching among the footmen to discover where you'd moved to."

"Oh, I beg your pardon. It never occurred to me that someone might come looking," Archer said, indicating that his lordship go into the drawing room.

The man paused just inside the door, taking in the threadbare sofa and spindly chair. There was no carpet on the floor and just one low scratched table in the center of the very small room. At least Archer had removed the remains of his breakfast. He'd learned quickly that if he didn't clean up after himself, insects would do the job for him.

"Er... cozy," Lord Pennyston said, moving farther into the room.

"It's just temporary," Archer explained.

"Of course."

"I'd offer you some tea, but..."

"No, no. Thank you," the man smiled and sat gingerly at the edge of the sofa. "I, er, I'm here to give you some good news, actually."

"Oh?" Archer was afraid to sit in the chair. He'd done so once, and it had made some ominous creaking sounds.

"Yes. I've sold my building and am ready to invest in your company," he said with enthusiasm. "Um... perhaps we might want to go to Powell's to discuss this further? Maybe over a glass of port or something?"

This was the best news Archer had heard in a long time—and maybe Pennyston would foot the bill.

"An excellent idea!" Archer agreed enthusiastically. "Do I want to know the particulars?"

"I can't imagine that you do, but I certainly want to hear some more about this company I'm going to be investing in," he said with a laugh.

"I'll tell you all about Madras over a glass of port," Archer offered.

"Perfect."

They settled into the last two available seats in the reading room at Powell's and were soon served.

"Before I tell you more about the project, may I ask how you came by the funds? You'd said that your sale fell through. Did you find another buyer?" Archer asked, after toasting his new investor. Perhaps Lady Moreton had come through for him after all.

"No, actually, it's a little awkward," Pennyston told him.

"Oh?" Archer asked.

"I don't know if I mentioned that my building was being used as a hospital..."

"Yes, actually you did," Archer said before taking a sip of his drink.

"Right. Well, I couldn't really put them out, now, could I?" his lordship said with a little laugh.

"And Lady Moreton was volunteering there and feels very strongly about the welfare of both the men and the hospital."

"She is a very kind lady," Archer commented.

"Not only kind, but beautiful, sweet, funny..." He chuckled again, his cheeks turning slightly pink. "I'm going to ask her to marry me."

"Really?"

The man nodded. "She's er, going to go through a difficult time, but I'm going to do absolutely everything in my power to make it better for her. An opportunity has come up, and well, it's quite possible that we're going to be leaving the country."

"Really!" Archer shook his head in wonder. Lord Pennyston was going to upend his entire life for Lady Moreton, move to a foreign country. Archer was stunned, but it also made him think. How far would he go for his love of Cassie?

He could never go far enough, his heart answered immediately. Then why in the world was he doing everything he could in order to leave her and return to India? His heart didn't have an answer to that besides to tell him he was a bloody fool. But Cassie would never listen to Archer's heart. It was his mind that would sway his lovely, intelligent blue-stocking. That made him laugh.

"Is there something amusing?" Pennyston asked.

"What? Oh, I'm sorry! I realized that I, er, I'm going to ask that you keep your money. I don't need it after all," Archer said, surprising himself.

"What's that?"

"No. When you told me what you were doing for Lady Moreton, it made me think that I would do the same for Miss Benton. I would do anything for her—

I would give up my life, my... I'd even give up my dream of creating this business." He paused and took a sip of his port. "I love her. I don't want to leave and return to India."

"She could go with you—after you married, naturally," Pennyston suggested.

Archer shook his head. He'd asked her to do that once, and although she never did give him an answer, she took a great deal of time to think about it. It made him think she would have said no. "I wouldn't ask her to leave everything she's ever known," he told Pennyston. "And living in Madras is not easy. No, it's better that I give up my dream."

"Well, here's to love and future opportunities!" Pennyston said, raising his glass again.

"Absolutely! To love!"

~May 29~

Cassie paced back and forth in the garden, wondering whether Archer hated her now. Would he come? Would he respond to her note at all? It had been nearly an hour since she'd sent the footman off with her message. As far as she knew, he still hadn't returned.

She stopped her pacing.

Maybe something had happened to the footman! Maybe he'd been hit by a passing carriage. Or perhaps he'd gotten lost. Although, how one could get lost in Mayfair was beyond her comprehension. It wasn't a very large area of London.

Could something have happened to Archer? Was that what was taking so very long?

No. It had to be something else.

He was just angry with her, and who could blame him? She'd told him she never wanted to see him ever again! She'd yelled at him, and ranted, and raved, and behaved in a completely deplorable manner. Of course, he wasn't going to come just because she called.

With a heavy sigh of defeat, Cassie dropped to her knees in front of some tulips. The flowers had already wilted and died, leaving only the greenery, but even that was looking very yellow and sad at this point. The flower had had its moment of glory and now was simply waiting until next season to bloom again.

Maybe that would be her as well. Maybe she'd had her day, had her one chance at happiness. She'd bloomed and now was withering away. Perhaps she'd have a chance again next year if her mother allowed her a second season. Otherwise, she would simply hide away in a cool, dark place just like the tulip bulbs, only she might never be replaced in her soil to grow and bloom once more.

She would have nothing if—

"Are you studying a new flower?" Archer's voice came from nearby, making Cassie jump to her feet.

She brushed her dirty hands down her gown. "Archer, you came!"

"Actually, I was just stepping out to come here to see you when your footman found me and handed me your note," he said with the most beautiful smile. Really, the man was too handsome; it just made Cassie want to sigh with happiness.

"Really? You were coming to see me?"

"I was. I've been thinking..." he started.

"Yes?"

He looked at her, smiled, and came closer—close enough to run a hand down her cheek. Close enough to look deeply into her eyes. Close enough to make her heart pound wildly in her chest.

"You were wrong," he said softly.

Cassie giggled. "It won't have been the first time, and it probably won't be the last. What was I wrong about?"

He laughed. "I can't imagine with you it happens very often, but in this instance, you were wrong. I do love you. I love you more than anything."

"Oh," she sighed.

"I love you so much that I'm not going to go through with starting this company. I don't want you to think I wanted to marry you just for your dowry— I didn't, by the way. I proposed the first time when I thought I was fully funded, but then the Duke of Warwick backed out the following morning just before I came and proposed to you again. But I couldn't—I just couldn't rescind my proposal at that point. I was hoping I would find another investor before you found out, but unfortunately, I wasn't able to do so."

"And then I found out," Cassie said, feeling awful for all of her unfounded accusations. He had been trying to find another investor. Lord Wickford had been wrong!

"And then my first investor backed out as well."

"I'm so sorry!"

He shook his head with a rueful little smile on his lips. "He's offered to come back in, but I told him that I wasn't going to go forward with the company after all."

"What? Why?"

"I love you, Cassie. I don't want to return to India without you, and it was wrong of me to ask you to leave everything and everyone you know to come with me. So... I'm going to speak to my father and I thought... maybe with your knowledge of plants, you might know something of agriculture?" he asked hesitantly.

Cassie just laughed.

"If you do, then you could teach me. I could go and, perhaps, try to offer my services—or yours—to my father. I... I don't know. I don't know if he'll even speak with me after I sold the commission he bought for me. But I would do anything—and I mean anything—to be with you. I know this isn't well thought out. It isn't coming from my head, but I'm trying. Please, Cassie..."

She put her fingers to his lips to stop his silliness. "No, it isn't well thought out. Not at all," she said, giggling. "But that's one reason why I love you so much—because you think with your heart. And it's why we make such an excellent match, because I think with my head. But you're trying and I am too."

His shoulders dropped a little as the tension within him relaxed.

"But I am still thinking with my head," she told him. "And you don't need to give up your dream. You can, and should, start your company."

"But—"

"I've used my head, and I spoke with someone who is an expert in the import-export business. We've worked out precisely how much it will cost for you to start this project, and there are shipping companies ready and eager to work with you on this. You will still need some investors—my dowry alone won't cover the costs—but I think we can do this."

Archer's mouth had dropped open a little. When she stopped speaking, he snapped it closed again. "Are you serious? You've... you've worked it all out?"

She could only laugh. "Well, I didn't. My friend

did."

"I can't believe you have a friend in the business, but that's neither here nor there. I... I don't know what to say." He truly seemed to be dumbfounded. It made Cassie laugh.

"You could ask me to marry you," Cassie suggested.

Archer dropped to his knees. "Cassia Benton, you are the most amazing, incredible, brilliant woman in the world, and I absolutely don't deserve you, but would you? Could you...? But wait, does this mean you would be willing to leave your sister? Your parents and friends? All you know? We'd have to live in India for some time while this company got started," he said, interrupting himself.

"I would," Cassie said, brushing back a lock of his soft blond hair that had fallen onto his forehead when he'd gone down onto his knees.

"But your roses..."

"Do you know there are many more varieties of roses in India than there are here?" she asked, still laughing at him.

"No, I didn't. Although, now that I think about it, there are a lot of flowers in Madras. And, my goodness, the smell! They're incredible!"

"I'm sure they are. I look forward to smelling every one of them and continuing with my attempts at creating a new type of rose to carry that smell back here to England. But it's going to take me years, I'm certain."

"Years... with me?"

"Years with you, my sweet heart-thinking man," Cassie agreed.

He jumped to his feet and took her in his arms, but then he pulled back and looked down at her. "I love you, my sweet brilliant botanist."

"And I love you," she said just before his lips descended upon hers.

A Token of Love

Can the Ladies' Wagering Whist Society help a scarred war veteran rediscover his ability to love?

Christopher Pennyston, the most beautiful boy at school, the most handsome man of the ton, returns from war horribly scarred by a sabre slash. Forcing himself to return to London to care for his injured batman, he is devastated by people cringing at the sight of his disfigurement. But his biggest shock comes when a beautiful volunteer nurse ignores his scar and ignites his heart.

Ellen Aston, Lady Moreton, has devoted her life tending to others. After being told that her husband had been killed in the Napoleonic war, she turns her energy to caring for wounded soldiers. But despite her devotion to her injured wards, she yearns to find a way to break out of her humdrum life. The spark comes from an intriguing stranger, who lights the embers of her heart.

The Ladies' Wagering Whist Society has to carefully play their hand, to help a woman eager to discover the world find love with a man who wants to hide from it.

About the Author

Meredith Bond's books straddle that beautiful line between historical romance and fantasy. An award-winning author, she writes fun traditional Regency romances, medieval Arthurian romances, and Regency romances with a touch of magic. Known for her characters "who slip readily into one's heart," Meredith's heart belongs to her husband and two children.

Meredith loves connecting with readers. **Sign up for her monthly newsletter** at http://meredithbond. com/blog/newsletter-sign-up/ to receive free short stories and get all her news before anyone else. And don't forget to find her online:

Website: http://www.meredithbond.com

Facebook:
https://www.facebook.com/meredithbondauthor

Twitter: https://twitter.com/merrybond

Pinterest: http://www.pinterest.com/merrybond/

Amazon: http://www.amazon.com/Meredith-Bond/e/B001KI1SNE

Instagram:
https://www.instagram.com/meredith_bond/

Bookbub:
https://www.bookbub.com/authors/meredith-bond

Newsletter: http://meredithbond.com/subscribe/

Please don't forget to leave a review wherever you buy books.

Follow all of the women of the Ladies' Wagering Whist Society

1806 Season
A Hand for the Duke
Featuring Christianne Norman, Lady Norman
The Jack of Diamonds
Featuring Miss Lydia Sheffield
The Games She Played
Featuring Miss Diana Hemshawe

1807 Season
A Trick of Mirrors
Featuring Claire Tyne, Lady Blakemore
A Bid for Romance
Featuring Alys Russell, Duchess of Kendell
An Affair of Hearts
Featuring Mrs. Penelope Aldridge

1808 Season
Love in Spades
Featuring Cynthia Montley, Lady Sorrell
A Token of Love
Featuring Ellen Aston, Lady Moreton
The King of Clubs
Featuring Joshua Powell, Lord Wickford

Other Books By Meredith Bond

The Merry Men Series
An Exotic Heir
A Merry Marquis
A Rake's Reward
A Dandy in Disguise
My Lord Ghost
My Gentleman Thief
Under the Mango Tree
A Spanish Dilemma
When Hearts Rebel

The Storm Series
Storm on the Horizon
Bridging the Storm
Magic in the Storm
Through the Storm

The Children of Avalon Trilogy
Air: Merlin's Chalice
Water: The Return of Excalibur
Fire: Nimuë's Destiny

Falling
Falling for a Pirate

Chapter One: A Fast, Fun Way to Write Fiction
Self-Publishing: Easy as ABC
"In A Beginning", a short story featuring Lilith

Acknowledgments

Every author is dependent on their publishing team, I know I certainly am. I also believe that I have the best people to help in this journey. They are invaluable to me. Without them I wouldn't have a book, let alone as many as I do have. So my heartfelt thanks go to Chris, the most amazing editor and Alex (Mirslav), my fantastic cover designer. Thanks also go to the incredibly sharp eyes of Sandra, Phyllis, Nancy, Allyn, and the others who were amazing at catching my typos.

Thank you, all!

Merry

Dedication

To my mother, Nessa, who lives forever in my heart, and who introduced me to the fantastic Regency romances of Georgette Heyer.

And to the man who will always be home to me no matter where in the world we are, my dearest husband.

www.ingramcontent.com/pod-product-compliance
Lightning Source LLC
Chambersburg PA
CBHW071423200726

48294CB00002B/492